AURORA

SYNDROME

By Julia Twaddle

Cover Photo by Thomas J Spence.

Cover Design by Rafal Kucharczuk and Agnieszka Wiśniewska-Kucharczuk.

ISBN: 978-1-967568-01-7 (paperback)
ISBN: 978-1-967568-00-0 (hardcover)
ISBN: 978-1-967568-02-4 (e-book)

Library of Congress Control Number: 2025912453
Published in Las Vegas, Nevada

For rights and permissions, please contact:

www.JuliaTwaddle.com
Dry River Publishing, LLC

For all my nieces, may you have the courage to always speak your truth.

AURORAL

SYNDROME

I never realized having a power could make me vulnerable. Vulnerable as a target, vulnerable to exploitation, even vulnerable to others of my kind.

When you're a child, you dream about having a superpower, being able to do whatever you want and shedding the limitations that hold you back. But this power is not a dream coming true– it's a nightmare.

I can't give this back.

I can't roll back time.

I never wanted any of this.

KLARA
Lutsen, Minnesota

The tangy smell of pine wafts up to me as my boots crunch down the path toward the shoreline. Waves of grief wash over me, just as the waves of the majestic lake crash up against the rock outcropping. My breath comes ragged, siphoning through my tight throat and chest, as a sob presses against the roof of my mouth, threatening to loose free. Tiny, needle pricks of water splash against my cold cheeks, a spiteful reminder that I am here, and he is not. Off in the near distance, a heavy fog is hunkered atop the water's surface, an unmoving mass preventing my view of the vast beyond. It's the reason I love to come here, to this precise spot, to feel how expansive the world is, and how small I feel in comparison.

Each crash of a wave against the shoreline is like a punch to my gut. I fold over, bending in half as I allow my body to be wracked with this pain. For the briefest moment, I allow myself to fantasize what it would feel like to jump in, to drop to the bottom of these icy waters like a boulder returning home to the bottom of this Great Lake. I imagine what it would be like to be numb from feelings, erased of memories and pain, and to cease existing. But I don't allow these thoughts to linger. I know the answer lies inside of me and in acceptance. I take a slow, deep breath to calm myself, and I speak aloud to the muffled foggy air, the mantra that has been with me for a while now, "attachment begets suffering." I must accept what is. Turning my back to the water, I walk back toward my truck, wiping from my face the mixture of fresh lake water and salty tears.

A few moments later, pulling out of the harbor parking lot, I ease the truck onto Highway 61, pointed south on the straight-as-an-arrow route. Alongside the roadway, bright splashes of orange and red leaves carpet the shoulder, the last gasp of fall, as she begins her farewell to welcome incoming winter.

My day at the art gallery has been typical. It is the end of season for fall colors, but still fairly busy as tourism is concerned. Weekends are always full of visitors enjoying a getaway to the North Shore, donning flannel shirts, quilted vests and cozy knit hats, often holding hands in a display of romantic affection typical of those enjoying time away from responsibility.

In spite of my sadness, and perhaps as a respite from it, I enjoyed answering shoppers' questions and helping them choose the right piece of art to bring home, envisioning the space in which it might be placed. Usually, the item calls upon something from nature or Native American symbolism, helping the visitor to remember their time by the Great Lake, in the wildness and freshness of the northern spaces. Today, I sold one of Ryen's latest items. A welded piece of sculpture more appropriate in a garden or on a front lawn, he had carefully crafted the project using scrap metal and found objects. The ribcage was made of bicycle spokes, spikes along the spine were crafted of old axe heads. It was meant to be an indistinguishable, non-specific creature. Designed to be both fierce and fragile, I was almost sad to place the sold ticket onto the creature's paw. Wondering if he was working on anything new, wondering if I'd ever see him, or his art again.

Driving homeward and away from the water, there is barely any fog here. Darkness seeps over the horizon, like ink spilling out onto a fresh sheet of paper. But it is still light enough to see the expanse of the lake spread out in front of me, appearing as if the highway will drive straight into it.

I find myself looking forward to the inviting smell of chili in the crockpot that will greet me. But as quickly as the warm feeling comes to me, it is replaced with a sharp ache. Tears prick at my eyes, and I don't bother to blink them back. It hits me suddenly that I am driving home to an empty house. No amount of comforting food or beautiful surroundings can take the sting out of the fact that I will be alone for another long, cold night. Beginning to sink down into the familiar pit of my grief, I hardly notice the thumping sound at first.

Scanning the dash, I recognize the low tire pressure alert. A flat tire. I sigh, wiping away the tears and pull myself back to the present.

I look out my rear and side view mirrors, as the truck angles over onto the sloping shoulder. The chili– and my grief– will have to wait.

I carry a full-size spare tire, not the little donut designed for temporary use. Of course, I recently verified it was in good working order, part of my usual checklist and upkeep. I have everything I need, and I take comfort in the fact that I will have the truck back on the road in a matter of minutes. I check the loaded handgun in my locked center console and slide it deftly into my holster. Making my way around to the side of the truck, I begin gathering my supplies. The dwindling daylight and desolation could be frightening to some. But not me. Self-reliance is the only thing I know anymore. These woods are as comforting to me as my cabin with its walls and locked doors.

Pulling out the jack, I hear gravel crunch behind me. An older model, non-electric F150 with small amounts of rust around the wheel wells slows to a stop on the shoulder. They're called "gas burners." Up here on the iron range and other rural areas it's not too difficult to find gas stations or refill from a neighbor's private fuel storage tank for these old model cars and trucks. But with a vehicle like that, you have to be prepared with extra canisters of gas. It's nothing but charging stations in urban areas after the 2030 Congressional ban. It's even getting difficult to find someone who can repair and get parts for these engines. But in these northern parts, gas burners still provide more range than fully electric cars when the temperatures regularly drop below freezing. And there are still many here who cling to the past.

"Need a hand, Klara?" With his head out the window, his not-trying-to-be-ironic mustache makes him easily recognizable.

"No thanks, Burt. Got everything under control here." I look back to my task.

"Two sets of hands probably will get you back on the road a little faster," he says, starting to open the driver's side door of his truck.

"No really, go on home to Deb." I wave my hands in a shooing motion, impatient to finish this task alone.

"It's no trouble at all," he says.

"Really, you know I like to do this sort of thing my way." I add an edge to my voice to make sure he gets the message.

"All right, if you're sure?" He tilts his head under the vintage TC Twins baseball cap, looking sideways at me one last time.

"One hundred percent," I reply.

"Well give us a call when you get home, just so we know you made it fine, will ya?"

"You bet," I say. "Everyone still going out for beers tomorrow at the Staggering Moose?"

"Wouldn't be a Saturday if we missed that, I suppose," he says.

"I'll see ya then," I say and wave as he pulls away.

Fifteen minutes later, the darkness has crept in as I head home. In spite of the sadness, a self-satisfied grin spreads across my face. Being self-reliant and capable is the thing that gives me the most comfort. Ryen may have disappeared, but I know I'll be fine on my own. I always have been. It's safer than having to rely on others.

Several hours later, heading up to bed, the third stair from the bottom creaks out a goodnight greeting to me. As I begin to think about what's coming next in the true crime book waiting on my nightstand, I anticipate climbing under the heavy piece-made quilt I just took out of storage. My great-aunt Heather gave it to me when I bought this house. Her skillful hands laid out and carefully pieced the sections together. Each square is a bird of Minnesota. There's a bright red male cardinal, a great horned owl, and a precious little chickadee. The speckled Northern Flicker regally claims the center spot. I yearn to smooth my hands across the quilt's surface, to feel the seams beneath my fingertips as the weight of it calms my body beneath.

But, just as I place my foot on the top step, feeling where the carpet is worn into a divot, I hear the distinctive "who cooks for you" call of a barred owl out in the direction of the driveway. Looking out the window facing northward, I see a faint greenish glow above the treetops. The sky is eerily bright, as if dawn has come early.

Returning to the landing, I grab my boots and flannel jacket, heading out to get a closer look. The familiar, sweet smell of pine needles welcomes me as I open the door. Outside, with a less obstructed view, I can see the sky is lit up. Green shifting shapes, interspersed with pink and red are waving in the northern sky above me. I feel a dizzying sense of vertigo, as if my body can't distinguish the ground from sky.

Over the sound of crashing waves in the background, I hear the owl call again, hooting low and earnest. Does the owl know something?

It isn't completely unusual to see the Aurora Borealis here so early in the fall season. Lutsen is in the weak Aurora zone, so we are treated to a northern light show on occasion. But, I'm a bit puzzled. This is the second time in a week, and happened twice last week. Tonight it's so bright I could go out for a drive without headlights. It's eerie. They aired a news segment on it the other night, speculating at causes, and interviewing astronomers. Looking up at the magnificent sight, my skin prickles. An unfamiliar tingling sensation spreads up my arms. I feel heat diffusing across my skin despite the cool night air. Even though it's cold enough to see the vapor of my breath, a trickle of sweat runs down my back.

Back inside, I strip away the flannel and realize my hands are shaking as I return it to the hook. Without its coverage, I can see the bare skin on my arms. Even in low light, I notice what looks like a rash across my forearms. I'm certain it wasn't there just moments ago when I left the house. Running my fingers across the skin, the heat radiates under my touch. Strangely, it doesn't itch. This is like a sunburn without the painful burning sensation. It's as if my skin is a heat source.

I consider fishing an ice pack from the bottom freezer when a wave of fatigue washes over me. It's like the pull of gravity just doubled.

Instead of heading for the freezer, I drag my leaden legs up the stairs. Distantly I hear the owl again. Crawling into bed, I reach to turn out the light. The waves crashing against the rocks on the shore of Lake Superior lull me off to a deep and heavy slumber.

Hours later, the sun glinting off the water wakes me. Given the sun's position on the horizon, I can tell it is late morning already and

I have slept much later than usual. My sheets and pajamas are drenched in sweat and tangled around me. Perhaps it was too soon to get out the heavy quilt, too warm for it. I flip the heaviness of it off me as I climb out of bed.

My singular thought is: coffee. Coffee will get my morning back on the right track. My head feels stuffed with cotton, as if I've been up late drinking tannin-rich wine all night long instead of sleeping twelve hours. Heading downstairs to the kitchen, I press the Start button on the coffee maker that I had prepped last night after dinner.

Taking out my favorite glazed pottery mug with its smooth, glossy ceramic, something catches my eye. Something off. I look closer and notice the clock on the microwave is dark. It is totally out. Not blinking like after a surge or outage, but totally dark. I make a mental note to research the cost of a replacement.

Turning back to the coffee pot, I listen for the familiar puffing and spitting noises, only to realize nothing is happening. It, too, is dark and unresponsive. The indicator screen and power button stare blankly at me, unlit. Disappointed and groggy, I set down the mug and sigh out loud at the prospect of a circuit outage.

By the entry closet, I find the panel on the wall containing the breaker box. I move my hand to flip the kitchen breaker, and that's when I notice. It's not tripped. Scanning down the list, I see that none of them are. They are all lined up correctly, together forming a visual challenge to my sanity. For good measure, I flip off and on the one marked "kitchen," but the appliances remain dark.

Walking over to the living room, I reach under the shade of a lamp on a side table, feeling for the switch and turning it on. Nothing.

Hurrying over to the landing, I try the wall switch. Nothing.

With more energy now, despite my lack of caffeine, I jog up the stairs to my bedroom, taking them two at a time. I grab my satellite phone lying on the nightstand and lift it from the glass charging plate. Frustratingly, there's no response as I tap the screen. I power it down, but nothing happens. I consider the possibilities. Forming an orderly little logic train in my head, I assume this is an outage at the nearby transformer.

Back downstairs, I rummage through the cabinets. Hallelujah! Just where it should be, I see my emergency stash of instant coffee, usually reserved for camping. A lightness seeps into my mood, blurring the edges of my annoyance. For every Plan A, the Plan B is just waiting in the wings.

It takes mere moments to light the gas stove and boil a kettle of water. But before I have even tasted a sip of delicious triumphant coffee, my moment of celebration is short-lived. As I approach my truck, I realize there is no beeping sound to signal unlocking of the outdated keyless entry system. This is really too much. Bent under the hood, I check a few things and momentarily pause to look upward at the tree which last night housed the owl whose call I heard. No sign of him now. I take a few deep breaths, then reconnect the battery.

The truck starts instantly, and before long I'm pulling onto the highway, a grin returned to my face. And it doesn't slip away this time. I roll the windows down and inhale the intoxicating aroma of nature, feeling the crisp air against my warm cheeks.

After a short drive, I pull into a parking lot. Smaller stones give way under larger ones, as gravel shifts and crunches under my tires. Muddy tire tracks in the lot are now frozen hard after the cold night, and I follow them to the edge of the clearing.

Pines and nearly naked birch stand like soldiers guarding the well-worn path. Sunlight attempts to poke through the treetops, but is thwarted by leaf cover. Cursing myself for not bringing gloves, I stuff my hands in my pockets.

As my boots crunch along the path upward, my body already warming with the pace, I start to remember something. Like a slow trickling of water, I begin to recall images from a dream. It floats at the back of my mind, slippery in my grasp like a brook trout wriggling on the line. I look down at my hands. I can't shake the recollection of a searing sensation, but looking at them now, I see no marks or indication of what I felt last night. Fear nibbles at the edges of my mind. My breath quickens as I recall a power, a flow of energy. Fiery, fierce and uncontrolled, I remember the sensation of being pulled into a current. At the edge of my memory, chaos and destruction. It was only a dream, but the guilt is real. I shake my head to dispel these thoughts, like brushing off the tickling spider silks that have caught against my skin.

A red squirrel dashes in front of me, chattering fiercely. He sits up on his haunches for a moment, accusingly, then dives headlong into the underbrush. The trail climbs ever upward, but with each footfall, the dream fades. The sensation of earth and stone beneath my feet grounds me to the present moment, tethering me back to the living universe all around. Pachamama, the indigenous name for Mother Earth, comes into my mind. And the earth feels like a mother to me, stretching out her comforting arms.

Relaxed, my brain shifts to logic and problem solving. What does the dream symbolize? Am I finally feeling the anger and rage I am supposed to feel? Anger was supposed to be part of the grieving process. An article I read stressed the importance of experiencing each emotion and phase of the process. The fiery emotion of anger would help numb the pain and give me motivation to move forward. But, try though I might, I haven't been able to feel any rage. Not even bitterness. Was the dream about anger or revenge?

Formed over a billion years ago, these mountains were once hot flowing lava, molten and liquid. I can almost envision the heat once held in the rock. I imagine it emanating up my legs and flowing all around me. Eerily, it takes me back to the scorching heat of my dream, sparking a connection. Neurons firing, I'm lit up from the inside, knowing in the moment that I will remake the burned ashes of my life into something new and better. A crackle of energy tells me that I am about to be reborn into a new life.

It is good to burn.

LIN
Heilongjiang Province, China

Russians call it the Amur River. Dark and mysterious, snaking its long course marking the edge of her country. To her people, it is called Heilong Jiang, which translates to Black Dragon. This is what Lin learned to call it as a child, and it is how she thinks of it now, a living thing, a real dragon.

Dry and frozen, the dragon hibernates. It waits for a time when the heat of summer and the monsoons return. When the rains replenish its former glory, it will writhe and pulse through the lush countryside.

But today, as Lin makes her way past its banks, the dragon sleeps. Pieces of her dark hair escape the knitted hat tucked under the hood of her parka. The loose tips of hair are frosted from the vapor of her breath as she plods carefully along the icy path. The ice grippers she wears over her boots make it awkward.

Lin focuses on her footsteps, as she ponders Plato's Allegory of the Cave and tries to anticipate the questions she might be asked on tomorrow's philosophy exam about the Theory of Forms. She looks out over the frozen river flanking her route, and imagines her future, what contributions she will make to society, what her role might be.

She feels a restlessness, an existential need for more. Her life can be so much bigger, so much more impactful. She's not sure how, or why, but the restless feeling tells her there is something else she needs to do with her life.

The exam will determine if she can progress in the philosophy program at the University. It will disappoint her father if she continues in the program instead of pursuing technology or science. He adamantly pushed her away from philosophy, viewing it as a frivolous waste of time that would lead to nothing more than meager earnings. But Lin excels at philosophy, and it feeds her imagination and her soul in ways nothing else ever has.

Lin wants to bring home high marks on this exam and a recommendation from her advisor to continue to the program in the hopes her father will finally see how talented she is. If he could only realize that she can become someone truly admired in this field, maybe he will finally support her.

She knows she was meant to accomplish great things, even though her choice of study is a disappointment to her father, the pre-eminent cardiologist. Her brother would have followed in their father's footsteps. Or, at least, this is an assumption that can't be refuted. Her twin didn't survive their birth, stamping Lin with a grief for someone she never met, creating a perfect landing spot for their father's misplaced ambition.

But Lin still believes there is more to her story than being a disappointment. This is because of how her grandmother told her the story of the eve of her birth, recounting it as lore in graphic and poetic detail. Even with the tragedy of a baby boy who didn't live to breathe more than a few breaths, her grandmother's rendering of the night as magical and fated has always been a balm for the grief Lin felt over a sibling she never met.

"The night of your birth was the last time I remember seeing the Auroras. We seldom see them in this area anymore, not the real Aurora." Her grandmother went on to explain how some of the villagers mistook the cold night lamppost phenomenon for Aurora Borealis. The lampposts are just ice crystals condensed from water vapor. The crystals capture and refract nearby light, tricking the human eye into thinking it sees something more than simple beams of light mirrored a million times over.

"That night, this was no lamppost activity, Lin. This was the real thing, and it was more spectacular than any Aurora I have ever seen in the whole of my life." Grandmother explained how she had only seen the Aurora a handful of times as a child and rarely as an adult. "The night of your birth, the northern sky put on such a show. I knew you had to be a special baby for the universe to come down and turn on those magical lights just for you. Five differently colored lights wandering in a lazy waving pattern across the sky. Purple, pink, green, bright chartreuse, and deep red. So many colors came out for the occasion of your birth."

Grandmother told her how their people, under King Zhao, were the first to record the phenomenon in ancient court records. On Bamboo slips of paper, the writers told of a "five colored light" appearing in the northern night sky. "You see, it's our ancient message, for our people, Lin. It's your birthright." Every time grandmother recounted the tale, Lin would be entranced by visions of dancing colors in the sky. Her father's harsh words faded into the backdrop of such a rich and meaningful scene.

Unfortunately, forgetting was not something her father could do. Since the moment of her birth, she hadn't stopped being a disappointment to her father, and a reminder of the child he deserved to have. When she was awarded first chair for the cello, and played in her first concert, the audience stood and clapped, mesmerized at her artistry and skill. But her father sat firmly in his seat.

Nothing Lin did would ever be enough. Her very existence fell short of his expectations. And while she felt in her heart it would never change, she couldn't stop herself from trying. Despite his harsh stance, Lin desperately wanted her father's approval for the path she chose in her life and placed a high value on his opinion of her.

The ice cleats make a light clacking noise under her feet as she crosses the road and makes her way to the train station. Low, dark clouds settle overhead like a heavy quilt. They are predicting another snow this afternoon, and she hopes to arrive at her apartment on campus before the worst of it comes through. She needs to be fully rested to excel on the exam and prove her father wrong.

Grandmother's gentle but piercing voice accompanies her as she boards the train, and as she looks out across the bleak landscape during the trip home. Lin knows her birthright is about something bigger than the misplaced expectations of a simple man in a small village. Deep within the cells of her body, she feels the pull of something bigger, something more.

KLARA
Duluth, Minnesota

My nostrils fill with the sting of rubbing alcohol as fluorescent lights strobe overhead. But the task light set up close to my skin is warm and comforting. The only other customer in the tattoo parlor today, a mid-fifties white man with a graying beard lies prone on his stomach as a small sprite of a woman masterfully works a Samurai scene across his shoulders.

After an outage lasting several days, power was restored to the area late yesterday. It's been plenty cold to put food outside and know it will stay frozen, but I only have the ski locker to keep my food safe from wild animals. Because I had been performing routine maintenance on my solar powered generators, I knew they had enough watt-hours to keep several space heaters and small electronics going until mercifully the power came back.

After the lights in my cabin flickered on rather unceremoniously this morning, I confirmed with the artist that he was still able to take my appointment before making the drive to Duluth. Already, the solar panels are set up on my front driveway and the batteries should be fully recharged when I get home later, ready for the next outage.

Pulling myself back from thoughts of purchases I need to make in town before I head home, I look down and find I'm staring into a pair of eyes. On the soft underside of my forearm, the piercing, hooded eyes of an owl begin to take shape. Shrouded in delicate feathering, a slim, sharp beak punctuates the center of the image. The needle burns and snaps, biting into my flesh. I look away.

A bittersweet memory comes to visit me. Just as a stranger on a train platform would place a hand on my shoulder, innocuous and unexpected, it implores me to turn and look. With no escape, I fall down the rabbit hole of memory.

***

Swirling sweetly and deliciously, the curtains move and take shape. I jump and scream. Ryen has launched himself at me from behind the curtains, growling as he grabs my waist. I hear the reverberation of my foolish, childlike scream in my ears, instantly embarrassed at my reaction. He is laughing so hard he is almost out of breath.

"Stop it you jerk, it's not funny!" I protest, wrenching his hands from me.

"You scream like a little girl," he says, playfully mocking me, clearly gratified by my predictable response.

I can't help but laugh every time, which only encourages him. Despite my feeble protests, he wraps me in his strong arms and hoists me up and over his shoulder like a bag of chicken feed. Bouncing over his shoulder up the narrow stairs, I catch a glimpse of bobbing images through the small window.

"Shouldn't we be out there shoveling?" I suggest, giggling as he flops me down onto the bed. The sounds of neighboring shovel scrapes and distant snowblower motors paint a white noise backdrop that is both comforting and chaotic at the same time.

"Nah, let the sun do some work on it first." He is breathless from carrying me as he reaches over to brush a lock of hair from my face. "I have other ideas for how to spend our morning." He levels his gaze on me, and a different kind of melting begins. Not the warm sun on a slippery sidewalk, but it may as well be for all the heat that

14

is rising inside my chest. Nuzzling into my neck, I feel his lips against the sensitive skin behind my ear. He huffs in my scent, lustily exhaling.

"It might all be melted by the time I'm done with you," he says, slowly unbuttoning my flannel shirt. "This is definitely going to take a while," he says.

***

"I'm sorry, what did you say?" I ask the burly tattooist at my side.

"This is going to take a while," he repeats.

"Are you fine continuing?" He looks down with concern in his eyes, handing me a tissue.

I swallow around the knot I hadn't realized was in my throat and nod.

"I'll spray a little more lidocaine," he offers, spritzing my arm before tenderly wiping blood from the image.

Laying back against the table, I close my eyes. Torn between feelings of wanting to fall back to that scene, I simultaneously want to numb my emotions and block it all out. If only there was a lidocaine spray for my mind, a way to erase the pathways back in time.

"What's the meaning behind this one?" he asks while his gloved hands work the needle methodically over his creation.

"Wisdom?"

"Owls have a discernment, they find prey under the blanket of snow, in the cover of darkness. They are keenly skilled at finding what they need, no matter the obstacle."

"I guess I can see that," he says.

Rather than succumb back down the tunnel of memories, I decide to continue here in the present, opting for a conversation with a real live person, instead of the one with a ghost in my mind.

"Owls can take the good with the bad. Have you heard of owl pellets?" I ask him.

He shakes his head silently, continuing his work.

"It's something they cough up. It's got bones, fur, claws, all the things that are not digestible. Sometimes you can find them on the ground near a nest. Owls digest all the nutrition and useful parts of their prey, then they just regurgitate out the hard, useless pieces. They go on with their life, taking the good, spitting out the bad."

"Gross," he says. "But cool too, in a sciencey-nerdy way." Laying back, a tear slips out of my eye and runs down the side of my face, pooling into my ear. It's tickling, but I don't move to wipe it off.

LIN
Saint Sophia Cathedral, Harbin; China

Settling the instrument between her legs, Lin gazes fifty-three meters up to the ceiling. She marvels at the Byzantine architecture of the cathedral swallowing up the sounds of their string quartet. While the interior is structured in the shape of a cross, the exterior features bulbous green onion domes, squatting like Christmas tree ornaments or fat green birds atop the building. Gilded cornices and curved archways adorn the ancient monument. Lin feels a light airiness looking up at intricate chandeliers suspended above.

A full audience is packed tightly into the cathedral. As the quartet plays one number after the next, Lin's dark eyes glow with pride, her pale skin stark in the low lights. Her prowess on the cello is magnetic. Her skill and artistry have refined into something truly masterful.

Deep and low, she releases the notes as her hands move deftly across the instrument. Hundreds of tightly strung horsehairs make friction, their microscopic crevices and protrusions raking across the metal strings, chaos and vibration generating a sound so beautiful it's almost painful.

The Nicolas church is especially hushed and reverent tonight with the falling snow muffling all external sounds and activity.

Later, when their performance ends, Yutai, the violinist, puts away his instrument then helps her maneuver the cello into its case. He holds out the straps so she can angle her arms through the loops and ease it onto her back. Pulling her hat tightly down over her ears, she exits the church as part of the foursome. Lin's gaze carefully focuses downward on the slippery marble stairs leading out onto the square. Fresh melting snow mixed with the dirt from scuffling feet has created a surface both slick and gritty, especially dangerous because of the unpredictable and uneven texture.

So focused is Lin on the careful placement of each foot on the stone steps, she barely hears the quiet utterance from the violinist. A gloved hand resting lightly on the handrail, he whispers up in awe. "What is that?" His other gloved hand points northward to the sky. As Lin pulls her eyes up from the steps, she looks around to discover the concertgoers have not dispersed. Instead, the throng of people bundled in winter coats crowds the square. Following their gazes and Yutai's upward gesturing, Lin finds herself facing northward.

With a gasp, she realizes what has captured their attention. Bright and intense, a light show is unfolding in the sky. Colorful rays of light splash across the sky, like a bruise beginning to form, blossoming up a yellowish green and purple from the horizon. The sky is miraculously painted with shape-shifting dragon tails of dark green. Stumbling, she nearly loses her footing for a moment, the subtle movement in the sky prompting a feeling like vertigo.

While she treasures all the details from grandmother's story of the Aurora on the night of her birth, until tonight she has never seen it with her own eyes. It always felt fictional, like fantasy. Something far away and untouchable. The Aurora Borealis rarely makes an appearance in this region. In fact, it hadn't been a regular sight even in her grandmother's day. At least not in this part of the globe. Lin assumed the story couldn't be real and was nothing more than an old woman's storytelling to a naive child.

But now here it is, right before her eyes. Just as her grandmother described it so many times. Not distant or imagined, but vividly real. It somehow clicks into place, the truth of grandmother's story, slightly shifting a piece of her identity on a deep, cellular level.

Lin feels a strong pull within her, something akin to the low vibrations when she plays her instrument. But this time, no music accompanies the sensation. Her fingers and toes begin to tingle, and warmth radiates up into her face, pulsing up from somewhere deep inside her.

"Lin, are you okay?" The sound of the voice is muffled by whirring white noise in her ears. A feeling somewhere between falling and floating overtakes her. With no chance to respond, a tunnel of darkness closes off her vision. Lin's legs give way beneath her.

AARYA
Burbank, California

"It happened again. This time it lasted three hours." Walton is standing a little too close to Aarya's desk, awkward in his eagerness to share the news.

She wants to drink her latte while it is hot and work on her agenda for the upcoming star party program.

He fidgets with the smart eyeglasses case on her desk, causing it to beep as the charge cycle is interrupted. He continues to share each painstaking detail from the latest update. "At first, I thought it couldn't be possible. A coronal mass ejection of this magnitude so soon after the others. But I verified the radio noise. There is a strong circular polarization suggesting intense magnetic fields. We're waiting for estimates regarding when to expect the storm's arrival this time."

Aarya knows, after a mass ejection, it could take anywhere from twelve hours to several days for the subsequent solar storm to reach Earth. The most recent CME, or coronal mass ejection, impacted Earth's atmosphere only fourteen hours later and wreaked havoc on satellites, cell phones and power grids. With some areas still recovering, another storm so soon after could be absolutely destabilizing.

Aarya often thinks of life in terms of Before the Event or After the Event. It was the kind of thing astronomers knew could happen as an isolated incident, but never imagined would occur in their lifetimes, and with increasing regularity. After the polarity of the Sun's magnetic fields reversed at the start of solar cycle twenty-six, the solar flare activity and coronal mass ejections escalated to a rate not witnessed since Lincoln's presidency.

When her colleagues and other scientists first started to understand what was happening, their meetings primarily focused on the Carrington Event of 1859, because it was the most extreme recorded solar storm impact on Earth. Until now. Her work lately has focused on a type of storm forecasting that involves predicting how storms coming in such close succession speed through the atmosphere and have greater impact if a prior storm has paved the way. Although it was thrilling when Auroras first started occurring in places like Cuba and Hawaii, the sightings quickly became a terrifying reminder of the destruction and chaos caused by both Borealis and Australis lighting up the sky in places previously untouched by their wonder.

Aarya looks at Walton, setting aside her latte. Her initial annoyance at being interrupted evaporates entirely. A new kind of tension is brewing in her, and all she wants now is to get to the observatory and join him in the monitoring, measurements and reporting, to record the latest event and all relevant statistics.

"Have you posted on the NOAA page yet?" she inquires.

"I was just about to but wanted to come tell you first." Walton's loyalty to her is endearing, despite his awkwardness.

"We'd better get over there before Leonard finds out and hogs the equipment," she says, heading for the door, latte forgotten and tablet in hand.

As they make their way through familiar passages within the immense facility, she looks out at the early morning through tinted windows. Despite the expanse created by high ceilings and yawning rooms, this building comforts her in a way usually reserved for closer spaces. It's her safe haven, the only place she has ever felt true belonging, a feeling of being home. As they scurry along the half-circle walls on their way to the telescope room, it feels to her as if the building is wrapping her in a hug.

Walton stops short.

"What is it?" she asks.

"Your sweater, Aarya. You forgot to bring it. You are going to be so cold."

In her haste, she had left behind the granny sweater she keeps at her desk. She found it in a local shop. The old yarns are out of fashion now with lab grown synthetics favored for being more environmentally friendly, and for providing warmth without bulk. Aarya finds many discarded for resale. She treasures the knobby cardigans and considers them rescues that she is re-homing. To her, each has a story and a past. She even goes so far as to assign each one a name.

"I'll go back for it. You get in there and make sure Leonard doesn't get to the equipment before us." Walton is already doubling back toward their office area.

"Thank you," she mutters.

Indeed, the room is cold as she enters, but thankfully she finds herself alone. As she calibrates equipment and cycles up software programs, her thoughts wander to the story she saw on the news. If the stories were true, would the young woman in northern China already be experiencing symptoms from this latest CME? Would she be frightened, or excited. Was it painful? Were they monitoring and measuring the girl closely now, just as Aarya and Walton would be feverishly capturing data from the solar storm?

Conjuring an image of the pale, dark-haired woman in her mind, she is pulled back from far-away thoughts to see Walton triumphantly entering the room. She notices half of his shirt is untucked, and frowns at the length of his pants riding short above his shoes and exposing his socks. In addition to retrieving her nubby charcoal cardigan, he also presents her with the forgotten latte. For a socially inept guy, he is awfully considerate.

The two work side-by-side in near silence, collecting the available data, recording it, and checking the upload speeds.

"I'm getting a better connection today," Walton says. "I've submitted about twenty-five percent of the data already and it's only taken an hour. They must be making progress on the undersea cable upgrades."

"Yes," Aarya says. "I listened to a radio program yesterday where they talked about the teams working around the clock to bring up transmission capacity. They're thinking that some ATMs may come back online in another couple of weeks."

She thinks back on the early days of the power outages and satellite interruptions, when cashless payments stopped for periods of time. Panic took hold as long lines formed at the bank to make withdrawals of cash. But as more people began to carry and hoard cash, muggings, burglaries and assault became more commonplace.

"I heard that a few, sporadic air flights are scheduled for next week, pending solar storm forecasts," he says. "Can you believe how long it has taken to retrain the pilots?"

"Considering how hard it is to get anywhere when the GPS systems are down, I'm actually surprised they are able to get flights going again so soon."

"Oh, that reminds me," he says, standing up enthusiastically from the computer. "I'm getting a road atlas from my granny!"

"Why? How?" she asks. "Aren't those selling for thousands of dollars?"

"Yes," he says. "This one could probably fetch over three grand. But she found it tucked away in some of my grandad's old books and said I could have it—for emergency purposes and not to be sold."

"That's pretty neat," she says. "But do you really need to leave the city these days? Isn't a city map good enough?" Even as she asks the question, Aarya knows how unsafe it feels to be stuck in one place. No air travel, limited ability to drive interstate, it's been a feeling of claustrophobia she never could have expected.

"I am a man of great freedom now."

Aarya smirks, then shakes her head, slightly bemused, but also jealous.

Four hours later, they've gathered and uploaded all the data they can for the day and decide to wrap up. There's an unspoken code that one shouldn't be out driving in the city past dark, so they're always careful to plan out the workdays, coming in on weekends to spread things around, and staying overnight at the observatory if the work requires them to stay past safe driving times.

Walton escorts her to the parking lot, as has become his custom.

"Did your car fully charge?" he asks.

"Eighty percent," she says, after checking the gauge. "Better than before, at least."

"True, and you'll be able to get home and back on that," he says. Checking his phone he adds, "Too bad the GPS is still down. I was really hoping it would be back up."

"Yeah, there were two accidents on my way here," she tells him. "It will probably take me an hour to get home at the speed I drive. I'm such a turtle!"

He laughs and wishes her a safe journey, then drives off, looking more comfortable behind the wheel than most of the drivers on the road.

But Aarya sits behind the wheel of the car for a few moments, to review her paper city map to confirm the best route home. She always needs to calm her nerves before taking the car out of self-drive. Sure, everyone is still required to learn some basics for "emergency purposes" but she's found it's actually terrifying to really do it outside of the test course. She's shocked at how difficult it is to judge the distance between cars, how much time is available to cross through three lanes of traffic, all while trying to read street signs and remember which turns to make. "How on Earth did humans do this without technology?" she thinks.

KLARA
Northern Minnesota

A chill creeps into my fingers. The toe on my left foot aches in protest- a warning I have been in the cold too long. "One more quick loop," I think, glancing at the horizon and the darkening sky. As puffs of air escape my nose, ice crystals form on my eyelashes.

I enjoy these times on my own. Solitude is as much a comfort to me as anything else in life. Looking down at the groomed track on the frozen lake under my feet, I notice the corners have degraded to an icy and hard pack. The ice creaks and groans. An unseasoned skier would think the noise was cause for panic. Instead, I move my skis quickly and rhythmically through the well-packed, glistening snow, enjoying the hum of satisfaction as muscle memory takes over. I love being outdoors, moving my body and feeling the harshness of the air on my face.

Off in the distance, a murmur, almost a rumble, picks up. I slow my pace and look in the direction, listening for sounds, looking for clues. A twig snaps and I jump, alarm signaling inside of me as I nearly cross my skis. Just then, a large six by six-pointed mature male elk strolls along the shoreline in the trees. He effortlessly navigates through the underbrush and dense snow. I regain my balance and exhale, laughing at myself for being so edgy. "Hi, big fella," I whisper. Our eyes lock for a moment and I feel a connection to the untamed that never ceases to fill my soul. I feel as if mother nature is leaning over and whispering a secret in my ear meant just for me.

I look ahead to gauge the height of the sun as it begins to kiss the tops of pine trees, marking the limited amount of daylight that remains. I look down at the track as it begins to turn a corner and I hear another, much louder creak of the ice. I smile, knowing the rock-hard lake surface will hold, and thinking of this as another one of mother nature's secret handshakes. Popping and creaking, even groaning sounds are not uncommon on a frozen body of water. I think of it as a wink or a whisper from nature signaling I am truly part of the mysterious natural world around me.

Swish, breathe. Swish.

The creak has also brought forth a memory, rich and deeply embedded within me. It was the first time I heard Mother Nature's language, but instead of gleeful wonder, I felt sheer terror. I had to be six years old, because I remember wearing the mittens I had gotten in first grade when Mrs. Jefferson was my teacher. She had given a lesson on penguins, after which I became obsessed for the next two years. When I saw the mittens with penguin faces on them, I squealed and begged my mom to buy them for me.

The rest of me was bundled up in a full body snowsuit, as I went with my dad across the frozen lake for a day of ice fishing. I ran out ahead of him, going fast then sliding on my knees across the cold and slick surface. I hadn't bothered to look for him, to see how far away I had gotten, just enjoying the playful moment, feeling intrinsically safe and happy. But the sound was like nothing I'd ever heard before. It sounded like a ray gun, like something from a science fiction movie. Metallic, boomeranging noises began zipping around me and terror gripped hold of my small body. When I looked for my dad, he was so far away. I found his eyes just as I started to cry, in the way a child of that age does, first self-conscious, not wanting to be a baby, but starting to wail after seeing the fear in an adult's eyes. He quickly closed the distance, rushing over to me and kneeling down. He removed his gloves, wiping tears from my face, his hands warm in spite of the freezing air.

"Don't be afraid, Klara," he said. The sound continued to reverberate around us, and I darted my eyes in all directions, looking for the source. Despite his comforting words, my small eyes grew even wider with fear.

"It's just the singing ice," he reassured me, a twinkle in his eyes.

"The ice?" I asked, terrified and questioning. "It sings?"

"Yeah, it's something about the thick top layer of ice and movement of water underneath that causes the strange noises. The lake is putting on a special concert, just for us."

"Adults are so weird," I said, thinking that if I had named the sound, it would be ice warning or danger ice. Singing made it sound like a sweet, angelic sound.

Swish. Breathe. Swish. Back to the here and now, on this lake not so far from the one in my memory, I move the skis under me, sticking the poles and pushing off. Back to reality, and utterly on my own.

It's been three full weeks since Ryen vanished, walking out the door, never to return to our life together. After I filed the police report, put up fliers, did all the things a person could possibly do, everyone told me to let him go. He made a choice to leave.

But did he? Why did he go? Is he okay? My anguish is interlaced with grief, and I wonder if I should be doing more to find him, or if I am in denial about what really happened.

Gradually, then more sudden, the murmur off in the distance picks up, vibrations mounting, growing closer. I wonder if another Alzheimer patient from the nearby nursing home has wandered off to freeze in a snowbank. This happened about two months ago. The Sheriff's chopper had circled neighboring areas looking for the old man before it was too late. My thoughts naturally turn toward Ryen, wondering if he will ever resurface and make contact. Wishing I could go find him as easily as a missing old man in the snow.

As my skis glide across the icy snow, the murmur develops into a thunderous roar. I look up to see a small black dot coming into view at the edge of the lake. The sound moves toward me before I can visualize it, the shape of a helicopter coming into focus. As the aircraft moves closer, I think my mind must be playing tricks on me. It almost seems like the vehicle is lowering. Small puffs of snow kick and dance ever so slightly from the top layer. Moving toward the surface of the open and desolate lake, the helicopter unbelievably lands about two hundred yards in front of me.

"Holy shit!" I exclaim. What could possibly be happening? I think of my child-like fear on that lake with my father all those years ago and attempt to calm myself. Our human minds fill in the empty, unknown details, with the worst we can imagine. But so often, just like that memory from my childhood, there is a rational explanation much less terrifying than our minds have conjured up.

It can't be what I think, but my gut says this is all wrong. A stark contrast to the white and gray landscape all around, heavily clad military personnel in dark gear emerge from the side of the helicopter and sprint toward me. I freeze in place, panic gripping hold of me.

"Holy shit," I say more quietly, the words bouncing off the inside of my ice-crusted neck buff. I look behind me and all around wondering if this is part of some military exercise I have wandered into. Or maybe a hostage situation at an ice fishing house, some domestic dispute gone too far?

Realizing there is no one else on this frozen surface, a deeper, more terrifying chill comes over me.

"Klara Dubkins," a voice booms over a bullhorn, not a query, but a statement.

"Down on your hands and knees."

A constellation of thoughts bombard me:

"They know my name?"

"How can I get onto hands and knees wearing skis?"

"Am I dreaming again?"

Using the tip of my poles, I quick-release the skis and drop the poles at my side. Lowering onto my knees, the ice is an unforgiving mass.

Bodies loom over me and my cheek scrapes against the sharp ice as I am pushed face down. A heavy object is thrown over my body, much like a weighted blanket, something I have no frame of reference to understand. Through chinks in the metal, the last vestiges of daylight barely glint through, and I realize the material is something akin to chain mail.

LIN
Military Base, United States

Lin reaches around her slim body, trying to pull the rough wool blanket over her shoulders to generate some measure of warmth. It's dark and so very cold. Her hip is sore, pressing her body weight into the thinly padded concrete slab. As she curls herself into a tight ball, she tries to remember how it felt, the blissful heat from the southern California sun, to remember the excitement of her trip to America, before it all went wrong. In her mind's eye, the palm trees sway in the breeze, and she tries to match their rhythm and rock herself back to sleep. They were so much taller in real life. She found herself transfixed, looking up at them instead of watching where she was going. She didn't even notice the athletic man, when he helped her pick up the sheets of music she had dropped after bumping into him. Flustered and uncomfortable at the prospect of having to speak English to an American university student, she hurried to collect the papers whispering "Sorry."

She tries now to remember any detail, anything specific. She inspects her memory for some nefarious look in his eye, a curve of malice at the edge of his mouth. But he was so very unremarkable, and she was mesmerized by the golden sunlight streaming through the palm fronds. It's all a blur.

"That might be the very last palm tree I ever see," she thinks wearily to herself, wondering if her days are numbered. Running a hand down the back of her arm, she can still feel the bruises from the forceful hands that tossed her into the back of a dark van. That part was exactly how the movies portrayed it, terrifying, anonymous and swift. Her wrists still bear the dark, tender circles from where the zip ties held her hands together behind her back. "Why me?" she thinks.

She fights the urge to cry, knowing self-pity will do her no good. The memory is only helpful if she can find details. Steeling her mind against the trauma, she goes back over it all again. She must have been drugged.

"Why me?" she thinks again, but this time with a critical eye. "What is it about me that would make anyone want to kidnap me? Someone doesn't want me being accepted into the university orchestra program?"

A flash of heat prickles her chest in a fevered wave that makes her shudder. She picks at the memory of the night prior to her audition. Remembering the rash of heat she felt that evening, just as it had happened outside the cathedral, she thinks, "It can't be. It's too supernatural, too strange." Occam's razor tells her that these events must be connected, it's the simplest explanation despite being supernatural.

She looks back at the events now through a different, much clearer lens. Reliving the memory of that night, out on the restaurant terrace, is that the same athletic young man sitting at the corner table? When she, along with the other patrons abandoned their meals and glasses of wine to clamor at the railing and look up at the bewildering light show, were two large men watching her from a distance? Was it a coincidence that she fainted again? And what about the power outage? Did the men cause it somehow as a distraction? It must be related.

Gingerly, she turns herself to face the wall, giving her pained hip a break, but her other joints protest all that she's endured. Repositioning herself under the blanket, her grandmother's words come to her. A whisper from somewhere in the past faintly brushes against her ear. "This was not lamppost activity, Lin. This is your birthright."

She knows it to be true down to the cells in her body. There is something special about her and it's tied to these new lights in the sky.

KLARA
One Month After Abduction

I am aware of my body as something separate and detached. Just barely awake, I can sense a gray tinge of light filtering through the small window on the door. Thought and awareness feel difficult. The energy it would take to open my eyes is more than I can bear.

I wouldn't exactly call it pain.

Pain would be preferable. It feels as if I have been running marathons for weeks, and a feverish chill rolls over me in relentless, undulating waves.

Am I alive? Am I dying? Already dead?

A loud noise at the door assaults my senses.

"You'd better eat. It's not going to get easier, you know," a voice barks, the decibels piercing through me.

I drift back into unconsciousness, no longer aware of my surroundings, no longer capable of physical feeling.

I dream. I fall backward into one of my earliest memories.

The first time I saw the Aurora Borealis, we were driving home from Grandpa Rick's, just outside of Beaver Bay. I remember having the cloth mask with bumble bees on it that mom had sewn for me. I took it everywhere during the pandemic. Dad didn't usually wear a mask, and neither did most of the people in our small town. But Mom made us wear them around Grandpa. I liked the feeling of protection it gave me. I liked that I didn't have to fake a smile at the adults. In the back seat of the car that day driving home, I fidgeted with the straps, folding them together then apart, attempting a braid that the looped ends wouldn't fully allow.

"Hey kids," my dad said, looking over his shoulder, a gleam in his eye. The sky was inexplicably green and so much brighter than it should have been.

"That's the Northern Lights. Pretty neat, isn't it?" he said.

I stared up, dumbfounded and confused. "Why is it like that?" I asked. "So green and wobbly?" It looked fake. The subtle movement in the sky played tricks on my mind, making me dizzy as if I was the one moving, not the other way around. I rubbed my eyes to be sure I was seeing clearly.

"You know, it's actually like an attack going on up there." Mom chimed in from her side of the car.

"Oh now, honey, don't you think that's a bit over-dramatic?"

"No, just think about it," she said. "The sun's particles are slamming so fast into our atmosphere. The atmosphere is protecting us by redirecting the particles. Basically, the light show you are enjoying right now is no different than your body's immune system response to a virus. Like a runny nose or a fever, the Earth is waging war against a foreign intrusion."

I was no longer listening to Mom as she went on about particles traveling forty-five million miles per hour, the earth's poles, and whatever other documentary film facts she recited.

I looked up, and I was utterly lost in that great big glowing sky. It wasn't just the color, painted in great swaths across the sky that pinned my gaze upward. Even the brightness at this late hour— though it was surprising— wasn't the thing that mesmerized me. The thing that pulled my attention to it like metal fragments to a magnet, the thing I never forgot, was how the lights in the sky danced. Shuddering silently, hypnotically, like a snake from the charmer's basket, the sky slithered with movement and expression.

I wonder now if that's when it all began, when something inside of me began to shift and change. Did my cells dance in time with the particles of energy and light overhead? Were my molecules striking a secret deal with the universe? Was something inside my body, some nucleotide buried deep, being hypnotized like the snake into behaving in an unnatural way?

AARYA
Los Angeles, California

Aarya puts her feet up on the coffee table, a pastel and inky blue pillow nestled beneath them for cushion. She's wearing wool socks reminiscent of oatmeal, which were a staple for her during the recent cold snap. A freshly poured glass of Rousanne, from her favorite organic winery awaits her on the side table, but she reaches around it for her phone. Switching on the TV, she scans the latest news stories available in her queue before deciding on a recent local newscast. Just as she clicks to start the video clip, Bumbu, her twelve-year-old ginger cat hops onto her lap, arching his back for affection. She strokes his soft fur, and he curls into a ball on her lap.

"SatPhone coverage was returned to California early this morning, marking the longest outage to date since the November storm," the journalist reports. "The recent wave of solar storm activity has caused disruption on the West Coast and locations in the East China Sea. This, we understand, is due to the timing of the atmospheric impact. I'm here now at a local San Fernando grocery store that was hit hard during the power and satellite outages. You can see behind me that looters broke most of the windows and the manager tells me they made off with most of the shopping carts.

"

These shelves were fully stocked before the outage, but as you can see, sections that once contained pantry staples like rice, beans and canned goods have been picked clean."

"Now this store recently hired a private security firm to secure the premises given the recent rise in looting and property damage. But what we are hearing from store management is the security detail was just too small in number compared to the overwhelming size of the groups that swarmed in and overpowered them. The work will now begin to board up windows and secure the premises, but the manager tells me he will not be able to accept delivery of new items until the refrigeration units are fully cleared out and the property is safe for customers to return."

"Back to you, Jenna."

"Thanks Marco, stay safe out there. We turn now to local astronomer Leonard Pakkala, a professor of astronomy at Caltech, one of many scientists studying these storms and hoping to find answers."

"Leonard, thank you for being with us today."

"Thank you for having me, Jenna."

"Tell us what astronomers like yourself, those in the academic community, have been doing to understand this solar activity."

"He looks so smug," Aarya says out loud to Bumbu. Leaning in, she examines the screen more closely. "I think he even dyed his hair!"

The cat mews a response as she takes a liberal sip of wine.

"Well Jenna, we have been working around the clock since all of this activity first began, which was even before the November storm, if you can believe it. You see, there was a series of smaller solar storms detected in October which essentially paved the way for the atmospheric effects of the November storm to get through and have such disastrous impact."

"I see, so this first began in October?"

"Yes, that's right. And here we are months later experiencing continued events with no understanding of when or how relief may come."

"And scientists like yourself haven't made any headway?"

"I certainly didn't say that." Leonard is getting agitated, red splotches of color appearing on his cheeks. Aarya thinks he is possibly the worst person from their department to have been chosen for this coverage and wonders about the selection process.

"I have actually been testing several theories myself in the last two weeks which may prove incredibly useful. However, I cannot reveal too much at the moment, pending additional testing."

"I see, very exciting. Are these theories related to somehow preventing outages and getting our lives back to normal?"

"Yes, a remedy or methodology for mitigating the storm's effects has been my focus since this all began. I want nothing more than to bring about a return of normal societal functioning once again." His eyes wander a bit during these last two sentences and Aarya's bullshit meter is off the charts.

"Normal societal functioning?!" she says to her cat, as if looking for a response. Just yesterday Leonard was ridiculing the average American and their desire to return to normal. He mocked the term normal and droned on about how life evolves and changes.

"Well, we certainly will be following up with you to hear what you discover in your ongoing work. Dr. Pakkala, thank you so much for joining our coverage this evening."

Her phone pings an alert. Walton's name appears as the sender. She reads:

"It should have been you, Aarya. Why don't they recognize how brilliant you are and splash you all over these programs? You'd make them look a zillion times better than wormhole-faced Leonard."

She laughs out loud at his nerdy attempt to throw shade, then sends back a deflective response, too humble to accept his praise. Yet, privately, she agrees that it should have been her. And a warmth is spreading through her, maybe from the wine or maybe it's the feeling of having her talents recognized.

It's not long before their exchange devolves into discussion of Leonard's many weaknesses and character flaws, even his bad breath. Walton wraps up their messaging with TTYTMRW.

Returning to the news coverage, Aarya selects a clip from a national news program uploaded just twelve minutes prior.

A middle-aged man in an expensive suit with slightly orange skin tone sits behind a desk. A banner across the bottom of the screen declares in bold lettering, "Wyoming Reclaimed from Fringe Militia!"

"Good evening and welcome to our broadcast," the orange man says.

"We have all the latest coverage on the take-back of the Wyoming governance where leaders of a group known as the Triple Zs are now in custody, and where both the governor and state legislature have just today been reinstated.

"Caren Hartley is on the scene now in Cheyenne with the latest updates. Caren, what's the mood at the state capital today, and are there ongoing concerns of instability?"

"The mood can best be described as cautious optimism." A young woman with a perfectly coiffed blonde bob dons a parka with a fur-lined hood. "The people I spoke with today in the governor's office are of course relieved to have this chapter closed but acknowledge that it's a long road ahead to regaining the kind of stable government and social order that we once took for granted."

The journalists talk for several minutes about barricades in front of the state capital building, and the National Guard, and discuss other extremist group threats identified in the state. Aarya is struck by the seeming smallness of the capital building and how unassuming it all looks, even with the reinforcements and additional security.

Then it's back to the man in the suit at the desk.

"On the heels of the Wyoming incident, we are hearing about similar efforts in a number of other states, as well as renewed efforts taking place to overthrow the White House. As the growing national concern mounts, we are joined today by a panel of legal experts weighing in on the President's recent extension on the declaration of martial law, and how much longer we might expect to be living under a construct that was never meant to be in place for an extended period of time."

As the anchor introduces his panelists, Aarya hears the beeping of a keypad at the front door. She looks out the window to see Ravi's black BMW x9 parked in the drive.

"Pizza, glorious pizza!" Ravi exclaims, pushing through the front door with an elbow, balancing a reusable pizza box in his other hand.

"Let me help you with that," Aarya pushes Bumbu off her lap and runs to him. She brushes her lips on his cheek in greeting as he hands his prize to her. The box is hot and smells like it will be the best thing Aarya has eaten in a long time.

"You can't believe how hard it was finding a place that was open for business. I paid a mint for this. And if Melanie hadn't stashed an extra ReTake box in a closet at the office, my whole plan would have gone to rot."

Ravi brushes a hand through his expensive haircut and Aarya wonders at his ability to make things happen, no matter the price. His handsome looks and natural charm pave the way for so many things in his life. But, when those are not enough, his financial situation proves to be the best remedy for any challenge that comes his way. She often thinks he is too good-looking for her. He belongs with someone who is more focused on appearances with expensive manicures, decked in the latest in SynthiWear, and oozing the kind of polish and finesse that Aarya lacks.

She realizes she is wearing a baggy funnel neck sweater that covers her from chin to knees. She quickly pulls her hair loose from the bun on her head, shaking her dark, glossy locks free around her shoulders. Her hair is her one really glamorous feature, but she doesn't wear it down around her face very often.

"And how are things in the office?" she asks as he gets out the plates and reusable linen napkins.

"We are off the generator and back to full power, full Internet. Of course, clients are freaking out and we had a couple more today come in to liquidate their holdings. Probably going to buy gold bars or start their own private bank, lord knows," Ravi says. He works in a posh investment firm on Newport Beach.

"I'm just glad we can get back to work and try to return to normal. We're on the waitlist for a bigger generator so we can be better prepared for the next go-round." He reaches over to refill her wine glass, taking a sip for himself.

"This one is not bad." He usually turns up his nose at the organic wines and ethically sourced food items she prefers. "Too granola," he usually says, his refined palate seeking the best and richest items that his budget can afford. During recent events, she has had to lower her standards, taking any food available at the market. But her stockpile of good wines has been a saving grace in these dark times. She thinks about a tea towel she saw advertised the other day proclaiming, "The end of the world is not the time to start drinking bad wine!"

End of the world memes, products and themes have been circulating with increasing intensity. She doesn't mind the humorous ones, but some religious groups and extremists are taking the humor out of it.

"Any thoughts on when the next event might be hitting?" he asks, raising an eyebrow.

The scientific community recently launched a solar storm prediction alert system on par with severe weather alert capabilities. It's not hard to predict when a storm might hit based on observation of a solar flare or CME, since it's really just a matter of time. Even the severity of the storm can be predicted with relative accuracy based on the activity precipitating the storm. But until now, there hadn't been a need for an alert system on the national level, at least not for the general population. Aarya's colleagues at a sister program actually were part of the team leading the efforts and she celebrated with them when it was officially launched.

What's less predictable is the solar activity itself. The Sun, a magnetic variable star, has been especially variable lately. While she has always spent some amount of effort focused on the closest star to Earth, her work at the observatory has narrowed in recent months to now almost entirely focus on monitoring and measuring solar magnetic fields and all manner of solar activity. That's been the case for almost every astronomer she knows, and while it's not surprising, she sometimes worries what other observations and advancements have been pushed aside. At what cost does this shift in focus come?

She checks her SatPhone briefly to see if there are any new alerts from work before responding to his question: "Well nothing in the next twelve hours, at least." Ravi's shoulders noticeably relax, and he reaches for another sip of her wine. A twelve-hour window of stability is the best anyone can hope for these days, and between the slight wine buzz, and the celebratory mood Ravi brought in the door with the pizza, Aarya almost feels like her old self again.

"Leonard was interviewed on a Channel Five news segment tonight." She glances up and, seeing the look on his face, instantly regrets telling him. A discussion of her workplace with Ravi never puts her in a good mood. She braces herself for his usual tirade on how she needs to show more ambition.

"That mindless ape? Couldn't they find someone better than him?"

Aarya cringes, wishing he'd said it should have been her. She wishes Ravi understood just how good she is at her job.

"I have no idea how they decided on him. It's not like anyone asked me."

She pours herself another glass of wine and finds herself thinking about how Walton ran back to her desk and returned with her latte. Knowing she shouldn't, for the first time, she compares polished, handsome, accomplished Ravi to the awkward sweet-natured Walton. Ravi is considerate in the obvious, everything-for-appearances ways. That much is certain. But she wonders now how much he really gets her and how much he understands what she wants or needs.

"I actually submitted a paper today to the NOAA with a new hypothesis I am developing," she rushes to tell him.

But instead of praise, she is met by a disappointed frown.

"What?" she asks, hearing her voice come out like a timid mouse.

"We are in the greatest crisis of our lifetimes, and you are in a position to really do something." He looks at her like she is a child who needs to be told how to properly hold a steak knife.

"Thank you for that stunning realization. What's the problem, exactly?"

He reaches over to take her hand to soften the growing tension.

"I want you to think about how sharing your ideas on an open forum is going to undermine your ability to take credit for helping to solve this. I can only dream about being in the position you're in right now. And you are just throwing it away."

"Sharing my ideas with the scientific community in an effort to quite literally save the society we know, is not throwing anything away!" She has raised her voice now and tears are threatening at the back of her throat.

"How can you even say that, Ravi? This is all I have ever wanted. To be able to share my expertise with the world and do some bit of good with it. This is at the very core of me."

He blinks his eyes and sighs deeply.

"I just think you shouldn't forget yourself in all this selfless behavior. Please, for me, next time you have some new good information, before you post it openly for others to capitalize on, would you consider keeping it to yourself until you are ready to properly publish and get recognition?"

She's explained before to him how long it takes to get something published, the peer review process and editing, and everyone needing to lift their leg on it. She can't imagine sitting on the good news of a promising hypothesis while waiting out the administrative and laborious process for publishing. Most especially, she'd feel morally obligated to share findings that could save lives, or jobs or at least preserve the organic food supply chain.

To appease him and hopefully bring an end to this pointless fight she concedes, "Sure, I will think about that next time." She lays a hand on his arm affectionately. "You are so much more strategic about these things than I am." Stroking his ego is always a reliable play to end an argument. She reaches into the pizza box to signal the end of the conversation.

Yes, Ravi is strategic, she thinks, wiping some excess grease from the crust. But he is also cunning and selfish. She has already made up her mind. She will think about it next time. She will stop and pause and consider. But not in the way he intends. She will think about keeping information to herself. Not her scientific findings; her plans and feelings. In that moment, she realizes it would be best to withhold some information from Ravi, to avoid the feeling that has taken root inside her.

KLARA
Two Weeks Prior to Abduction

I walk up to the counter, thrown off by the glare from the plexiglass making it difficult to see the expression on the face of the uniformed man behind it.

"What can I do for you, miss?" His voice is matter of fact, not unkind, but professionally distant.

"My boyfriend, he's disappeared. I think something must have happened to him." As I say the words, they sound like someone else's story, someone else's voice. I sound hysterical even to my own ears.

I look down and see my hands are shaking.

"Ok. How long since you last saw or had contact with him?"

"Um, it was Friday night, around 8:00." I envision Ryen's face, just before he left. "We had a fight, and he left. I thought he was just going to blow off steam and drive around, but he never came home."

"Hmm," the man utters, the corner of his mouth drawing inward as if he's taking back a small portion of his interest.

"He's not answering his phone, none of our friends have heard from him either. I have this awful feeling." As I've been talking, a big, fat tear has slipped off my face and splattered onto the top of my boot. Apparently, I am crying. A lot.

I grab the hem of my sweatshirt and sloppily wipe at my face unable to feel embarrassment with the weight of the heavy emotions swirling within me.

"Please, what do I do? You have to help me find him!"

"He's an adult, and I take it he's not mentally disabled or anything of that sort?"

I shake my head.

"We can't take a report at this time, since it hasn't been forty-eight hours. It sounds like he just wants to be by himself, honestly."

"Can't we check with hospitals, or look at jail records?" I'm a little frantic.

"Yeah, those are good ideas," he concedes. "I just can't really do any of that for you at this stage. But you're welcome to make inquiries."

Frustration is starting to get the better of me. I need to focus. This all just feels so insane.

"Ok." I take a deep breath. "Do I just Google for hospitals nearby? Or how do people do this?"

"Yeah, here, let me have Mary get you a list." He softens a bit now.

"Tell ya what. While she's doing that, I'll check detox and jail intake. Write down his name and DOB here." He slides over a slip of paper and a pen.

"Does he have a record?"

"No, he really doesn't drink much, and I don't think he's ever been arrested."

"Any mental health problems, past suicide attempts?"

My mind is racing, thinking of his hunting guns and whether he seemed upset enough to hurt himself.

"Uh, no, nothing like that. He's a pretty stable guy. This is just so unlike him."

"Then I'm sure he'll turn up by tomorrow. Sometimes people just need a break. Especially us loners."

Within a half hour, I am back in my truck in the parking lot. I'm running the engine with the heat turned up. Heavy, gray clouds sit low in the sky and it's as if I can feel the weight of them on my shoulders. I'm no closer to answers, and I haven't even been able to file a report. I feel like I'm drowning. I'm useless and alone. This is such familiar territory for me, I don't even know why I'm finding it so hard. I've never really had someone there for me when things got hard. I guess maybe Ryen was the one exception to that, and now he's gone. I bury my head in my hands and let the reality of it all sink in. The sobs come in waves until I run out of tears.

I rummage around for my refillable water bottle and decide to check in with all of our friends again. With Ryen's parents having died before I ever met him, there's not much in the way of family. He doesn't even have siblings. I call my little brother Ben and tell him I'm going to drive around to Ryen's favorite hiking and hunting spots, just to make sure someone knows where I'll be. I can hear the sympathy in Ben's voice, but I make it a point to remain calm while I talk to him. It's always been my job to protect Ben, and I'm not going to burden him with my problems now.

As I pull out of the parking lot and head north, I hear Ryen's voice in my head.

"If you want to let the past control your future, that's your choice but I'm not doing it anymore. I need a fresh start. I need to get out of this isolating town."

"I can't leave Ben, you know that. He needs me. We've talked about this."

"You've talked. But you haven't listened. We've never had a real conversation about this, and honestly I don't think you can do that. You'll never allow yourself to live your own life, will you?" I saw tears glistening in his eyes.

As he reached the door, he turned back. "I need more than this, Klara."

It was the last time I saw him.

KLARA
Military Base, United States

"Wake up, Sleeping Beauty."

The hard voice has returned and is talking to me through the slot in the door for food trays.

I groan and roll over, trying to assess how long I have been here.

"Where am I? What is, this place?"

"That is on a 'need-to-know' basis, and you don't need to know."

I flip him off and roll over, so my back is to the slot.

"Suffice it to say you are safely in the custody of the U.S. Army, on a military base."

Then he adds, with a little honey in his voice, "If you cooperate, you might even have a nice time here."

"How long do you plan to hold me?"

"That's going to be up to you to some extent."

"I want to go home" I say to the wall. "Don't I have rights? I want an attorney."

"Maybe you have selective amnesia? We are still under martial law. You have the right to stop asking questions and start making yourself fucking useful."

I roll back over to face the sound of his voice.

"Helpful how exactly?" I narrow my eyes, a knot forming in my stomach. I know what can happen to young female prisoners. I'm not sure I will like his version of help.

"I'm so glad you asked. We have a few ideas. Maybe with your assistance, we can prevent the loss of more military lives and bring this war to an end."

"I am like the others then?"

I was worried when I heard the stories of women being rounded up. Women who suddenly held the power to damage electronics, cause power outages, erase computers. I had hoped my episode was unrelated to the outages in my area, I had hoped it wasn't my fault.

"We are pretty sure you are an Aurora, Klara."

"Are the others here, on this base?"

"Whoa there, slow your roll. Save your questions for another day. Today we need you to eat something and participate in a few tests. We need to know for sure what you can do. Then, if you play nice, I'll answer your questions," he says. "Some of them."

As if realizing that the thought of undergoing tests may sound unpleasant, he adds "Nothing invasive. Not terribly invasive." He adds emphasis on the word terribly, like it's a word he enjoys saying, and I get the sense he is more than a little sadistic. He is trying to put me at ease, but there is a malicious undertone that seems to run as naturally through him as a creek through the forest. Try though he might to suppress it, the darkness oozes out of him.

"Just some standard medical tests, the usual stuff to make sure you are healthy. And then we get to have a little fun."

"Fun?" I ask, a tremor sneaking into my voice.

"We'll spend the rest of the day on aptitude tests." He pauses, considering something. "It's time to see just how powerful you are, Klara."

Three hours later, having reluctantly eaten some oatmeal that could barely be considered gruel, and feeling a small measure of strength returning, I find myself seated in a laboratory, a two-way mirror on one side of the wall for unseen others to observe. Oddly, there is a metal looking fabric, almost like chain mail coating the walls and floor. It covers the door and even the mirror. I am reminded of the blanket that was thrown over me when I was abducted off the lake, and I'm unable to suppress a shudder at the memory.

I spend the next three hours undergoing medical testing. He didn't lie about most of it being pretty standard. There was a blood draw, urine sample, EKG, ECG, blood pressure, weight, height as well as vision and hearing.

But there was more intensive testing too, tests I would not consider standard or routine. There was a CT scan which I had never undergone before. And ultrasound on several parts of my body.

Now I am looking at a piece of computer equipment that looks like an oversized computer drive. There are various sensors and machines placed around the room. Some of them are beeping, others ticking. Three laptops are positioned on a table next to my chair.

He enters the room and reaches out his hand. "Sorry for not properly introducing myself before."

I lean forward and take his hand out of reflex. It is large and rough, the calloused hand of a man who knows his way around a tool bench. Despite the harsh way he spoke to me before, his face is now open and kind. He leans in, green eyes intensely inspecting my face, trying to read me.

"I'm Luke. But everyone calls me LT," he says, firmly gripping my hand.

"And you already know my name," I say, accusingly, dropping his hand like it's the handle of a hot skillet. I can tell he is trying to get in my good graces, and I plan to keep him at a safe distance.

He looks military. Everything about him is standard issue, like he is playing a role in a movie. From his shaved bald head, muscular build, the tattoo of tire tracks around his bicep, right down to his combat boots, he is a living, breathing GI Joe.

"So, what now?" I ask.

He takes a seat in the empty chair across from me.

"Let's start with something simple." He points to the computer equipment on the table. "This is a fairly small server tower for shared workspaces. You familiar with the concept?"

I nod.

"In theory, it should be rather easy for you to disable it with a brief electromagnetic pulse. Nothing outside the room should be affected," he says, pointing at the chain mail coating the room. "We have enclosed this space in a large Faraday cage. We just want to see what you can do to a single piece of equipment with a contained exercise. Can you control the power?"

I shake my head.

"From what we have learned in working with the others, you have the ability to decide when to use the power or not. Was it a conscious decision when it first happened?"

I shake my head again. I don't dare speak. I am certain my voice would tremble, and I can't show him any fear. But I am afraid. Terrified is more like it. I don't want this to be real. I don't want to repeat what happened before. I want to go home to Minnesota. The big lake, the one I call "Mother," will be nearly frozen over, with plate ice layering up around the shore outside my cabin. The tinkling sound it makes reminds me of wind chimes, lulling me to sleep on even the harshest and longest winter nights. I miss the familiar comforts of nature and home. Wherever this is, I don't belong here. I haven't seen daylight since I arrived and there is no fresh air. I would have no idea if I'm in the middle of a desert or on a snowcapped mountain. Everything in this building is concrete and sanitized and closed off from the outside world.

What happened before, I wasn't even conscious. I was dreaming. Dreaming of Ryen and my dad. It was both memory and fantasy. I was protecting myself in the dream. Fighting back against the hurtful awful things that happened in a way I've been too afraid to do in my real life.

In the dream, I was powerful. I caused damage. I brought forth energies from the universe and called upon them to do my bidding.

"It was more accidental?" he asks.

"Yes," I utter. "It wasn't real."

"It was very real, Klara, even if you weren't awake for it. You took out a sub-station. Power to the area wasn't restored for an entire week. From studying the others, we have learned that it can be controlled. Like flexing a muscle."

"How many others are there?" I ask, eager to find out more, to understand this strange isolating thing that has happened to me; to know I am not alone.

"Hold your horses. That's a conversation for another day. Let's focus," he says, pointing now to the equipment.

"I want to teach you how to channel this power, so you can control it. So it can be a decision next time."

"What is this power?"

I see a gleam in his green eyes. Something excited or even greedy.

"These solar storms that have been happening, the auroral activity extending farther from the poles than ever before?" he asks.

I nod my head, leaning in.

"Something has happened to other young women like yourself. Women from auroral zones all over the globe, all born on January 7, 2014."

"Same as me." A sisterhood of women bound together by an unusual happening simply for sharing their birthday.

"What is it, what happened to us?"

"We don't know. No one does. We can't understand, but somehow, you are able to emit electromagnetic pulses or EMPs. From what we can tell, it started to happen after the November storm."

The November 2038 solar storm was a major world event three months ago. They said it was the most powerful solar storm since 2003. It caused power outages on the east coast, grounding of flights and destruction of satellites. In some areas, satellite phone coverage was down for almost two full weeks. In a strained effort, some phone providers briefly started attempting to revive the old cellular network, but without any real success.

Ever since, there have been more and more solar storms with outages becoming more regular. Reliance on GPS has become spotty because storms regularly disrupt it.

"What's the result of these EMPs?" I ask.

"Well, it causes damage to electrical devices, computers, and stuff like that."

"Is that what the Black Dragon has been doing?"

Following the November storm, there were reports of electrical substation outages that they speculated were the result of targeted attacks, rather than mere solar storm fallout. They talked on the news about attacks from China on the infrastructure. A young woman, dubbed the Black Dragon, was blamed for outages and blackouts that had occurred in recent weeks. They flashed surveillance video images of her on the screen, her dark hair and pale skin striking in contrast. She didn't look malicious or evil to me. Just a young woman carrying her musical instrument case, going about her business. I wonder now if it was an accident for her too. Is she in a room like this undergoing tests like me? Instead of thinking of her as an enemy, it occurs to me that she is one of my birthday sisters too.

"Yes, we believe that Lin Zhao is behind the attacks. They call her the Black Dragon because of the region she's from. We have information that suggests she is being helped by Auroras from China and their allied countries."

"Auroras, is that what they are calling us?" It's a strange thing to say out loud, 'us.' To connect myself in one tiny word comprised of just two letters to this thing that is so big it feels like it is going to swallow me up. Somehow, I have become part of this, whether I want it or not.

"Yeah. And if you don't start helping me real fast here, you can kiss all of this goodbye. We are about to go into an all-out war. It could turn nuclear in the blink of an eye."

"How exactly am I going to help?"

He points again to the piece of equipment. I take a seat next to him.

"I'm listening."

"Have you ever meditated, Klara?"

"Like, focus on your breathing kind of stuff?" I ask.

"Yes, that is part of it. But going further, blocking out everything else and wiping your brain clean of all conscious thought."

He instructs me to close my eyes and take a series of slow, deep breaths. Then, walking me through a guided meditation, he tells me to visualize from my head down to my toes an emptying of each space within my body. When my breathing has reached a steady, normal rate and I'm feeling calm and weightless, he says, "I want you to find it, the power. It's there with you. Look around. Do you see a door, or a latch, a handle? Something you can open?"

Within the recesses of my mind, inside my conscious self, I search. There is something, I can feel it. The knob of a closet door. The kind that you pull out and the door panel splits down a seam on a hinge, folding back on itself. The handle a round, cheap piece of metal shaped like a concave disk. I slip my fingers over it in my mind's eye feeling the slight lip at the edges.

"Open the door, Klara."

I pull outward and instantly feel a searing heat. It's as if the door was holding back the flames of a roaring fire. Dry waves of heat fan my face, baking my flesh like a piece of meat. But it doesn't smell like food. It smells like melting plastic. Rancid, chemical burning smells waft up to me. I'm stunned out of my meditative state when I hear a popping sound and then a hiss like steam escaping from an overheated car radiator.

I open my eyes to see LT beaming with something akin to pride, but laced with a greediness, something dark and excited running in an undercurrent beneath it.

"You did it, Klara." He opens up the computer server and attaches an instrument to various points on it. "Totally fried!"

I feel that prickling heat again on my arms and chest. Looking down, I see the red markings streaking up my arms just like the night of the Northern Lights and the owl — the night of my dream when the power went out. Suddenly, I am extremely tired, barely able to keep my head up.

He is looking at the instruments on the table, taking down measurements and making pleased murmuring sounds. I am hardly able to hear him. It's as if I have been plunged underwater, deep down to the bottom of a pool. Sound is muffled and my senses are dulled.

"Please." I hear myself ask. "Please, I need to lie down. I'm so tired."

"Not yet," he snaps angrily. "These numbers are remarkable. We need to try a few more things. I am going to get a full report sent up the chain of command. You can rest later."

Out of the corner of my eye I can see a woman in military fatigues enter the room. She is wheeling in a cart with computer equipment on it, which she places squarely in front of us. She exits the room as silently as she entered.

LT grabs me roughly by the shoulders, shaking me from the depths of the pool of fatigue. I blink my eyes and try to focus on him.

"Did you open the door all the way, Klara?"

I shake my head, trying to find my voice. My tongue feels dry and sticky. I try to peel it off the roof of my mouth to say "Didn't." But it is pasted in place, fastened and unmovable.

"How far did you get it open?"

'D-didn't." I say again, the letters sticking in my mouth where saliva no longer provides the lubrication needed for words.

I try again, "Didn't. Get. It. Open."

I had attempted to pull on the knob, to pry the door loose in my mind. But the handle was hot, and the waves of hot air pressed back at me.

"My god!" LT exclaims, reverence in his voice. He is looking at me like a bobcat that just discovered a nest of fresh rattlesnake eggs.

"We've got to get the door open. Klara, you are the key to changing all of this."

MACK
Cambridge, Massachusetts

"A cellular mutation. That's all it could possibly be." Mack puts down the newspaper and reaches for the steaming mug of coffee in front of him. Georgia butters her toast, looking sleepy and disinterested as she pushes butter across then back over sections already well-coated. Still dark this time of day, the light above their kitchen table bathes her in a warm glow.

"What's that dear?" she asks.

The salt-and-pepper haired physician is already dressed in a crisp button-down shirt and khakis, his usual choice for a workday. He sets down his reading glasses and leans in. "This young girl from China, the one who supposedly emits an electromagnetic pulse, an EMP. It's so far-fetched. I figured it for a hoax. But now that they are saying there are others like her…"

Georgia, still in her robe and slippers at the breakfast nook yawns and blinks. She is a young fifty-five, trying to adjust to early retirement and finding it more difficult than she had imagined. Her short dark hair grazes her chin, with wiry pieces of gray poking rebelliously out from the otherwise smooth fringe.

Mack loves the way his wife's hair looks in the morning. She keeps things tidy and orderly. Later before going out of the house, she will smooth herself out and tame those troublesome hairs. But for these private moments, he enjoys the intimacy of seeing her like this, in a way she would never let the outside world see.

Gazing out the window, taking in the shadows painted across the snowy landscape by the early light, she speaks in the direction of the window, a crumb of toast in the corner of her mouth. "I heard about the one in Northern Minnesota. Awful how they abducted her. Is that legal now?"

"They are reporting another was discovered late yesterday." He rubs thoughtfully at the gray hairs in his cropped beard, as if to wipe them away. "I have to wonder how they are able to locate these women. It makes you think that all the military science and experiments we assume are happening must be real. They can do so many things we are not remotely aware of."

Mack and Georgia have been having discussions like this more frequently. When they started hearing on the news about spikes in Auroral activity occurring in the weak Aurora zones and even farther south, it was a curiosity they found amusing. But in recent weeks, the reporting has taken on more of an alarmist tone. And then, the special powers were uncovered.

"The biological effects on these women must be absolutely crippling," Mack theorizes.

There is a reason he focuses on this aspect of the situation. In his work over the years helping patients suffering from electromagnetic hypersensitivity syndrome, the medical community has never recognized EHS as a legitimate medical diagnosis. Some head-in-the-sand physicians still record it as microwave syndrome, using a now outdated term. Relegated to the realm of psychosomatic conditions, patients reporting vertigo, tingling and illness from a nearby cell tower or neighborhood radio station have been shuffled off to receive therapy. To fix the problem in their minds, since modern science has deemed it nothing more than a mental condition.

He repeats his earlier theory, "It's got to be a cellular mutation. Similar to how a cancer develops, the cellular variation could explain not only how these women channel or emit EMPs, but also how their bodies can tolerate the effects on respiration, hematology and immune response."

Tuning out most of the medical jargon, Georgia asks, "You think women across the globe are developing a cancer that somehow causes these bursts of energy?"

He sees that she is fully awake now. He thinks back to her recent bout with breast cancer, remembering the terror they both felt at the initial diagnosis. He shudders as the image of the young woman's face enters his mind, imagining the whirl of emotions and physical sensations she must be experiencing. He tries to envision her face, how surprised she must have been as military personnel plucked her from a previously normal life.

The look on Georgia's face reminds him she asked a question.

He says, "Not exactly a cancer in the sense of tumors, at least not that I can surmise. But in the way cells divide irregularly and begin to take on unexpected properties. I have to think they are already examining specimens from the poor woman as we speak. It must be connected to these recent solar storms. It could explain disruptions in how some patients' cells replicate. Could be enough to cause changes in their DNA sequence."

"Would it be... terminal?" Georgia asks.

"I can't see how it wouldn't," Mack replies, using a double negative to avoid the unsavory answer head-on.

He adds, "I think the only way they survive is if a treatment can be rapidly developed. But who would even be thinking of that, when they probably aren't being viewed as cancer patients?"

The scrape of a snowplow blade catches their attention, cutting off the conversation. The outside world slices into their dark reverie, bringing them back to their own lives.

KLARA
Military Base, United States

I am escorted out of the building for the first time since I arrived. So far, all I know for sure is that we're on a military base. I must still be in the United States because I have not heard any of the guards or staff speaking another language besides English. The signage on doors and corridors is printed in English. Now that I'm outside of the facility, I am awash in details of my surroundings. The fresh air is a welcome relief to the staleness inside that oppressive place. This is probably the longest span of time I have gone without being outdoors. Without the connection to weather and air and daylight, I've felt like a part of me was wilting, stagnant and sick. Something inside me stirs a little now, remembering how alive I feel being exposed to the great big sky above.

There is no snow on the ground, and I'm sufficiently warm in the flak jacket they provided. I am guessing it is in the high 50s or low 60s. I can feel humidity in the air and green treetops line the perimeter in the distance. I conclude that we are somewhere in the southeastern part of the U.S. I have a vague recollection that there are a number of large military bases in that part of the country, definitely more than in my Midwestern region. But while I feel freer and more alive being outside in the elements, it's anything but a bright or refreshing day. The cloud cover is a concrete ceiling, hanging low and flat. Instead of being fluffy or blanketing, these clouds sit heavy as if conspiring with this place to hold me hostage and prevent my spirits from soaring high. I feel an inch shorter, compressed down by the weight of that gray expanse.

The guard who came to get me makes no attempt at eye contact, his face an unreadable mask of duty. I follow him through exterior gates, along corridors of heavy fencing topped with menacing loops of razor wire. Aside from a few distant chirps of birds in those far-off trees, it's a quiet day. No airplanes overhead, no sounds of traffic in the distance. It's so quiet I can hear the new military-grade boots on my feet creak with each step. For some reason, just the left boot creaks, so it's a footfall then a creak, a half-time step of rhythm. I think about my well-worn Danner hiking boots sitting in the front closet at home and wish for their familiar comfort. Where these boots are heavy and stiff, like bricks on my feet, the Danners are light as slippers, an extension of my feet rather than something other or separate. I think I understand now why my cousins used to joke about military-grade in a derogatory tone.

The guard leads me into a gated yard where a berm of dirt is built up against the long end of the fencing. Lined in front of the dirt are sections of plywood, interspersed with numbered cards. I follow over to a section of folding plastic tables beneath a wooden shade ramada. Another man in military fatigues is setting out gear and rearranging various items on the table.

He snaps the clasps of a hard plastic case closed and I flinch involuntarily at the harshness of the sound. Just as I get close enough to see what's on the table, the guard tips his head in a slight nod, signaling to me this is our destination.

"Mornin' Jonah," he barks in the direction of the man. This other man at the table places the case on the ground and looks up at me, scanning my face, as if he is looking for clues to solve a riddle only he knows about.

"I'll take it from here, thanks," he replies, his tone less serious than the guard. There's a warm confidence in his voice and I'm struck by how young he looks and how different his demeanor is from everyone else here.

He smiles at me revealing dimples that surely have gotten him out of trouble and into beds. He runs a hand through wavy, sandy brown hair that looks out of place against the military fatigues.

"It's nice to finally meet you, Klara." He reaches out a hand, offering me a firm but brief handshake. He's intently looking at me and the eye contact is a little unnerving after the arms-length distance I've been treated to by most others here.

"Finally?" I ask, a challenge in my voice.

"You're already becoming something of a legend around here. News of your abilities has spread excitement through the ranks. Quite frankly, you are giving us all the kind of hope we have needed to keep our efforts going."

I bristle at the implication that I am some savior or holy grail. That I'm somehow responsible for other people I have never met and know nothing about. The mantle of imposed obligation causes a shudder to go through me. I wonder about the 'us' in his statement and the history behind their efforts to locate me.

"What's all this?" I ask.

"Ever fired a gun?" He spreads his hands out to display the arrangement of handguns, long guns, ammunition and protective gear.

I roll my eyes.

"I'll take that as a yes," he says, eyes twinkling as if this is some sort of game. "Guess we've got a head start over the others with this part of your training."

At the mention of others, my mind calls back to what LT said, and I hungrily scan the windows of the building, as if a simple glint of light off the windows might silently pass me information. I wonder if they are in their cells now, secluded and guarded in their own version of captivity. I wonder how many there are and how long they have been here.

"These other Auroras, they don't have experience with guns?" I probe, hoping for any crumb of information he might inadvertently drop.

"Let's talk about your experience with guns, Klara," he deflects. "Hunting or self-defense?"

"Both."

"Great, what do you shoot?"

Currently, I have six different guns at home. I have strong feelings about gun safety and worry about how we are going to ever stop the mass shootings. But guns have been a part of my life since childhood. And guns have kept me safe, kept me alive, on more than one occasion. I am not ready to tell Jonah about that part of my past.

"For daily carry, it's my Ruger American, 9 mil. I have a hard time carrying the Glock 21. That I keep at home and use mostly for target practice. I'm not fond of hunting myself. But I was raised in a hunting community, where duck hunting is part of the culture, so I'm comfortable with most shotguns. I've shot rifles at the range now and again, but definitely less familiar there."

"Great. That will be a good start. Let's get your eyes and ears and see where your baseline is."

After about an hour of shooting weapons that fall squarely in my comfort zone and impressing Jonah with my marksmanship and quick reloading abilities, he suggests we advance to some new guns.

Pulling off the ear protection headphones, I adjust the safety glasses that are digging into my temples. Jonah leads me over to a table farther down the ramada. It's lined with semi-automatic shotguns and fully automatic rifles.

"You may never have to fire any of these in the field, but I want you to have a comfort level handling these guns since they'll be used by those who accompany you."

He picks up a sleek shotgun and hands it to me. "Benelli M5," he states, holding it out like a rare artifact.

The gun feels expensive in my hands.

"The Marines rely on this beauty so it's something you could definitely come across."

Next, he walks me through the short-barreled M5 carbine used by SWAT operations. The automatic assault rifle is shorter and lighter, and I can see why it makes sense for close range situations like those he describes.

He carefully explains how a gas-operated gun works, and what to watch out for in terms of fouling, improper cycling and debris accumulation.

We spend another hour together as he guides me through adjustments and handling as I shoot at various distances, trying a different grip and getting comfortable reloading.

When we are finished, I feel accomplished and capable.

Jonah turns to me and says, "I think that was a good first day." He is loading the weapons and gear into a secure box on the back of a side-by-side ATV.

"What's the end game here?" I ask, hoping that the time we have spent working together built enough rapport to get information out of him.

"End game?" he asks.

"Yeah, what's the point of all this? All the problems here on U.S. soil aren't going to change regardless of this tension with China."

"Tension? This is so much bigger than you realize."

"Well enlighten me. Don't I deserve that much?"

"It's classified."

"Put yourself in my shoes. Wouldn't you want to know what it was all about?"

He softens at this idea, seeming to realize the difficult situation I face.

"Ride with me over to the armory," he offers. "I'll fill you in on what I can, but don't press me on things I can't."

"Deal," I say, hopping up onto the passenger seat.

We ride bumpily along the crushed gravel path, and I revel at the sense of freedom that washes over me. It's the first time I haven't felt like a prisoner since they abducted me off that icy lake.

"Can you tell me where we are?" I ask him, holding onto the side rail with one hand and brushing hair off my face with the other.

"I assume we're in the Carolinas, maybe Fort Liberty?" I offer.

"I can't say yes or no. But you seem to have a good sense of these things," he says, impressed at my deduction.

"What's the plan? Go to China and take out key targets, bring down the power grid somewhere as a tit-for-tat to get back at what they've done here?"

"It's much more strategic than that. Don't you understand that if we take out the power in the right place at the right time, we can cause significant financial harm and destabilize an entire region?"

We are pulling into the armory now and he drives us right up to a work bench.

I help him transfer the weapons onto the cleaning station and consider the strategic importance of causing such damage.

"We are at war," he explains. "This is not the kind of war we've ever experienced before. This isn't drone attacks, missiles, and sending troops. This is taking out your enemy at the knees and setting them back a century kind of warfare."

"China has taken out key substations to disrupt power from being distributed out to customers. And that doesn't just mean residential customers like you who want to watch TV or keep your frozen foods from spoiling. This impacts commerce and industry and robs us of revenue."

"But I thought the outages were caused by the solar storm activity."

"Some were, sure, but that's mostly a cover story because the government doesn't want people freaking out. A lot of this is China and their allies. It's because they discovered their Auroras first and realized the opportunity they had."

"Have you ever heard people talk about how the entire electrical grid in the U.S. could fail by domino effect?"

I nod my head. I've heard it vaguely mentioned in news stories.

"Well to put it simply, the whole system truly is a grid. It's all interconnected. So, when one major node is taken out, the load redistributes and causes a strain elsewhere. If 'elsewhere' is another place being attacked at just the same time, now you have a situation where remaining nodes are overloaded enough to cause them to fail by virtue of the strain on the system. And it's a cascading effect."

"And it's kill or be killed?" I ask. "They are coming for us and we're going to retaliate? That sounds like mutual assured destruction to me. How is this different from a nuclear war in that sense?"

"You're not too far off the mark, actually," he says, eyebrows raised.

"Don't look so surprised," I say. "I'm not some hillbilly from 'up on the range' who makes maple syrup all winter."

"They told me you had a high I.Q., but I guess I didn't realize how much real-world knowledge you had. I admit, I'm impressed," he raises his hands in a gesture of surrender.

I tilt my head slightly in his direction, accepting the praise like a cat leaning into an outstretched hand.

"You're right. This is very much like nuclear warfare. The hope isn't to continue escalating until every involved country's grid is decimated and their G.D.P. has tanked. We just need to strike back a handful of times, enough to show that we have our own Aurora weaponry and we're not afraid to use it. Flex our muscles," he says.

Relief seeps into my bones and I feel something unclench deep inside me. There's a reasonable end game, I realize. And it's near-term. Before we know it, we can all go back to what life used to be like. And maybe I can go home.

"That makes a lot of sense." I look into his dark brown eyes, seeing him differently now, appreciating the risk he is taking in sharing all this with me.

"I know LT isn't the warmest and cuddliest," he offers. "But that guy is a tactical genius."

"You've known him a while then?" I ask.

"About four years now. He's like a father to me at this point. If you listen to him, let him guide you through all of this, he will keep you safe. And he will bring this to an end."

I consider this. Following the momentary relief at understanding where things are headed, I feel a heaviness returning. Once again, just like so many other times in my life, it falls to me to do the unthinkable, to take on an enormous task. To set aside my wants and needs. Already I know somewhere deep inside me that I'll be a good little soldier. I'll do what needs doing and I'll hope that this time is the last time.

He scans my face for a moment. As if he is reading my mind, he ventures, "Speaking of fathers, I know about yours." His voice drops significantly now, almost to a whisper. I can tell he is trying to be sensitive to my story. I wince at the mention of my dad. It's no secret what happened, but somehow this information feels too intimate, too personal to be known by someone I just met today.

He looks me square in the eye before continuing. "It's not the same at all, but my dad ran off when I was twelve. The bastard had a mid-life crisis and decided that parenting was too much responsibility for him."

We finish locking up the guns, and he motions for me to climb back onto the side-by-side. As we roll out through the garage doors, I find myself squinting in the bright sun.

"Looks like those clouds finally cleared away," he says, smiling over at me.

We are off again. With my hair whipping wildly around my face, I make no efforts to hold it back this time. I close my eyes and feel all the sensations. The heat on my face, the wind, the grit of sand being kicked up as the vehicle lurches onward. While the vehicle bumps me along and back toward the main building, I let the memories bubble up inside of me. For once, I don't try to push them down.

Suddenly, I'm eight years old again as we jostle across the grounds. Jonah is silent as if he knows what he has stirred up from my past. And we drive straight into it, turn a corner right up alongside that horrific night. I reach out my hand and I can almost touch the memory. I can hear it.

I can hear the gasping. The awful sound of sucking air.

That's exactly how I began to relate the story to the social worker all those years ago, describing the sounds that pulled me from sleep.

She had wiry, gray hairs escaping around her face from the loose bun she must have quickly attempted in her rush to meet me. Her eyes were kind but guarded. She had a look of someone who has heard too many tragedies for anything to be shocking or new.

I go back to the house in my mind, as my eight-year-old voice tells her all of this.

Half asleep I knew that sound. I would know that sound today.

I am eight years old again. I am there.

I hear the gasping. The awful sound of sucking air. It's the sound of my mother unable to breathe. I can hear it from rooms away. Terrible recognition sets in. I sit up in my bed and clench the sheets around me. "Please don't kill her," I whisper.

Ben is still asleep. He is splayed across his bed, covers thrown off. He wears a frown on his face, like he is fending off a bad dream, or maybe just smells something he doesn't like. He is wearing his favorite robot print pajamas even though he is too big for them. The pant legs graze above his ankles in a high-water look.

I can picture my father, hands clasped around her neck, squeezing the last breath out of her. I count, holding my own breath, wondering if this time will be the last time.

Time passes. Here is where the memory, the story of that night is blurry. The edges of the night's events go soft and hazy in my mind.

But when a loud bang startles me, I jump. Finding myself in the doorway of my parents' room, I'm met with a scene that's too much for my mind to comprehend.

"No!" I beg to an unseen god. I take in the gore. Dad is covered in blood; the bedding and mattress are soaked in it. I take in the sight of my mother standing at the foot of the bed.

Moments later, when my mom is shouldering a rifle, I've curled into a ball, not wanting to look.

"Do it, Hannah," My father glares at her, wheezing with mouth agape, his chin held high in defiance.

My mother squeezes the trigger.

His head flies backward into the wooden headboard. It lands at an awkward angle, his chin unnaturally resting against his chest.

The ghost of smoke appears, swirling in the space between his body and my mother. I smell pennies and retch on the carpet near my feet.

PENNY
Hobart, Tasmania

"Don't you think you've had enough?"

Nick leans over the bar, muscled forearms against a worn-smooth surface. A neon light behind the bar casts a bluish glow against his hair. The soft light illuminates dull fingerprints and smudges in the brass beer taps.

A loud crack interrupts the chorus of a song playing on the vintage jukebox. Groans and jeers float over from the pool table in the back.

"It's been a long week." Penny pushes her glass forward, insistent.

"Penny for your thoughts?" He repeats the joke that would irk her if it came from anyone else. His eyebrow raised, it comes off with disarming intimacy. Genuinely interested in her thoughts, he's an old-school bartender who may as well be a local therapist, for all the listening he does.

But her thoughts are her own tonight. It happened fourteen years ago on this day, and she is terrified of the images that will haunt her dreams tonight. Whiskey oblivion needs to knock all conscious thought from her mind, and it needs to happen fast.

"Come on. Just a dribble." She waggles the glass at him, ice tinkling.

"Ah honey, are you coming onto me?" a voice saunters up behind her. Through the leather of her moto jacket, she can feel the unwelcome weight of a meaty paw settle on her shoulder.

"This idiot must be new to town," she slurs to Nick without turning around.

"You're not exactly her type, buddy."

She feels an arm snaking her shoulders like a boa constrictor carefully assessing its opportunity. With a possessive grip, the man leans into her. His toad-like face mere inches from hers emits enough tequila vapors she can almost taste the Cuervo.

In a moment of vivid sobriety, her reality becomes sharp. Her senses are heightened. A woman's piercing laugh from the other end of the bar signals to the room she wants to be noticed. A faint whirring sound from the wine fridge under the bar vibrates up to her. Time slows. Something unfamiliar and frightening rages up. Searing heat courses through her.

Nick's face takes on a sudden look of surprise. Just as quickly as reality around her sharpened in, everything outside of her fades. Her heartbeat is a thundering pack of horses.

Red curls flying, she whips around and pivots off her barstool, turning away from the grabbing hands. With the force of a freight train, her two hands press into his barrel chest thrusting forward. As his neck whiplashes forward, his eyes widen in horror. Penny feels a powerful burst of something unknowable surge from her. Before she knows it, the man's pudgy shape T-bones into the pool table. Sparks fountain off the overhanging light fixture as it explodes, just before a curtain of total darkness descends.

Amid sounds of confusion and surprise from bar patrons, a crackling sound fizzles out. Penny is loosely aware of the fact that she has landed on the floor. A scalding sensation is the last thing she remembers before consciousness slips away.

When she awakes, she has no way to know if it's been hours or days since she landed on that bar floor.

Distant sounds and a familiar sanitized smell tell Penny she is in the place of her nightmares. Back in a hospital bed where she once spent more than a month of her life in a medically induced coma. Fourteen years ago, she was small and frail and nearly died twice in this building.

The terror of recognition swells up within her, taking her breath away. Gasping, she launches upright in the darkened room, feeling her left arm catch against something. Handcuffed to a hospital bed, she realizes there are sensors hooked up to various parts of her body. She has to get out of here before anyone knows she is awake.

Pulling up the bedding, she threads her right hand alongside the plastic bed rail, feeling for a joint or connection point. Coming up empty, she decides on another approach. Removing chest sensors and ripping out an IV, she climbs up over her left arm and onto the floor. Pulling all her bodyweight from the opposite side of the bed, she hears a crack. Something gives way.

Sensors are beeping all around her as the bed groans. The door flies open and a middle-aged woman in scrubs rushes in.

"Don't make me sedate you," the nurse says, advancing.

Penny's backside is entirely exposed as the hospital gown gapes open behind her. The nurse puts two arms under her armpits and hoists her up.

"They'll do a lot worse to you than I can if you try that again." She is helping Penny back onto the bed, nimbly settling the sheets and reattaching sensors.

Defeated and out of breath, Penny resigns herself to lay back. Handcuffed, there is no way for her to fight out of this. She will need to wait for another opportunity and come up with a more solid plan.

"How long have I been in here?" she asks woman.

"A little over twenty-four hours. You made a real mess over at Nick's Hideaway. The electrical is totally destroyed all the way to the nearest transformer station. And Gerald had to get ten stitches, not to mention two broken ribs and a punctured lung."

"Is that why I'm handcuffed?" Penny asks.

"I'd imagine so. But you can ask the officer when he comes by in the morning. He's been waiting 'til you were alert enough to talk."

Calming a bit under tending from such gentle hands, Penny tries to put her thoughts together on what happened and why.

"It's all over the news, you know. Not just here and the mainland, it's on international media. They are saying some electrical phenomenon occurred."

Penny's thoughts race with memories of another time she was in this same hospital. So many years ago, the news stories featured a different horrific event.

"Did anyone die?" There's a tremor in her voice and she doesn't look up when asking.

"No. And TBH, Gerald had it coming." She smirks at Penny, glancing up with a mischievous twinkling in her eyes, tucking the blankets around her.

"He hasn't been here long, but he acts like he owns the place. Mainlanders…" she says, shaking her head.

"You know, if it wasn't in your file, I wouldn't have known the burn was so bad." She pauses, and there is a sadness in her voice when she continues. "Your tattoo is beautiful, and I'm surprised how much of the scarring it covers. Whoever did it for you has got real talent." Penny feels exposed, realizing this nurse and whoever else has provided care would have not only seen the tattoo of a magnificent phoenix covering most of her back and shoulders, but also would have seen the details of her past, written in scalding detail within her file.

"I'm sorry hon, but they are definitely going to have a lot of questions for you in the morning. Best to get some sleep now." And just like that, pink scrubs shuffle out of the room, an arm deftly turning out the light while exiting.

Penny knows sleep won't come easy, wondering about the event at the bar and anxious with thoughts of what awaits her in the morning. She's terrified of another media frenzy and the inevitable questions she can't answer.

In her sleep, she hears a banging sound. The heel of hand against a glass window. Someone is trying to get in. No, they're trying to escape. Crackling flames and searing heat well up around her. Penny lurches upright swatting at the sheets to put out the flames.

Drenched in sweat, she takes in her surroundings. There's no fire. Just early dawn trickling through the hospital window. It feels like she was sleeping only a few minutes, but somehow, it's already morning.

Reaching for the call button, she hears the door creak open. A bald police officer pushes a wheelchair through the door, smiling up at her. "Time to break you out of this place, Miss Penny."

"Why? Where are we going?" She eyes him suspiciously as he reaches over to unlock the handcuff and re-fasten it to the chair.

"I'll explain all that on the way, but don't worry, you're not in any real trouble. You're more of a celebrity. Now do you want to help yourself into this chariot, or shall I get an orderly to come assist?" He offers brightly.

She shakes her head. Carefully holding the back of her gown closed, she climbs out of the bed and into the chair.

"You'll probably be wantin' a good cup of java first thing. Want me to make a stop at Island Espresso along the way?"

Penny beams up at him and says "Careful, I may fall in love with you. Coffee is a direct path to my heart." The automatic doors swish open as the chuckling pair wheel off into the morning light, the officer moving a little more quickly than necessary as he piles her into the unmarked vehicle.

As they drive off, she notices the blue and yellow checkered markings on a police cruiser heading in the opposite direction.

LIN
Military Base, United States

She is awakened by the sound of a metal tray of food, the same sound at the same time of day, for weeks. She eases herself into a seated position, contemplating the bland food and the circumstances of her life. She had been calm and even a little excited when she realized she was connected to the Auroral activity, that something inside of her was special and linked to something bigger.

But now that she has been in custody for so long, she worries if she will ever get her freedom back. She can't understand the purpose of it all. Despite having a newfound power, she feels utterly powerless. She has demanded an explanation every day for weeks now and gotten no response, except in some cases a sneering laugh.

"Let's go, you know the drill," a voice barks at her from behind the heavy door. She has finished her meal and is dressed and ready. Reluctantly, she waits to be led through the secure passageways and into the training room where she will be asked to use her power on various pieces of equipment and in escalating ways that exhaust her.

Yet today, as her footfalls echo along the corridor and she turns left toward the room, the guard leads her to the right. He stops at a window with a counter and a uniformed guard seated behind it.

"Leaving the premises today?" he asks the man standing at her side who is now activating his smart glasses to sign onto the tablet on the counter.

"Yeah, time for a little field trip." Reaching around, he grabs Lin's wrists and places them firmly in handcuffs. He is not rough or overly aggressive, but he handles her in an authoritative manner.

As alarms are disabled and locks disengage, she is led through exterior doors and through a fenced entryway. It's the first time she has seen fresh air and real daylight since she was kidnapped in Los Angeles. Her pulse quickens as her proximity to freedom dawns on her. Quickly her mind starts turning over the logistics of how or whether she could get away. How fast and how far could she run before he would catch her, before others would come?

The guard tightens his grip on her arm and swiftly leads her into the back of a bland service van. He politely but firmly places her into a seat and locks the seatbelt into place. He closes the doors and sits opposite her, then bangs on the grate separating them from the driver.

"Move out," he orders as the engine turns over and the vehicle lurches.

"Are you taking me to an attorney, or to the embassy?" she asks the guard, furtively trying to catch his gaze.

He doesn't bother to look at her and snorts in reply, as if her question is so ridiculous it isn't worth answering.

After half an hour of driving, the vehicle pulls down a gravel road and stops short amid heavy cover of trees and bushes.

The guard points in a direction over Lin's shoulder. "Over there" he says. "About eight hundred meters in that direction, there's an electrical substation. Can you sense it? Do you have a good read on it?"

"Why would I tell you?" she spits out the words.

Lin sees his hand moving toward her an instant before she feels the sting of the slap. She has been handled roughly and not treated with any dignity during this captivity, but this is the first time someone has purposefully and physically harmed her. The shock of it throws her off guard.

"Answer the goddammed question!"

"Yes," she replies.

"I want you to channel all of your strength into that substation."

Lin ponders her options, thinking about all that has happened and what could happen next.

"I know my rights. I want to speak to an attorney."

He openly laughs in her face, replying, "Hasn't anyone told you? Your rights are a thing of the past. The world is a very different place now. You're going to do what I say or I'm going to have a lot of fun rearranging the features of your face. You understand?"

The side of her face is still hot and stinging from the slap moments ago. Feeling hopeless and humiliated, Lin lowers her gaze and enters the secret area within her mind where her power is stored.

She opens the doorway and unleashes her ability. She channels a small amount of energy into the substation. Off in the distance, smoke streams up like a lazy finger above the treetops.

The guard is looking down at a device in his hands.

"Nice try, weak-Lin. But I know you can do far more than that."

She's already feeling a touch of fatigue from the limited damage she has caused. Her reflexes are dulled just enough that she doesn't see his arm move this time as he cuffs her across the side of her face where it is already swollen and red.

Her eyes fill with tears and there is a ringing in her ear.

"You are going to hit that substation with everything you have. Or so help me God, I'm going to hit you with everything I've got. Do you think this is a request? You think I have time for these games?"

His eyes glimmer with malice as he grasps her wrists tightly and pulls her inches from his face. He's so close she can smell his aftershave. She can see the flecks of gold in the bright green irises of his eyes.

"Do it," he commands. "Do it now, with everything you've got."

Lin lowers her chin and levels him with her gaze. She considers her options. In an instant, she clenches her fists and lets out the most visceral, guttural scream that pierces through the air in the van. She channels with everything she can muster, screaming and contorting her body. The windows on the van shatter, the tires explode. Roughly eight hundred meters away, a series of loud booms and crackling can be heard.

Lin falls limp in her seat, secure in place only by the seatbelt.

She faintly hears the guard ordering a new vehicle to arrive "pronto" to get them out of here as she slips into a deep and dark state of unconsciousness.

KLARA
Military Base, United States

Morning light trickles into my cell, painting long and delicate fingers across the blanket. I've been awake for a while, but with nothing to occupy my time, I haven't bothered to get up. I long for the comfort and weight of that quilt back home on my bed. I wonder when I will return to my old life.

I hear a scuffle of noise and look over to the door where I see Jonah's face through the glass. The latch on the door grinds open and he is standing before me with a goofy grin.

"Good morning sunshine!"

Skepticism raises the alarm, curling its fingers around my mind in a protective grasp.

"Good morning?" I reply, a question rather than a greeting.

"I pulled a few strings; you are getting your wish."

"And what is that, exactly?"

"A sisters' reunion is planned for you today. A real kumbaya and all that."

Excitement, nerves and fear well up in me, a delicious and terrifying brew of emotions. The others? There is so much to learn, to understand. So many unanswered questions that I have turned over in my head during the solitude and waiting. In this moment, I feel something tugging at me, almost physically pulling me toward the unmet strangers. These women are somehow knitted to my story, woven into the unknown future before me. And I too am a piece of their puzzle, a clue to the unraveling of their stories.

Jonah leaves me so I can briefly freshen up and dress. My hands shake as I tie the laces on my boots and rake them through tangles in my hair. Moments later he is guiding me through corridors and gaining entry through locked doors. As we enter the room, I recognize it as the laboratory where I first tested my powers with LT. I follow Jonah through the doorway and look around to see the faces of three women, three sets of eyes trained on me. Hope, fear, aggression, it's all here. A kaleidoscope of emotion swirls through this room.

"Okay, introductions," Jonah curtly calls out as I take a seat.

Leaning against the far wall, aggression looks over at me, arms crossed protectively. A mane of flaming red hair coils past her shoulders and her eyes are narrowed.

"Over here is Penny," he points. "Penny is from Tasmania. She can be a real devil." He laughs at his own terrible joke "A Tasmanian devil, get it?"

No one laughs. Not even a smile. Penny's eyes are shooting daggers at Jonah.

"Ouch, tough crowd," he says, throwing up his hands in exasperation. "Well, moving on. This is Luz."

Seated in the chair where he has pointed is fear. The dark eyes of a petite woman are slightly obscured by the curtain of dark hair hanging down to her chin, angled asymmetrically and cropped short on the other side.

"Lucia, who goes by Luz, is from Bariloche in Argentina. Spanish is her primary tongue, but as you'll find, English is not a problem."

Next, he turns his gaze over to the one who embodies hope, the only positive emotion in the room, and she is sitting cross-legged on the floor. She looks up at me with all the openness of a flower after morning rain. Her white-blond hair is pulled back in a partial braid that encircles her face, the rest of it hangs loosely down her back. Her pale skin is accentuated by the bright blue pools of lapis that are her eyes.

"Aino is from Finland. Most of her classes at the University of Helsinki are in English, so you all should have no trouble."

"And this is Klara," he points to me.

"She is from the U.S., a state in the north called Minnesota."

I smile weakly and awkwardly at the others. If they are aggression, fear and hope, what am I? What do they see when they look at me? Am I just a jumbled and confusing patchwork of emotions on the outside, like I feel inside?

"Right, well we didn't bring you all together today to make friendship bracelets and find common interests. Let's get down to business." The others move to chairs, and we are all seated now, with Jonah closing the circle.

I want to know everything about these women. Yet I know that Jonah's remarks about us bonding were nothing more than his attempt at humor and we are clearly here for some other purpose. I look around at the electrical equipment similar to what LT has used in my practice sessions.

"Let's start with something that should be pretty simple." He wheels over the cart with equipment and sensors on it. "I want each of you to channel together at the same time. We will gauge the combined strength of your powers to see how they can be multiplied."

The only one who looks eager is Jonah. The others must feel the same way I do about this, unwilling participants plucked from their lives, never choosing to have this new power.

"Okay, ready? I will count you down. Three, two, one!"

I reach inward and open the door, now familiar with the process and able to decide when to use it, or how much. But this time, something unusual happens. There are other doors, other knobs and handles. Each one has a different color and feel. I search briefly for one that might be familiar. I take a guess and grasp.

Before I can even turn the handle of the door, a force like a strong wind or a wave of energy blasts into me and I'm thrown off my chair. I land hard on my hip, then shoulder, arms splayed out. I lie there on the floor in darkness, disoriented and immobile. Finally, after what seems like an eternity, I open my eyes to look up and see the group standing over me in a circle.

"What- what happened?" I ask, stunned and afraid.

"You tell us," Jonah says, a concerned skepticism playing at his eyes.

"I- uh, I'm not exactly sure." I say.

"There were other doors to open this time. I wasn't sure which one was mine. Did I choose the wrong one?"

Luz and Aino are each on other sides of me, hoisting under my armpits to get me back into my chair.

"Okay, let's just unpack this." Jonah interrupts, his hands gesturing for us to slow down. When we are all seated, he asks, "What did you see, Klara?"

"Well, I sensed other doors and handles to open. I got confused and wasn't sure which one was mine."

"What about you, Penny?" he turns to face her. "What did you see?"

"Nothing." She admits, coolly, accusingly.

"Ok, Luz, Aino, what about you?"

They both shake their heads, and Luz says, "It wasn't there."

"Klara, how many doors did you find? All four?"

I think back and almost inadvertently open the pathway. I catch myself and just try to remember without actually going anywhere. "More than that. It was a corridor of doors. I didn't pay attention, but maybe ten?"

"This is unexpected." He runs a hand through the waves of his hair, pushing it off his face. He starts pacing, looking around at us, then at the ceiling, trying to piece the information together.

After a few moments, a look of resolve comes over him.

"I need you all to try again," he says. "Klara, maybe just start out on the floor in case something happens. We don't need you crashing to the ground again."

I sigh and look down at my hands, not sure how to feel, but slightly afraid of this new terrain. I nod my head, and he helps me brace my back against the wall in as comfortable a position as I can find. The others move the chairs to my side of the room, encircling me once again. Jonah remains by my side on the floor, the weight and warmth of his hand a comfort on my shoulder.

"Everyone ready?" he looks around to nods of agreement. He counts us down again and this time as I close my eyes, I'm more prepared for what I find. I slow my breathing and focus my concentration. Without the surprise I felt the first time, I find myself intrigued. It's much more expansive than I realized. I explore the hallway of doors within my mind, seeing doors on my left and my right. Behind me the hallway turns left, and up ahead it comes to a "T" veering off in both directions. I touch nothing, making no move to open any of the doors. I explore for a while, counting as many as I can, attempting to make a mental map.

When I open my eyes, all four of them are looking intently at me.

"What happened?" Aino asks first.

"There were hallways with doors lining up in all directions. I counted at least seventy-eight but was worried I might get lost, so I stopped."

"More than seventy-eight?" Jonah whispers, his eyes roaming left and right as he processes the information.

"Do you think each door is another Aurora?" Luz asks, her deep brown eyes querying him like a child with intense curiosity.

"Yes, most certainly," he responds nodding vigorously.

"But why can she access all of 'em?" Penny asks and I note her Tasmanian accent for the first time.

"I'm not sure. Maybe something about bringing you together has unlocked the corridor?" He looks around, chewing his bottom lip as he thinks.

"Did any of you do anything?" he asks.

"No," Luz responds, the others shaking their heads. "It was the same as always, but no door this time," she adds.

He steps out of the room to consult with other personnel behind the two-way mirror. Then, for the next twenty or thirty minutes, he removes the other women, one at a time, asking me to try again and see what I find. We continue like this until only Aino remains, with the same result. He then interchanges Aino for Luz, then Penny. Always, it's the same corridor with no less than eighty doors regardless of which of them is in the room with me during the exercise.

He asks more questions about the colors, shape, lighting, and other details. Then he goes so far as to ask me to draw a map as best I can recall of what I saw. In the end, he concludes that, stunningly, I can access the collective power of all the Auroras, so long as just one of them is nearby.

We are back in a circle again as he finalizes some notes. "I have to tell LT so he can report this up immediately." His face is flushed and bright with the excitement of the discovery. He pauses meaningfully before asking "Do you understand what this means, Klara?"

I shake my head. "I guess… not really," I admit.

"She can stop 'er," Penny interjects. "She can stop the Black Dragon. None of us can access our power if she's by us. Same's true for the one in China."

Understanding dawns on the other two as a grin spreads broadly across Jonah's face, revealing those gorgeous, dangerous dimples.

As the idea begins to sink in, I'm not sure if I should feel special that I'm the one, for whatever reason, who can do this. Or if I should feel burdened once again by responsibility I didn't ask for. Why can't I sit on the sidelines and just be normal? But a part of me is excited. We can end this sooner than anticipated. We can go back to our lives.

This is the most hopeful I have felt since that helicopter landed.

***

The next morning is crisp and cool. A slight hoar frost on the grass is glistening and beginning to melt in the warmth of the sun. My boots crunch across the field as I join Aino and Luz under the ramada.

Penny has a large rifle shouldered and is making easy work of a target. Jonah stands by her side, providing pointers and redirection, but honestly she is a natural. I look over at Aino, her whitish hair pulled cutely back into pigtail buns low on her neck. I'm struck by the contrast of her sweet and childlike face paired with the severity of the goggles and ear protection. Looking over at Luz, I see dark circles under her eyes and wonder how much sleep she has been getting. I haven't been able to sleep much myself. The exercises and practice leave me constantly drained beyond anything I ever previously experienced. It's a miserable combination of exhaustion and insomnia, and I wonder if it shows on me as much as on Luz's face.

In the quiet pause after Penny lands a final round in the target and begins to reload, I hear a strange almost tinny whine off in the distance. Aino hears it too and removes her ear covering to listen more closely.

Just over the treetops, one then two, then more, maybe twenty drones appear flying in a formation and heading in our direction.

"Oh shit!" Jonah sees them too. He places a hand on Penny's shoulder, pointing to the sky. Aino's eyes widen in shock, and she looks to Jonah. "What is this? What should we do?" Her delicate voice is pinched and constrained.

"Take cover!" he commands, pulling Penny to the ground under a table and motioning to the rest of us to join. He deftly pulls a handgun from his waist, taking aim at the lead drone as the swarm grows louder and narrows in on our location.

He fires a round and misses, then fires again and clips the wing of a single drone. It falters, then maintains formation, as the pack moves closer. Aino and I are making our way toward the table to join Penny when I hear a cry from just behind us.

Luz is on the ground; her right hand is pressed against something sticking out from her right thigh. I see her eyes growing sleepy and then close. Mere seconds later, a drone dives to her position, landing on her briefly, then departing.

I'm still frozen between the table and Luz when the entire swarm makes a 180 and veers back over the treetops. Jonah gets off another round, taking out the rear drone and causing it to tumble and cascade through the branches of a large pine tree at the periphery of the clearing.

"What the hell was that?" Penny demands, cautiously crawling on hands and knees, coming out into the open. Jonah, Aino and I are already hovering over Luz, inspecting her and attempting to rouse her.

"She's out cold. Breathing and pulse are stable; she's just been sedated." Jonah runs a hand over her thigh where a dart-like object still protrudes from her. Aino reaches to remove it, and he interrupts her. "Don't. I don't want this contaminated. Go back inside and tell Darrell to bring evidence bags in a hurry. And ask him to call for medical."

As Aino springs up from her position like a jungle cat, eager to take some action, I am able to get a better look at Luz. There is a small cut on her neck, just above the collar of her jacket, and a few drops of blood are making a lazy trickle as they pool in the dip of her clavicle.

"Penny, go locate the downed drone, but don't touch it or move it." Jonah instructs, as he retrieves a first aid kit from the table. He is already wiping the blood off Luz's neck when Darrell and several large men come running out.

"Drone swarm from the northwest edge of the clearing," Jonah explains. "Luz has been sedated, and I'm not sure but I think maybe a specimen was retrieved from her."

Darrell eyes the scene, ready to perform whatever duty is required.

"Penny is over at the edge of the clearing; you can see her red hair just near that dead tree." He points, then instructs "Go help her bag the drone, then get everyone back inside the facility. You two," he waves at the burly men "I need your help transporting her into the medical bay."

Aino and I are ushered along by Jonah as Luz is lifted and then carried. As we reach the entrance of the facility, I look back and see Penny also making a return with the guard who has bagged the drone.

I wait in my cell for what seems like hours, wondering what is going on, and worried about Luz. But I know it probably hasn't been as long as it feels, judging by the height of the sun in the sky. I didn't have the stomach to eat my lunch, and I jump at every noise.

I've turned the details over in my head a million times and ways. Someone knows we are here. Someone wanted a specimen. Are we in danger?

After I've just about given up on learning any news today, I hear a scrape at the door and Jonah appears.

"What's going on?" I demand, launching up from my bed.

"Calm down," he replies. "Everything is okay. Let's regroup in the training room with the others. Luz is awake and she is fine. She's resting now."

We make our way to the room as I pepper Jonah with more questions. His only response is "just wait" wanting to fill us all in at the same time.

Once we are seated in a circle, all eyes are on Jonah, but he doesn't get a chance to say a word before Penny says "It had the U.S. Army logo on it."

"What?" I tilt my head in her direction. "Why would the Army spy on and steal a specimen from another U.S. military operation? That doesn't make any sense." I shake my head and look to Jonah for answers.

But instead of a look of surprise or shock, he looks unphased.

Aino juts out her chin and asks the question we are all thinking "Aren't we part of a U.S. government program here?"

"Well, no, not exactly." Jonah says. "Our Project is privately funded. We are a commercial enterprise." Seeing the look of shock and concern on our faces, he goes on.

"We are doing this on behalf of the government. It's our job to figure out how to protect the U.S. from these attacks and ultimately to restore order. I know none of you volunteered for this, but we are the good guys here, I promise. The federal government works with private firms on a contract basis all the time. This is very standard."

"What about all that stuff with rights being suspended and martial law?" I ask. "Doesn't that only apply to the actual military?" Jonah and I have been chummy for a while now, sharing snippets of our life stories and opening up to one another. I felt like I was starting to respect him in a lot of ways, and I thought he saw me as an equal. Now I begin to turn all of that over in my mind, looking for clues or red flags. He looks hurt that I would challenge him like this in front of the others.

"Listen," he says. "You've got to understand that the world is not what it once was. Society is not the same. Things are not as black and white as they used to be. This is a private conscription for the sake of national security. It's all been approved by Congress as a new wartime mechanism to propel our efforts in a conflict like this. You won't be here forever; this is just a short assignment and then you'll be released to your former lives. Heck, you'll be heroes when it's all said and done. Featured on the news and all that. You'll be famous. And maybe, because of you, life can go back to something like normal."

Penny is shaking her head, eyes narrowed. She hasn't bought into this "good guy" speech.

"How do we know we aren't the 'bad guys' here? What proof can you give us?" she asks him.

Jonah looks around at each of us, getting a sense that this is not going over as well as he had thought. He backpedals, "Yeah, that's fair. Let me see what I can share that will help with your concerns." He stands. "Just give me a little time. I've got to go up the ranks."

Somewhat calmed by this response, or at least having no other demands, Penny nods her head and takes a seat.

"Let's skip the rest of today's exercises, okay?" Jonah suggests. "I think you all deserve a break from the hard work. Besides, the whole thing with Luz this morning was upsetting. Take some down time today and we'll regroup first thing in the morning."

As I make my way back to my cell, I think about the difference between my role here and that of a prisoner. Is my position all that different from thousands of men who were drafted into service to protect their country? It feels different, and I think the word prisoner has felt like a more apt label in recent weeks. But now I am not so sure. The lines are blurry. I think about Jonah's words. Nothing is black and white.

MACK

Cambridge, Massachusetts

Mack reaches down and scratches the fur behind the ear of his golden retriever, Lincoln. The dog sighs contentedly and curls up on the rug at his feet. As Mack rests his slippered feet on the ottoman, he selects a clip of the news coverage he's looking for. When the screen comes on, the volume is up too high, causing the dog to jump and look around with worry. "Sorry Link," he says, adjusting down to a more acceptable level, patting the dog consolingly.

"This is breaking news coverage we are bringing you exclusively this morning." The female reporter sits behind a desk wearing a chartreuse green jumpsuit and speaking with the kind of excitement that always feels inappropriate from news anchors when they report bad news but are clearly happy to have the scoop. Large, silver earrings dangle in the locks of her brown hair, bobbing slightly as she continues.

"Sections of Washington D.C. are without power today, as thousands of residents and numerous local businesses are waiting to hear when service can be restored. This comes after the latest attack on a power company substation near Foggy Bottom. And most concerning, we are hearing off-the-record reports from power company representatives who say they are being asked by government officials to keep quiet about this attack because it is believed to have been carried out by China." She pauses for effect, looking over at her colleague.

"That's right Andrea," the male newscaster's flamboyant pompadour wags with each exaggerated word. "And residents of the area are concerned about the potential for follow up attacks during an already weakened state. There is a fear this may threaten national security. We spoke today with Gary Landsome, owner of a restaurant supply store in the area who says a power company representative confidentially told him this was carried out by the Chinese Aurora they are calling the 'Black Dragon.' Apparently, they have her on surveillance cameras in an area nearby these latest attacks."

Mack pauses the coverage and searches on his tablet for "Black Dragon Aurora." Scanning through, he sees several pages of results. Setting down the tablet, he makes his way into the kitchen for another cup of coffee. He is going to need it. He plans to read every word of information he can find on the topic.

PENNY
Military Base, United States

Jonah holds a tablet, pressing pause after playing the news clip about an outage in Washington, D.C.

"I know it's unconfirmed and off-the-record at this point. But I wanted to share it while I work to get you more proof." He looks at each of them earnestly, concern evident in the furrow of his brows.

Aino's hand is on her mouth, fingers worrying at her lips. Her eyes cast about as she tries to absorb the information. Then Penny asks, "What's the big deal though really? Lack of power, so what? We are all dealing with that regularly from the solar storms anyway. Why should we care?"

"Right, yeah. I can see why you would ask that, I guess." Jonah says. "It's a lot more than a single outage. You heard them say they're worried about follow-up attacks, right?"

Penny tilts her head in a conceding gesture but doesn't respond.

"The reason they are so concerned is that if other substations in the area are also attacked before this one comes back online, then we will start to see grid failures in the area. That can start to impact surrounding regions outside of D.C. If China is being strategic, they'll next attack stations that are taking on the overflow from this outage. It becomes a domino effect. Once that happens, we aren't talking outages for several days and maybe even weeks. We could be out for months. And during that time, think what else they can do while we are in the dark, without power, just sitting ducks."

Penny sighs but still doesn't respond to him.

"There's more, if you want to see it." He looks at Luz who nods her head vigorously.

When the clip restarts, the anchor with the big hairdo is speaking again. "Andrea, what can people do, to be prepared? And, more importantly, what is being done to prevent future attacks?"

"Great questions! First, authorities are cautioning not to panic. They say it's wise to revisit your emergency plan and ensure provisions are kept on hand just as you've all been doing since the start of the solar storms. But in terms of prevention, this is where it gets really interesting. They say that any young women exhibiting signs of this Aurora power should come forward. They are looking for Auroras who might be able to thwart the Black Dragon and help restore order."

"Interesting, thank you Andrea. We will continue to follow up with the latest developments on this story."

Jonah pauses the video again and takes a seat in a chair, crossing his legs.

"You see?" he asks. "They're looking for more volunteers like all of you who are going to help us. With more Auroras, and just a little more time, we can tip the scales and prevent one of the most significant terrorist events in your lifetime. This is on the order of 9/11. If any of you had known about that in advance, and had some ability to stop it, wouldn't you have done so?"

The women cast glances at one another. Penny is the first to respond. "First of all, we weren't even alive for 9/11, so we couldn'ta prevented it." She rolls her eyes. "And besides, no one has lost their life in all of this." She is eyeing him with skepticism, challenging what he has just said.

"Yet." Jonah adds. "Not yet. But I guarantee you that is where this is all headed."

LIN
Military Base, United States

The air in the room is stale. Lin is eager for the exercises to end so she can leave and go back to her cell. She doesn't necessarily mind using her power, even when it leaves her drained and useless. But what she can't take any longer is being forced to do what they want, without understanding the bigger picture. She also can't imagine they'll just release her when this is all over. She's a prisoner here, and when they're done with her, that's when she'll be in the greatest danger.

Every day, she has scanned about on the walk to the room, looking for patterns, data, details she can use later. She has made up her mind. She will escape.

The frightening thought is wondering how she will prove, once she gets away, that she was compelled to act. Will she ever convince the authorities that she was held against her will and didn't choose to cause the damage? She has decided that when she is ready to make her escape, she will need to provoke a beating. She will need visible proof, on her body, of what has been done to her in this place.

And what is this place anyway?

The female guard she has been working with today is professional and detached. She has a kind face, but clearly knows better than to offer any kindness or human connection to Lin. Still, it's been more pleasant with her than the bald guy who seems intent upon crushing every bit of human dignity she has left.

While the guard has been finalizing tallies and entries into the record, Lin carefully observes the lanyard that attaches the key card to her belt. Without being obvious, she looks to see how the clasp wraps around the belt, and how the thin piece of woven fabric loops through the opening on the card itself.

As the woman gathers up the equipment, Lin realizes with relief that it is almost time to return to her cell. She has avoided any punishment today, and she is not overly exhausted from the exercises and testing. It's been a better day than most.

Just when she has made this assessment, the door to the room swings open and there he is: the guard from the van, the bald-headed asshole. His chest is puffed out more than usual and he takes up so much space in the room that it suddenly feels half the size. He marches over to the table where they are seated.

Lifting her chin in defiance, she looks up to make eye contact. Even in spite of what he did before, what he made her do, Lin refuses to be cowed or show fear. And on top of that, she has made it a point to memorize every detail about him. She will give the most perfect description of him to be sure that without a doubt; he will be identified and caught.

"How goes it?" he asks, a casual friendliness in his voice that belies the malice in those familiar green eyes.

The female guard who has been working with Lin looks up and responds in a measured but positive tone. "As we had hoped, the recent solar storms have strengthened her ability."

"Well, isn't that just peaches and cream?" he mews at them both. Lin is never sure what sort of reaction he wants from her. She stares back at him.

"But. There is a new problem," the woman reports. She hands him a tablet displaying various trend lines and calibrations. Pointing to a dip in the graph she says, "Around 10:00 a.m., for a period of about thirty minutes, Lin wasn't able to access the power source."

"Looks like you're withholding on us again are you Weak-Lin?"

Lin remains cold and impassive, staring at his boots, refusing to interact with him on any level.

Instead, the woman speaks for her. "No, I don't think so this time." She places the tablet on the table and crosses her ankle over a knee. "Lin was already in the room, just building up the power and the meter had started to register, when very suddenly it dropped to zero. We haven't seen that kind of activity before."

He glances at Lin, carefully assessing her face, weighing the veracity of this information, attempting to discern some deception or scheme in all of this.

Responding to the woman rather than him, Lin says, "I was kicked out. I couldn't get back in."

The woman then adds, "Thirty minutes later, she was back in and stronger than ever. I'm fairly certain it was a temporary block of some kind. Almost like interference. Could Project Faraday or some other team be running tests that would cause this?"

The bald-headed man ponders this information, thoughtfully rubbing his thumb along the edge of a tattoo on his left arm. His calloused thumb traces along the lines of tire tracks peeking out from under his T-shirt sleeve. Lin clocks this information too, taking care to make note of the measurements of the tattoo, the details.

A dark cloud rolls over his face as he chews on the question.

"I'm not sure, but I have an idea. Keep going at it for now and I'll return in a bit to check in."

He turns on his heel and marches out the door, leaving Lin with an uneasy sense of foreboding, knowing he will return, and knowing the safety of her cell is not coming so quickly after all.

KLARA
Military Base, United States

"It's clear the recent storms are enhancing your power." Jonah looks up at me, setting aside the tablet. Taking a big bite of his sandwich, he looks over and raises his eyebrows chewing vigorously.

"I guess that's good news, right?" I ask, signaling with my hand to the corner of my mouth where he has mayonnaise on his face.

He wipes his mouth with a napkin and finishes chewing. "One hundred percent. This is good news. More power means we have a stronger weapon in this fight."

I bristle at the word weapon. Jonah and I have had more of these private sessions lately, and I've learned a lot about his childhood. His dad wasn't dead, and his mom was still around, but the similarities in our circumstances have given us a lot to discuss. I envy that closeness with his mother. I only got to see my mom on rare occasions when Uncle Jeff made the drive to the Twin Cities and took us along for a visit to the women's correctional facility in Shakopee. Every time I saw her, it seemed she had aged a decade, and I feared she wouldn't be around whenever my next visit might happen.

I look over at Jonah's deep brown eyes and feel a warmness as I think about the connection forming between us. Maybe I'm imagining it, but I sense that he is feeling it too.

"What will you do when this is all over?" I ask him. "Will you be reassigned to some other facility or how does that work?"

"Why, you think I would want to come visit you up on 'The Range' and freeze my ass off ice fishing or something?" He teases me, poking at my leg in a playful way.

"I just mean is this 'it' for you? Following LT around to the next assignment? Or is there more in the books for you?"

He smiles, giving me the megawatt dimples, and says, "This project is my magnum opus. The AI technology to detect your presence, and the presence of others like you was groundbreaking. I was the only one who could figure out how to train the models to learn to eliminate interference in the surrounding environment and extend the range enough to allow for a broad sweeping coverage area."

He is glowing with pride, and I can tell it must have been a pretty big deal when he figured it out.

"I can write my own ticket after all of this. When this project is completed, I'll take my patented technology to the highest bidder. The applicability of it can be far reaching."

It's my turn to raise my eyebrows.

"Then you'll be handsome and rich?" I tease, returning his earlier poke on the leg with more meaning.

"Yes, I suppose I'll be one of the most eligible bachelors when all is said and done." He takes another bite of the sandwich and nearly chokes as the door flies open with a clang.

The heavy metal door smacks against the doorstop. LT marches in, red-faced, a finger pointed accusingly at Jonah. "Wipe that stupid grin off your face!" Jonah jumps up from his chair, still swallowing, coughing, and looking guilty at having been caught fraternizing.

"Have you been running tests today?" LT asks.

"Yeah," Jonah responds, wiping his off crumbs from his pant legs. "Why, what gives? You sure are in a foul mood."

"We agreed that Mondays and Wednesdays were off limits. You said you would abide by the schedule." LT is still pointing his finger at Jonah, nearly stabbing him in the chest with it now.

"Sure, I have been sticking to that for our extensive program. But with the recent solar storms, I thought we'd just pop in for a few minutes today and get some updated readings. We're not doing full scale testing or exercises. Just a quick calibration. We're already done anyway. Just having a little lunch before heading out."

LT gives me a quick look before turning back to Jonah.

"Well, follow the goddamn schedule next time, even if there are storms. You're really messing up some other projects here."

"Okay, sorry." Jonah offers up, clearly wounded at being chastised by his mentor. "I didn't think it would be a big deal. It won't happen again." He's shrunken down, almost wilted as he folds into himself.

As LT reaches for the door, he turns back as if remembering something.

"What time did you run the tests?"

Jonah looks down at the tablet, running his finger along some of the data on the screen. "Uh, looks like we started at 10:10 a.m. and were finished around 10:35."

At that, LT turns and leaves.

I look at Jonah, who looks as confused as I feel.

LIN
Military Base, United States

Lin is starting to hope the man won't return today after all. The woman is getting restless. Lin hasn't had lunch, and her stomach is audibly growling as she listens for sounds in the hall outside.

She hears a shuffling, then a beep of the keycard reader. The door flings open and there he is again.

"Glad to see you finally made it back, LT." The woman addresses him by name.

"Yeah well, the Project Faraday team is over there fucking around and not following the schedule. I had to get all the way over to them and back. Sorry if I interrupted your plans for a pedicure or whatever girly shit you had planned."

Listening to the way he addresses the guard, Lin is struck by the fact that he hasn't been singling her out for mistreatment after all; this is how he treats everyone. He's an equal-opportunity-asshole.

"Don't be a dick," the woman replies, still measured in her tone, but clearly unwilling to take any crap from him.

"Is that it? Are we done here?" she asks.

"Yeah, fine, but, next time that happens, message me ASAP. We need all the units to follow orders and stay on schedule."

"Got it." She turns to gather her things as the man exits the room. His departure has returned some air back to the room, and back to Lin's lungs. Not surprisingly, the woman is now visibly relaxed.

And now, Lin thinks, she has another crucial piece of information to tuck away. She has an identity, a name. LT with the bald head, bright green eyes, and a tattoo on his left arm.

She returns to her cell that afternoon, exhausted and hungry, but also pleasantly satisfied. She thinks back on all the details, the key card, LT, the woman. She stores everything in her memory and sends a silent thank you to her grandmother. Wherever she is, she must be watching over Lin. "Thank you, Grandmother. I will make you proud. And I will claim my birthright in all of this somehow."

AARYA
Los Angeles, California

A cat paw lazily stretches forth, claws spreading wide as if attempting to grab at the slice of sunlight streaking through the window. The paw clenches, then stretches, lazily grasping at the air. It's a meditative, rhythmic movement, accomplishing nothing.

"Bumbu, have you been in the catnip again?"

Aarya inspects his pupils, wiping a patch of drool from his furry chin. She cautiously attempts to stroke his belly only to be swatted and nipped.

Rejected, she leaves the cat in his stupor on the rug and tiptoes over to the kitchen island to see if Walton has responded yet. Picking up her tablet, she sighs in disappointment seeing that no message has come through.

Tapping her fingers on the counter, she looks around the space. She takes a moment to rearrange a beautiful bouquet of flowers, removing a few dead stems. She carefully pours out the cloudy water and refills the vase with clean, fresh water. She doesn't dare look at the note Ravi sent with the flowers. She doesn't want to think about their fight again. The flowers were a thoughtful apology, and his taste is always impeccable.

She needs to do something to get her mind off the waiting. News from the latest solar storm assessment should have come in by now, and she can't understand what could be causing the delay.

To get it off her to-do list, she decides to place a video call to her parents, hoping secretly they won't answer.

"Hi Aarya love!" her mom yells into the device.

Dang. She is on the hook now.

"Hi Mom, glad I caught you." She masks her disappointment, casually brushing her hand over the messy tangle of her hair. Seeing herself on screen, she sees a woman who has gotten too little sleep over the past week. She sees someone who is frustrated, distracted, working too hard, and failing to take care of herself. She wishes she had thought ahead to clean herself up a little.

"Let me get your father, he is out in the garden of course. He was just saying how we never hear from you anymore, now that you are saving the world and all this."

The screen wobbles and bounces along with her mother as a sliding glass door whooshes open.

"Harish, wipe that mud off and come inside. Your only daughter is calling to talk."

Aarya fidgets with the tag of paper on her tea bag, waiting for her parents to collect themselves.

Her father's kind face appears, his hands busy wiping on a rag.

"What a treat to have a visit from you!" he crows happily at her over her mother's head.

"How is Ravi, how is work? How are people surviving lately in California?" He drills her with questions, not stopping to let her answer.

"Slow down and give the girl a moment," her mom chides him. They both chuckle in a good-natured way. Aarya is struck how they never seem to get upset with each other. Could she ever talk to Ravi like that without him bristling at her?

"Ravi is good, you know just busy lately opening the new branch."

"Oh, yes up in Long Beach, the swanky office. We are so proud of you both, soon to take over the world. Such successful children."

"And your T&S project, love, how is that one going?" her mother asks sweetly.

"It's S&T, ma. Homeland Security S&T." All three of them chuckle at her mother's usual way of bungling up acronyms and technical terms. If it wasn't so endearing, it would be annoying.

"We saw on the news that you were going to get us up to at least sixteen hours of advance notice now. They said that people will know before going to bed if they can sleep soundly, you know. It's a big deal."

It's been weeks now that they have been reviewing data and providing recommendations to the latest project for the Homeland Security Science & Technology Directorate. Solar storm forecasting has vastly improved since the start of the Solar Surge, sometimes referred to as only "the Surge." In the beginning, they were lucky to have a mere five or six hours' advance notice. But the recent advancements in techniques and tools has given them up to twelve hours advance notice for the past few months.

"Yes, we actually are thinking we can get it up to twenty-four hours' notice by the end of next month."

"Wow!" her parents sing the word together, looking at each other in awe.

"Aarya you really are saving the world!"

Seeing her parents' enthusiasm gives her a new perspective on everything. She has been so focused on the daily grind, she hasn't taken stock of just how meaningful the work really is.

"You know, we also are finding ways to pinpoint the location where ground currents will have an impact. On top of the longer notice period, we can give a warning to the power grid locations likely to be impacted. It means resources can be shifted to the most vulnerable spots and harden our defenses."

She's not sure if her parents understand all of that, though lately the average person has gotten significantly schooled in the science of current events, so it wouldn't be out of the question. They give her a knowing, appreciative look, but she can't be sure if they are faking.

"Now you can start to plan the wedding then, right?" her mom asks, eagerness in her smile.

"Uh, yeah, we aren't sure yet. You know, things are still really unstable. Travel is still out of the question, for who-knows-how-long."

Her father gives a disapproving grunt.

Backpedaling as fast as she can, Aarya adds, "Of course we have been talking about maybe in the next six months."

Actually, Ravi has been pushing for sooner. Aarya has valid reasons for delaying, amid the current crisis. And, besides, she doesn't want to rush something when she is in the middle of the most significant work of her career.

It was the cause of their recent fight. They seem to have many causes over which to fight lately.

"We just are so pleased you found a good Indian boy to marry who supports your career." Aarya is not fooled by the last portion of her statement about Ravi supporting her work. She knows this is very much secondary to the fact that Ravi is from a good Indian family. Both sets of parents were thrilled they got together and have been pushing lately for them to set a date.

Switching topics, she asks about her father's beloved dahlia's, herb garden, and other horticultural projects. They talk for a bit about how many people are growing their own vegetables now given the supply chain concerns, and her parents elaborate on their plans for a community garden supported by local seniors.

Out of the corner of her eye, she sees a flash of fur a moment too late. Bumbu pounces on the tablet, then scampers across the kitchen island.

"Naughty cat!" her mom exclaims. "He is still up to his old tricks?"

"He still acts like a kitten sometimes." Aarya smiles, thinking of how he launched himself at her father those years ago when her parents visited.

She remembers the day. They had been sitting in the living room of her old apartment, just finishing some tea.

"Crazy little monster," her dad said after Bumbu jumped ferociously at him. "Where did he come from? You never seemed like a cat person."

Aarya picked him up, stroking his back. "Craig got him for my birthday."

She looked up to see her mom's lips pursed in a tight line, a reaction to mention of her then-boyfriend.

Ignoring the tension in the room, little baby Bumbu had curled into Aarya's lap and started to purr. She found it remarkable he could so quickly switch gears, but his presence calmed her.

Back on that day, her father had asked "I thought you two had broken it off?"

He wasn't wrong. They had. Well, Craig had.

It was awful, and Aarya's cheeks grow hot just thinking of it these years later.

Sitting in her living room at that time she had explained, "He didn't want me to be lonely. I guess you could say Bumbu was a parting gift." She gave a wry smile, but inside she felt rotten. His kindness in gifting her a cat had only made the whole thing worse, made her feel like more of a selfish coward.

"You and Greg are really over then?" her mother had leaned in slightly, seeking confirmation of what she had hoped since the start of their relationship.

"Craig. His name is Craig," Aarya had insisted, those years ago.

It was definitely over. Some bridges could never be rebuilt after you let them burn to the ground while you looked away from the awful scene pretending you weren't the one who lit the match.

She hated herself even with her parents' approving glances.

Craig had slammed the door that day when he left. He had hated her for making him decide for the both of them.

"I can't live in limbo like this forever, Aarya." His words were seared into her memory.

"You say you're not ready. But will you ever be?" His eyes accused her of something she was terrified to admit. He had asked her to move in with him. He wanted to share his life with her.

Aarya always had an excuse, needing more time. The truth was, she wanted nothing more than to take the next step. She loved him in ways she had never thought possible, and she knew he saw in her all the things she liked most about herself. He was someone who would love the way her wrinkles looked around her eyes as she got older. And he had been so patient with her.

"I'm tired of being your dirty little secret. I have given you time to tell your parents how you want to live your life."

There had been several phone calls that left her in tears. "He's not Indian," her mother had said, almost as if somehow Aarya wasn't aware of this fact.

"I don't understand," her father said.

They couldn't understand. They wouldn't.

"If you meet him, you'll see it differently," she pleaded with them.

"Out of the question!" her father had boomed.

When Craig came over that night, she had to tell him that he wasn't going to meet her parents after all.

"Give them time to come around."

But time hadn't changed anything, except to drag out the inevitable and to build a resentment between them.

"I see how hard it is for you to choose." His eyes were kind. "I think, actually, it's impossible." His voice broke. He cast his eyes downward, his shoulders dropping in defeat.

"But I can't live like this, and I won't put you through it any longer."

He met her gaze then, something between them connecting, one last time, something breaking. Understanding and acknowledgment passed silently between them.

She wished she had been stronger, had fought for him.

She still wonders about him, sometimes. Did he find a woman who had no trouble choosing him, proudly introducing him to family and friends? Was there someone who appreciated the details he put into everything? Did he ever think about her?

Back in her kitchen, in present day, she looks now at her parents' faces on the screen, loving them both, still desperately wanting their approval. Yet, she finds herself stuck on the fact that their love and approval come at the cost of her being untrue to herself. Is their love conditioned on her living the life they have chosen for her?

Just then an alert notifies her of a message from work. Adrenaline courses through her body. She is honestly relieved to have an excuse to end this call.

"Sorry, I've got to wrap up," she tells them. "Duty calls. I just got an update from work."

"Maybe we will hear about it on the news later?" her mom tilts her head to the side in a conspiratorial way.

"I hope so." Aarya gets ready to sign off.

"We love you so dearly," her dad says. Her mom blows a kiss at the screen and then the call is over.

Sure, they love her. It should feel good. But it feels insidious too. She wonders for the first time in her life if the cost is too high.

MACK
Cambridge, Massachusetts

"How is it possible that the coffee here has actually gotten worse?" Mack sets two paper cups of steaming brown liquid onto the table in front of him. Lynelle looks up from her phone and brushes back a lock of smooth, silver hair that has escaped her stylish chignon.

"I think it must be an experiment of some kind," she reaches over for the cup, with a mirthful tug at the corner of her mouth. "Testing the impact of long-term exposure to abuse on taste receptors?"

They share a chuckle as Mack winces after sipping his drink.

"You still owe us fifty bucks from last Friday," Lynelle proclaims. With her hand out she says, "Pay up."

"Eh, I'm out of cash at the moment. But you know I'm good for it." He waves her off. "Anyway, you and Grady were using coded signals to cheat. All that talk of your mushroom leather selection for the sofa, you think I can't see right through it? Eight years of playing bridge against you two and you think we're too thick to catch on?"

"Oh, it's always the same complaint, we must be cheating if you can't beat us?" she says.

Lynelle pours a packet of sugar into her cup and swirls around with a stir stick. "Something tells me you didn't ask to meet for horrible coffee only to gripe about losing again." She quizzes him with her keen eyes, taking a sip of the drink. If they weren't long-time friends, he'd be intimidated by that look.

"How did Georgia's recent scan go, is everything ok?"

"Fine. No news and no scan for another twelve months now." He shifts his weight in the chair, crossing his ankle over his knee. "But thanks for remembering. The time leading up to the annual scan is always fraught." He fidgets with his shoelaces before diving into it.

"I was wondering how much you've been following these news stories on the young women?"

"The ones with EMP powers?" she tilts her head like a bird, clearly not expecting this line of discussion.

"Yeah, these Auroras. I don't suppose you have any theories on what's causing it?"

She pauses for a good moment, taking him in. Fixing him with that signature stare of hers, she says, "I know you well enough to see through that." She narrows her eyes. "You're asking about my theories because you have one."

He raises his eyebrows as if to deny it, but she cuts him off. She shakes her head dramatically, punctuating each word with a wag as she says, "Cough it up."

He clears his throat, and they chuckle at the pun.

"I've been noodling on what could cause this physiologically. I suppose there must be a cellular mutation allowing the women to channel the electromagnetism through their nervous system."

"It's a reasonable theory," she replies, her eyes thoughtfully gazing upward as she turns it over in her mind, researching her mental library for facts and clues to support the idea.

"A cellular mutation in only a select few women in certain geographic zones it would seem?"

"Yeah, about that. I looked up where they each came from. They are in Auroral zones, but mostly weaker zones, not the areas with strongest activity."

"And do you make anything of that?" she asks.

"It's puzzling to be honest. The weaker zones are more heavily populated, so I guess it could be something to do with the recent increase in Auroral activity coupled with a larger population pool maybe."

He continues, "In some respects, it could be similar to a cancer in how the cells are mutating, taking on novel properties."

"It just feels so unusual," she says. "We've never seen anything this supernatural occurring through the natural mutation process. And it's happening so quickly and in such an extreme manner."

"You think this is a result of some intervention? Like gene editing?" he asks.

Lynelle raises a hand to her mouth as if to keep any thoughts from escaping, as if she could put the genie back in the bottle.

"It's been ten years since those human gene-editing programs were decommissioned," he says.

She nods at him to continue but doesn't dare speak.

"You and I both know the guardrails are easy enough to circumvent. There's never enough regulation and oversight, even for the labs that operate above-board. After Trump cut all of those positions in the '20s, we have never regained the necessary regulatory posture."

At last, she opens her mouth. "An unsanctioned human experiment causing mutations of a—what—supernatural nature?" Her eyebrows are raised so high that a row of skin furrows across her forehead.

"I hadn't gotten that far, to be honest. But now that we have talked it through… yeah." Mack stares down at the now-cold cup of coffee. He blows out a puff of air, as if attempting to expel the noxious idea.

"Where would we report our suspicions? What agency could even look into this? It seems to be occurring on an international scale."

"We know at least one of them is from the U.S., though."

"Right, true."

"Do we go to the Office for Human Research Protections? Don't we need specifics and evidence?" Mack rubs his hands over his face then rests his fingers at his temples. "It could be military, right? Humanized weapons?"

"Well, if that's the case, you know OHRP is already investigating." She gestures with her hands in a resigned way.

"You want to go on faith that someone is looking into this and is actually going to prioritize protecting these women over the advancements this represents?"

"I'm just not sure what we can do." She shrugs. "Two average citizens with ideas about something that we can't prove and that doesn't really have anything to do with us. There are most certainly agencies and committees with the resources and authority to look into this. It's been on the news; it's not exactly a secret."

"People always want to assume that some sort of benevolent Big Brother would stop harmful activities from endangering the average person. But we know better; that it comes too little too late." He's getting worked up, indignation simmering in his voice. "Progress and profits win out every time over protecting the little guy. Especially when that 'guy' is a group of women." He nods his head at her slightly when saying the word woman, as if to remind her of the plight of her gender.

This hits close to home for Mack. He has been at the center of several large lawsuits against major corporations whose operations and products were later discovered to have caused cancer, disease and death. He investigated syndromes dismissed as stress-related or psychological in nature, or just plain fictional. But he and his colleagues persisted and were able to prove the conditions resulted from chemicals, or wavelengths or by-products. In most cases, women were more severely impacted than their male counterparts, but their symptoms were routinely dismissed as psychological, emotional, or psychosomatic.

"You're right. Of course you're right." She concedes, exhaling. "We have to get involved, to do something." She fidgets with a bead on the chain of her reading glasses, pondering what that something might be. "Would one of the law firms you've worked with have an avenue to pursue this?"

He thinks for a moment. "There's one attorney who might. She never takes for granted that someone else is doing the right thing."

They both sip their terrible coffee in silence, both having the same bulldog of a woman in mind.

Lynnelle purses her lips to squelch the taste in her mouth, before stating the obvious: "Time to call in the Queen of No."

KLARA
Military Base, United States

I wasn't expecting it the first time it happened. Sure, we hadn't exactly been treated like VIPs at a luxury resort. Or even like prisoners with rights. I really shouldn't have been surprised. But I was. And that made it so much worse.

"Girls," LT addresses the group of us in his Texas drawl. It grates on me. Girls implies we are children. That we are lesser somehow. It's a term that a man-of-a-certain-generation would use to refer to his typing pool. "The girls will have it ready by morning," he'd say, leaning into the boss' office, pointing his glass of scotch in confirmation.

I want to scream. My head is still pounding from yesterday's practice. I look over at Luz whose eyes are puffy and red. I'm sure none of us got much sleep. LT should have given us today off. A break would be such a blessed relief from everything that has piled up on top and around us since this all started. We've been in survival mode since day one, and now it is somehow actually getting worse. There is a limit to what we can tolerate.

LT is setting up electronic equipment in the middle of the room, fiddling with cords and devices.

"Luz, over here." He points to a spot on the floor in front of the equipment, commanding her to him.

Without any argument or hesitation, like a zombie she walks over to him. Her eyes stare blankly ahead, not registering her surroundings or focusing on any particular thing. A deep fear, a worry for her swells up inside of me. How can she take any more of this? She is broken, empty, unthinking. My mind starts racing, scanning, strategizing, trying to think of what I might do to protect her from this today, to just give her a temporary relief from it all.

But LT is bulldozing ahead, "I want you to channel into this device and destroy the processor. Completely obliterate it."

Luz looks wanly at the equipment, then up at LT. The effort of focusing on him appears to take all the energy she has. How will she possibly channel when she is so completely broken down?

Making no attempt to follow his orders, Luz walks over to a chair by the wall and sits down, breathing heavily.

Taking the opportunity, I jump in. "She needs a break. We all do, LT," I say, stepping in front of Luz and toward LT.

He turns his head in my direction, eyes like those of a raptor seeking its prey. Anger flashes up in them when he responds.

"War doesn't take a break, girls." He draws out the last word, accentuating it. He must know how it disgusts me.

"We have mere weeks to perfect this technique before the attack. If we take a break now, we might all be under the thumb of the Chinese government by the end of this year. Not just me and you, but your parents, your families, the entire nation. Is that what you want?"

He spits out the last question as if we are the enemy. As if this is exactly what we want, and our goal is to undermine him every step of the way.

"How do you expect us to be ready for the attack if we can't restore our energy?"

I walk over to Luz and put my hand on her shoulder. She's not even looking at me, just staring at the floor, head hanging as heavy as a boulder.

And that's when it happens.

He comes over to her and with no warning kicks the chair out from under her.

I try to catch her fall, but because he kicked out the chair leg opposite me, she falls away in the other direction. I didn't have time to prepare. Neither did Luz. Rather than her hands bracing the fall, her shoulder and the side of her face slam full force into the concrete floor. The sound of bones on stone, and the hollow skin of her cheek slapping the hard surface will haunt me in my dreams.

There's a heartbeat or two of deafening silence before she cries out. It's a mewling, broken cry. Not powerful or angry. It's an anguished sound absorbed by her body. It's almost as if she is trying to pull the pain inward. To soak up the agony of all that has happened and put it into the same box where everything else gets locked up inside of her.

Even if I'm wrong about what mentally is happening for her, I can tell that physically she is absorbing the pain of this situation. Her eyes are squinted shut, and her body is curled tightly into a fetal position.

I rush to her side, Penny just seconds behind me. Eyelids fluttering, I can see she is still conscious as the shock sets in. Blood begins seeping from a nostril. From behind my left shoulder, I hear a sharp inhalation and then a howl of anger as Penny registers what this means. She is running her hand over Luz's short hair, comforting her at the same time her fury is rising up. Her soft, nurturing side has come out at the same time her warrior rages to the surface.

That's when it hits me. A bold and obvious realization that suddenly makes me feel ridiculous. We should have expected this. The fact that I have been caught unawares by this is its own perverse shock. I have been such a fool.

I'm caught up in the one-two punch of this shock, both the violence and my complete lack of preparation when a sudden movement flashes in my peripheral vision. While I was frozen, LT was one step ahead of me, ahead of us all. He must have had an idea how Penny might react, realizing the situation could turn on him if he lost control. At the precise instant Penny lunges at him, he pivots.

From behind, he grabs her arms in a hold, forcefully twisting them, restraining her upper body completely. Her face is twisted in fury, and she kicks her legs out and back, bucking like a wild horse.

In a sequence of moves so deft and effortless as to be second nature to him, LT brings her to the ground and is pressing her face into the concrete, pushing her entire body into submission with the weight of his own. She spits, but it is futile given the angle of her head and his position behind her. The slick moisture of her saliva smears against the concrete where her cheek has slid against it.

I look over at Aino to see how she is reacting to all of this, and I see her backing further into the corner, arms wrapped tightly around herself. Her eyes are wide and round, displaying a mixture of surprise and fear.

While I'm looking at her, before I can even think what to do, guards rush into the room. In a flurry of activity, several sets of hands are helping LT hold Penny down while a syringe is plunged into her neck. It's barely seconds before her eyes flutter closed and her limbs hang loose and lifeless. As the guards drag her backwards out the door, LT turns to face us, Luz now crouched holding her head. Wiping blood from her face with the heel of her hand, Aino is at her side, protective and comforting.

LT's chest is heaving from the exertion, though I detect maybe also from a sick kind of pleasure. He has a glowing, excited look in his eyes. He slowly wipes his hands down the front of his cargo pants, as he exhales in a deliberate and controlled manner.

"Anyone got anything else to say about that?" His voice is smooth and controlled.

Aino and I remain completely silent, not making eye contact with him or each other.

There's a low rumbling of energy inside me. I feel a fierce animal instinct waking up. Some part of me that was hibernating has taken notice of the circumstances and like a sleeper cell, I feel myself activating.

AARYA
Los Angeles, California

Aarya rushes from the platform and onto the train car seconds before the doors close. She saw him. She's certain it was him. Those grey-green eyes pierced through the crowd jostling on the platform and found her. The train is so crowded today, she can barely press between the bodies, forcing her way toward the window. She has to know, she needs to see his face. A backpack slung carelessly over a passenger's shoulders blocks her path and she pivots to thread between an overweight man in an ill-fitting suit and an elderly woman. Tripping on the man's shoes, she catches herself and pushes onward.

"Excuse me." A hand on her shoulder presses, insistent. "Sorry," she mutters, not turning to look. She can't be bothered. She's not even sure she could speak to him, isn't sure what she would do, but she needs to know if it was him. She wades through a group of teenagers in school uniforms, laughing and looking down at their phones.

"Are you there?" The hand is pressing. She swats it away.

"Earth to Aarya!" This time the hand, the voice cannot be ignored.

She jolts up in her chair, awake. Walton is hovering over her.

"What are you doing here?" she asks, confused and flustered.

"You asked me if I'd come into the office remember?" He looks at her with a skeptical, wry smile, taking in the empty coffee tumblers scattered across her desk.

Aarya looks around, realizing for the first time where she is, and that the sighting of Craig was only a dream. She wipes across her lower lip with her thumb, finding traces of drool. She's still half out of it. The feeling of having been on the train, the feeling of closeness to Craig is so real, still very present.

"I must have fallen asleep. What time is it?"

"11:45. I got here as fast as I could, but traffic was pretty horrendous." He's wearing a bow tie and burgundy leather dress shoes she has never seen before.

"Oh right, the party. How was it?" she asks, genuinely interested.

"It was fun, but honestly I was glad for an excuse to get out of there. People were starting to get pretty drunk and talking about skinny dipping in the pool." He has a scandalized look on his face and fidgets uncomfortably with his tie.

"Have you been here since last night?" he asks, a look of sincere concern on his face.

"Yeah. I am so exhausted, but we are really on the verge of something here."

"The Underground? Have there been updates?"

"Lone Wolf and Sir PB&J just posted some very surprising calculations." She points at her computer monitor as Walton grabs a chair and rolls it over to her desk. Members on the Underground never use their real names or any identifying criteria since they don't want to be sanctioned by their employers for sharing intelligence with the Underground community.

The computer monitor comes to life and Aarya clicks the avatar next to the name Lady Catnipernicus, her own alias. "Here," she points. "It's honestly so simple, it seems ridiculous. But if you layer our data points across this calculation, the pattern is obvious."

Walton scratches his chin for a moment, then looks at her skeptically. "You can't throw out the first three events though…"

She interrupts him, "The baseline events, right. We thought they had to be aligned to the start of the series. But Lone Wolf theorizes they might be unrelated to the solar activity. We'll have to prove his hypothesis, but assuming we do, pull those off the charts and look again. Now do you see it?"

Walton's jaw drops and he turns to look at her in surprise. Their eyes lock, and for a moment the recognition of what might be possible hits them both with a shock.

"I never would have thought to segregate the variables like that. It's a little insane!"

She nods her head vigorously, sipping stale coffee from a half-empty tumbler. "I thought my lack of sleep was making me see things. But you see it too, don't you? I'm not seeing things?"

Shaking his head, he replies, "No."

Aarya scrunches up her face, tilting her head to the side. "You don't? Oh, could I have gotten it all wrong?"

"No," he repeats. Very slowly, he adds, "No, you aren't seeing things, Aarya." Then he bursts out laughing, an awkward cackling sound that's a cross between a donkey braying and the hiss of a broken lawn sprinkler. It sounds like "Cah-Caaah, Cah-Caaah." He's pointing at her and holding his belly, mirth bubbling out of his eyes.

She barks out a single laugh, surprise, exhaustion and relief all tumbling together. "Oh, you got me!" she admits, conceding his victory. Then more laughter gurgles up, one after the next until she is in a full roar, the two of them laughing in unison, gasping for air, wiping tears from their eyes.

After she has regained her composure, she asks "I see you've been working on your humor?" shaking her head incredulously.

"I got you so good, Aarya. I see why people do that now." His self-satisfied comprehension is palpable, a wistful look in his eyes. "All my life I thought it was so cruel. You don't hate me for it do you?" He is looking at her now with genuine concern.

"No." She smiles warmly at him, wondering how many times in his life this nerd-man must have been the butt of someone else's joke.

"It's not cruel when the other person wants to laugh with you."

She pauses. "When you laugh together as friends, it makes everything in the world feel okay."

She reaches over and squeezes his shoulder, and he nods his head like it's the most obvious thing, as if laughing and touching is such a natural sequence of events for him.

"Speaking of things in the world not being okay…" she swivels in her chair to face the monitor. "I think we have to do something about this, we have to find a way to get our hypothesis and our data to the Underground."

"You heard what Leonard said the last time," he cautions. "No more sharing information without it going all the way up the chain for top-tier approvals first. We could get fired this time if we don't follow his directive."

"But the approvals will take months," she protests. "We can't wait that long."

Walton sighs deeply, weighing his thoughts, then a grin slowly spreads across his face, as gradual as the first rays of sunlight seeping over the morning horizon. "Some days I really hate this job anyway."

"What are you saying?" she asks, excited and appalled at the same time.

"We could track down Lone Wolf, bring the data to him."

"No, that's crazy," she looks at him, hoping he'll agree. "It's crazy, right?"

"I don't know, I have that highway atlas in my desk drawer. It might even be faster to bring the data to him in person, than trying to get it uploaded with our current transmission speeds. And at least there won't be a digital trail connecting us to it."

Twenty minutes later, they are heading to the break room to load up on snacks as a self-guided wheeled case trails them, carrying laptops and various electronics. Aarya doesn't remember saying yes, but she has watched, almost from outside her body, as she prepared to leave with him.

"What if we can't convince Lone Wolf to share his precise location? Jackson is a pretty large city, even if it is small-town compared to here," Aarya asks. She is on her tip toes reaching to the back of a cabinet for an unopened jar of peanut butter, her voice muffled into her outstretched arm.

"I have some theories on where to find him, based on his profile details," Walton says.

Aarya exhales as she grasps the peanut butter jar, then hugs it to her chest. She looks over at him, impressed. "You continue to surprise me, Walton. Do you know that?"

"I'm just glad you're willing to take the gamble on a wild card like me and head off on this crazy adventure," he says.

"I think six months ago, before all of this started happening in the world, I never in a million years would have thrown away my respectable, stable job, on a hunch. But it just feels like the right thing. And honestly, I'm starting to wonder if I've ever in my whole life followed my heart." She's thinking of Craig now, wondering how many of her life's choices were made for others, for their perception of her, or to gain approval.

"If that's how you feel, we are definitely throwing caution to the wind now!" Walton says, raising his eyebrows with exaggerated animation.

"Oh no, what did you do?"

Walton holds up a car key fob, attached to a golden, shiny letter "L" glinting in the light.

"Not his new E-Lexus! Oh, he will kill us before he has the chance to fire us!"

"We don't have time to wait until the car rental shops open. The next outage is coming, and we have to get on the road now."

"We really had better get out of here now, so we have a good head-start when he gets into the office tomorrow." Aarya is throwing bags of instant coffee into a grocery bag with the other snacks and heading toward the hallway.

Walton pauses in the doorway, hesitating, something holding him back.

"What's wrong? What is it? Are you worried about driving after dark if the GPS goes out?" she asks.

"Your sweater!" he cries out, running toward her desk.

In less than five minutes, sweet, surprising, nerdy Walton reappears near the front entrance of the building, knobby sweater in hand, ready to commit grand theft auto, and maybe, just maybe save the world.

PENNY
Military Base, United States

She rolls over, slowly, her body aching as she comes out of a deep, medicated sleep. Rubbing a hand over her face, Penny feels a lump near her temple.

The memory comes back to her at once, realizing why she is here, why she was sleeping during the day. She feels along the side of her neck, finding a tenderness at the point of injection. She pictures Luz, remembering her beautiful face twisted in pain, unconscious on the floor. The thought is bittersweet, at once bringing up the most buoyant, delicious feelings, as she thinks about Luz. With her big heart, deep brown eyes, and sassy, mischievous smile, Luz is someone Penny can't seem to get out of her mind. Whenever she needs something sweet to take her mind off all this awfulness, all she has to do is think of Luz's warm smile. But this time the thought that Luz's memory conjures up is a painful one. The memory of what LT did to her, pinning her to the ground, it's almost too much.

She scowls and pushes herself up into a seated position on the thin mattress. Penny knows she's not exactly an open book, making it hard for others to find their purchase onto her rocky shores. She wants to be different. She's tried to change. It's just that somehow, she always reverts back to self-protection. Being open to love, requires too much vulnerability. People never understand what it's like for her. They think they do. They make assumptions. But in the end, they reject her, tossing her aside like unripe fruit.

She strokes her hand along the scars on her arm, as memories from her past flicker, but refuse to take shape. She presses them down, sending them back to their dark recesses in her mind.

She sees a shadow flicker past under her door. Then, she hears a dull, tentative knock. Metal scrapes against metal and the door grinds open. Peering out from behind is Jonah's sheepish face.

She glowers at him. If looks could kill, his face would melt off like the Nazi at the end of Raiders of the Lost Ark.

"I'm really sorry, Penny. If I could apologize on his behalf, I would." Jonah's boyish good looks are really working to his advantage here, making him look young and innocent.

Penny wants to believe he is sincere but reminds herself that he's aligned with that monster.

"Why do you help him, then? Why don't you leave?"

"It's not that simple," he says, shrugging his shoulders helplessly. "But it doesn't mean I'm okay with how he treats all of you. I've tried to talk to him about it. I think he knows how bad it is. He's a complicated guy, he has his demons." Jonah says this last word with a sort of wistful, regretful tone of voice, almost pained to say it. "He suffered tragedy too, very similar to your story, actually. In a twisted way, it's what motivates him now."

She blinks up at him, withholding response while she assesses him just standing there in the doorway.

"Well, I brought you this," he hands her an ice pack. "It should help bring down the swelling."

She reaches out and takes the cold compress from him, then presses it gingerly to her head.

"How's Luz doing?" she asks, hungry for information.

"She has a bad headache, probably a mild concussion, but nothing too serious. I just checked on her a few minutes ago. She'll be okay."

He shifts his weight from one foot to the other.

"Is there something else?" she asks him, more harshly than intended.

His eyes snap to her face. "They took you to the infirmary to stabilize you first, before bringing you back here."

She shrugs. "Yeah, so what of it?"

"I, uh, might have read your medical file," he says, the last words tilting up like a question, guilt and pity written all over his features.

"Oh that." Penny looks down.

"It must have been awful; I really am sorry."

"Right. Anything else then?" she asks, abruptly putting this line of conversation to bed. Jonah takes the hint and quietly leaves. It's not lost on her that in some ways he is their jailer, making sure the door is locked on his way out.

Penny leans back against the wall, propping a pillow behind her shoulders. She tenderly holds the ice pack to her forehead, thinking again about Luz, how much worse her head must feel right now.

As she adjusts the ice pack into a more comfortable position, the tip of her finger grazes against the edge of something, coarse and fibrous. She inspects it closer and finds a slip of paper tucked inside the liner of the ice pack.

Although she knows she is alone, she finds herself checking to see if anyone is looking. Pulling the sheet open, her eyes are met with a dancing, almost floral penmanship. The handwriting jumps off the page, dynamic and alive. Just seeing it, Penny feels she knows another piece of Luz's personality and it makes sense, like a piece of a puzzle snapping properly into place.

> *Penny,*
> *Thank you for trying to protect me. It meant a lot to me*
> *when I learned what you did. But you should be careful*
> *not to put yourself at risk.*
>
> *You are headstrong and stubborn. You, they will*
> *punish and try to break. Me, maybe I am already*
> *broken, hardly worth much effort on their part. I might*
> *not be worth the effort on your part either. I feel myself*

retreating so far inward here that I fear I may never come back to my former self.

I love you for trying, but please just let the wolves have me. Save yourself and the others.

-Luz

Penny reads and re-reads the note several times, soaking up the meaning. Luz really has given up, she thinks. She traces her finger delicately over that word, "love." To see it in writing, feel it tangibly under her fingertip, just makes it that much more real. She feels determination bubbling up within her. She has to find a way to get Luz out of here.

She folds the paper carefully and places it beneath her mattress. As she tucks it in, next to another object hidden there, her memory takes her back to another piece of paper she held in her hands, twenty years ago.

She was so excited to show it to her parents. A cheap, bright blue ribbon clipped to the sheet of paper announcing Penny had won the third-grade science fair. Her dad helped her with the final adjustments only the night before and she couldn't wait to show him. As she climbed into the back seat next to her best friend Gemma, she told Gemma's mom about it. She went on and on during their ride toward her home, barely breathing between words, talking nonstop like a little jabber box, describing the 2nd and 3rd place projects, why she thought her project was selected as winner over the others.

She was running her hand over the folds in the blue ribbon tucked into the pocket of her denim overalls when it happened. She first heard Gemma's mom gasp, then saw her turn the steering wheel sharply. She caught nothing more than a fleeting glimpse of the truck barreling down on them as she felt her body go weightless momentarily. The car careened over toward the ditch, pitching and rolling. The vehicle flipped multiple times, but Penny wasn't counting.

It all happened so fast, she thinks now, recalling the event. It's the same thought she has every time she allows the memory to come to her. One second she was mid-sentence, exuding the most childhood joy she ever possessed, and the next instant her entire life's trajectory was forever changed. Her ability to feel that kind of joy forever gone.

There's the sound a heel of a hand makes against a glass window. Someone is trying to get in. No, they're trying to escape. Crackling flames and searing heat well up around her.

Penny lurches upright swatting at the sheets to put out the flames. Drenched in sweat she takes in her surroundings. Just like that morning in the hospital, just like so many other days, she realizes it was just a dream. She is safe, in her cell, but they are not. Gemma and her mom both died that day. She looks down at her hands. Penny had tried to drag them from the fiery vehicle, but she wasn't strong enough. Passersby came and pulled her away, wrapping her little body in blankets to put out the flames. She hadn't even realized she was on fire.

The scars on her arm are nothing compared to the ones on her back and shoulders. The skin grafts were painful, but she felt she deserved pain, to be punished. She should have saved them. It's not to say she didn't suffer, or that she wasn't punished. For three years after the accident, she underwent nearly one hundred surgeries. During that time, she lived with a tracheostomy which allowed her to breathe, until she was strong enough to have reconstructive surgery of her trachea. She swallows hard now, thinking about it.

Years later, she endured a different kind of self-selected pain to have a phoenix tattooed across large sections of the scarring on her skin. The colorful, magical bird caught up in a swirl of vicious flames is draped expertly across her shoulders. It's a badge of honor and a constant reminder.

Reaching under the mattress for reassurance, she feels the piece of paper from Luz, reminding herself it's real and that she is not alone. She needs to feel it in her fingers to reassure herself that it still exists. The other item is there too. A glob of melted, congealed blue ribbon, it's just a deformed lump of blue, entirely indistinguishable.

That was the last time she excelled at anything. It was no surprise that after the accident her grades fell. Initially, her parents understood and expected it. But, as the months and years passed, their patience grew thin, and they became worried. Penny knew exactly why her grades were bad. She didn't deserve to do well. She deserved to be punished. If she were to succeed, and worse, to celebrate, then more bad things would happen.

As she grew into a young woman, the depression, guilt and grief sent her down a path of alcohol, drugs, and rebellion. When she wasn't trying to numb the pain, she was punishing herself in some manner. Always this extreme paradox of one or the other. Never in between, never letting go. Somewhere deep inside, she felt that if she allowed herself to heal and to move on, it would mean their lives weren't worth remembering. The tattoo helped her in some ways to feel they were always with her, that she'd absorbed their memories onto her body, along with the scars.

She reaches under the mattress and pulls out that lump of blue plastic, turning it over in her hands. She's had it with her all these years, a reminder that she didn't deserve to live. She thinks again about the note from Luz and the fatalistic the message contained in it. What happened to make Luz think she wasn't worthy of saving? It's a hard question for Penny to ask herself, like looking directly into a mirror reflecting back her own wounded soul.

As she wipes a tear that has suddenly appeared on her face, she confronts the painful realization of how Luz must feel about her, how she'd want Penny to be saved too. Because of the love, that powerful little word on the page. She saw it with her own eyes. She looks again at it now, confirming.

And then she knows exactly how to save them both, how to redeem their irredeemable and broken souls. If it's the last thing she does on this earth, she will find a way to get Luz out of here. She won't let her be destroyed the way she allowed Gemma and her mom to be. This is her chance to right her wrong, to pay back the debt she has carried all this time. If the flames on that phoenix tattoo were real, they'd be flickering and waving with anticipation for all the determination flowing through Penny. This is her do-over, and she won't fuck it up this time.

KLARA
Military Base, United States

I hear a noise, like the sound of a cat trapped somewhere. I look up at Jonah, and he is holding a tablet in his hands, looking at me with concern.

Putting my head in my hands, I lean over and process what is happening. I realize the sound came from me.

"I don't understand," I say.

"Klara, he didn't leave you," Jonah responds.

"He's been alive all this time?"

"He's been looking for you since the day he came out of that coma." Jonah has just finished explaining to me that Ryen had been in an accident in Canada and had been in a hospital at the same time I was calling around trying to find him. But he was unconscious in a coma for two weeks. When he came out of the coma, the outage prevented him from getting any communication through. He was in no position to travel and by the time communications were back up, I had been abducted.

"Can you play it again for me?"

Jonah plays the news clip again, my heart leaping and churning at the sight of Ryen's face. His real, live face, the one I held in my hands so many times, speaking into the camera, it looks like home to me. I reach out and touch the tablet, as if to touch Ryen's face and feel the warmth of his skin, to find him there alive and well just under my fingertips. Looking into his face, I feel a sense of hope I haven't had since this whole ugly thing began.

"What he's doing, Klara, is dangerous," Jonah cautions. During the news clip, Ryen explained that he organized a group with other family and friends of Auroras who disappeared. They are appealing to the government, working with private investigators, doing all they can to bring us home.

"Dangerous how?" I ask, thinking about how brave and loyal Ryen is, feeling proud of him for being the one to spearhead the effort.

"You know better than anyone, Klara, that there are powerful forces at work right now. He doesn't understand what he is up against, and how dangerous it would be if they took you out of the mix right now. You are all needed to end this conflict and put our world back in order." He says this last part with such conviction, I find myself believing him, in spite of myself.

I squeeze the knuckles of each forefinger into my eye sockets, pressing deeply. I want to go home. I want to press my face into Ryen's chest and tell him I was wrong. I'll tell him every day how wrong I was. I'll tell him he can point to any spot on the map, and I'll go there with him, no questions. I know now that my home is wherever he is, and my cabin is just a place. I was holding too tightly to a false sense of security, and it caused me to push away the one person who actually wants to protect me and keep me safe.

But as strong as that pull is, to find a way back to Ryen, Jonah's words ring true to me too. As much as I want out of this place, and to regain my freedom, I feel a sense of obligation. Deep within me, I know I'm connected to the others and to this story. This thing has momentum; a chain of events has been kicked off that can't be undone.

I sigh deeply.

Looking up at Jonah, I can feel the hot tears in my eyes.

"How do we get word to him?"

Jonah's eyes have a warning in them, and I add, "Not for what you think. How do we make sure he knows I'm okay and to stop looking?"

I can see Jonah's shoulders relax, recognition that I'm committed to this fight seeping over him. He gives me a reassuring smile.

"I might be able to arrange something. We'd have to be super careful. We can't reveal any details. And if I get caught, I don't know what they'd do to me."

For the next several hours, I wait in my cell, wondering what Jonah is up to, turning over Ryen's story in my mind. My heart is racing. It is a lot to digest. Not only the realization that he is alive, and incredibly, he still loves me, but also the fact that I've made a choice. I've picked a side. I feel at peace with the decision, but also surprised by it.

I trace my finger along the creases between the blocks on the wall. Should I - will I - tell the others? They have people who are desperate to find them too. But how would that news impact them? We are all so different, with different motivations and fears. It's a big responsibility, this information. And it is dangerous too.

Drawing my knees into my chest, I hug myself tightly. What does it mean that I've decided this is my fight?

LT is an abusive bully, that much I know. I'm ready to attack him the next time he tries anything. I've made up my mind and I'm prepared. But even so, does that mean he's on the wrong side of this? Could he be a bad guy fighting for the good guys?

I know so little about the bigger picture, it feels impossible to sift through the tiny fragments of information available to me and somehow discern the right path to choose. Still laying on my side, curled into a tight ball, I turn my mind's eye inward. Slowly, I gain control of my breathing, lengthening the exhale, deepening each breath. I count each breath as it comes and goes, like gentle waves cresting on the shore. Thinking of waves reminds me of the shore on Lake Superior outside my cabin. But those are raging, forceful waves, crashing into jagged, iron-hard rocks. For a moment, thoughts of home and Ryen and the weight of so many conflicting emotions threaten to overwhelm me and tug me out of this state.

Gently, I push those thoughts aside, refocusing again on breath. There is nothing I can do now but to trust that my intuition will guide me. It's imperative I pause my conscious mind and trust that the truth will reveal itself to me. My inner wisdom will know when the time is right.

I have no idea how much time has passed when I hear a scraping outside the door of my cell.

"Klara?" Jonah's voice pierces through my reverie.

Lifting myself off the bed, I walk over to the door and press my face against it.

"I called off the dogs," he says, somewhat cryptically, in a whisper.

For a moment, I want to cry. I want to rage. I want a hero to come save me. Why do I have to be the hero again?

AARYA
En Route to Jackson

The sun is barely peeking up over the horizon, as the vehicle signals to exit and pulls off the exit ramp, autonomously taking them to the pre-programmed stop. The GPS came back online about an hour after they left and has been reliable.

The car smoothly pulls into the charging station, while Aarya saves the updated calculations to the analytic model. She looks over at Walton, his head lolling to the side, mouth gaping open. He's been sleeping for the past ninety minutes while she made the updates to their calculations. She remembers road trips as a kid when her parents had to actively drive the car, pressing down the pedals and turning the steering wheel, as she has recently relearned how to do. She wonders now, how anyone got work done or when they caught up on sleep.

She waits for the ChargeBot to plug in and service the vehicle as her mind wanders to Ravi. She wonders how and when to tell him she has gone on this adventure. He messaged her last night before she'd even decided to leave with Walton. She had been working feverishly on her new assumptions and missed the message when it came in. By the time she saw it, she realized it was too late to respond. She and Walton were in a mad scramble to "get out of Dodge" as they kept jokingly saying. Maybe she'll casually respond to him a little later in the day, not mentioning the trip or their ridiculously naive plan.

Lately, she finds herself wondering if Ravi is actually concerned about her, for her well-being and her best interests, or if he is concerned with how her actions reflect on him. It's the same train of thought that crosses her mind at times when she is interacting with her parents. She's not sure when it started to shift, but she has begun to hunger for a kind of acceptance she has only felt once before. This whole thing has made her question if she wants to be with a guy like Ravi, or if she just knows that is what her parents want for her. She's always done the right thing, the thing that gains approval, that says to the world she is on top of her game. She never stopped to question if it matters. What if others didn't see her as successful and having the right relationship or living in the right neighborhood? If she fell madly in love with a horribly unattractive man, or one without a successful career, but was truly loved and happy and secure, would others judge her for it, or would her own criticism be harshest?

The SnackBot is at their window now, offering a selection of refreshments. Just as she is internally debating whether to rouse Walton, his eyes flutter open. "Bathroom break?" she inquires as he smooths down his messy hair and sits upright.

"Where are we and how much farther?" he asks.

"We have about nine more hours to Jackson. We're in a sad little town called Mesquite, Nevada, just about to cross over into Utah. We could hit up a casino if you want to gamble? We already passed through Vegas so this would be your last chance."

"Hard pass!" He chuckles at her. "But we probably should take advantage of the facilities now."

After getting a few snacks and a bathroom break, they're back on the road. Instead of falling back to sleep or running more analysis, they find themselves engrossed in a deep conversation about the solar cycles and everything going on in the world. Walton surprises her by suddenly asking "What made you want to get into astronomy?"

She's caught off guard by such a personal question at this time and place. She thinks for a moment, realizing Ravi has never once asked her this question. She feels a warm, honey feeling ooze out from her chest and into her limbs as something deep in her starts waking up. She had forgotten what it's like to have someone truly interested in what makes her tick.

She fumbles with her sunglasses and awkwardly adjusts in her seat, looking off in the distance and noticing the way the sun has painted a hazy peach along the horizon. "My canned response has always been that I want to head up the Moon Colonization Program one day. Once that became a viable career path, half the kids in my school switched their course of studies. My parents were so proud."

She fidgets with an errant piece of yarn that has come loose from the sleeve of her sweater. "But you know the honest truth is, I couldn't care less about the MCP. I didn't even apply for the internship program when it opened up. By that point, I had realized I loved astronomy for how equations and math can explain the mysteries of our universe and the world around us. There's structure, something formal to it. And such a vastness to what's unknown or unstudied at the same time, it's like having a decoder ring for an entire set of encyclopedias."

He's looking at her now in a way that makes her feel he must know precisely what she is talking about. He nods his head.

"The beautiful, unknown, is that it?" He has a wistful, almost romantic look on his face.

"Yes, exactly!" she says. Being understood feels like being seen by someone else for the very first time. The air in the vehicle feels like it could crackle with excitement as they talk for another hour about their respective origin stories with astronomy.

After they've exhausted the topic, Aarya pivots back to the reality of their situation. "So how do you think we're going to locate Lone Wolf, let alone convince him to work with us?"

"It's so simple, you're going to laugh."

She nods, encouraging him to continue.

"In true science-geek fashion, I analyzed his posting activity on the site for the past several months. I mined for keywords and geo-location references."

She curls up her lip when asking, "Did you e-stalk all the posters on the Underground or just him?"

Putting on a face of mock offense he responds, "Hey, I had to know if we could trust these people, so I vetted them a little."

"Okay, fine, it's a bit creepy, but go on." She looks out the window at the scenery, and then ahead where the highway disappears into the face of a mountain. She glances at the interactive GPS map on the dash and notes the road definitely continues onward, at least on the map, even though visually it looks as though the road is going to dead end into the mountain.

"I assumed he must have some involvement with the Central Wyoming College in Jackson, since his posted city and state is Jackson, Wyoming. But there are too many students and professors to narrow it down."

He shows her the charts and data he compiled. "But then I saw something very unique. I saw that Lone Wolf made a few comments about findings that could only have been detected using infrared technology. That's when I started to wonder if it was someone connected to the Wyoming Infrared Observatory in Laramie."

"The WIRO?" she asks.

"Yeah, there aren't many other infrareds out there and being he is located in Wyoming, albeit the other side of the state, I was thinking it could be a solid connection."

"Wait, are we actually driving much farther than I thought today?" she looks at him over the top of the sunglasses, an exasperated look on her face. "I mean, that's all the way to the border of Colorado!"

"Well hang on, I don't think so. Let me finish."

"Phew!" she exhales. "I would definitely need more snacks if we were taking on that distance."

"Most of the observing happens remotely. Generally speaking, observing time is allocated to faculty and students at the UW campus in Laramie, but I recently read an article about a professor with Central Wyoming College of Jackson who was granted observation time through the WIRO for a special research project."

She raises her eyebrows, willing him to get to the point.

"I put two and two together, figuring he's probably the only guy in Jackson with access to infrared capability and that narrowed it right down!" He proudly shows her the article, complete with a photograph of Professor Larry Williams of CWC-Jackson.

"Huh," she says. "Larry Williams is Lone Wolf?"

"Not as unique as Lady Catnipernicus, of course," he demurs.

She nods smugly, looking out the window at the barren desertscape.

"Whoa, it looks like we're going to drive into the side of this mountain up ahead!" he says.

"I think it's an optical illusion because the GPS shows it going through," she points at the map.

For the next half an hour, their conversation is paused while they are distracted with the scenery. They marvel at the rock walls parting on either side of the highway to allow passage, pondering the amount of dynamite required to create the route. With the early morning sunlight, shades of rusty red, sulfuric yellow and the occasional cactus plant are highlighted and cast in shadow. When they drive past an idyllic stream abutted by greenery and standing cattle, the contrast is shocking.

After the break in conversation as they come through to a more boring stretch of road, Walton says, "I just realized something."

"Yeah?"

"Won't we be coming along the edge of Zion National Park along this route? I think there are some amazing spots on the next segment of our trip."

"Oh wow!" Aarya exclaims. "I haven't been to Zion since I was a little girl. It's completely magical."

"I've never been," Walton admits.

"We really should take a slight detour then and at least drive through the park. I was lucky enough to go on a school trip for stargazing and geology when I was in the fifth grade. It was one of those special moments in life that has stayed with me. It was the first time I looked at stars through a telescope."

She had forgotten this memory, realizing it was buried under the layers of adulthood and responsibility.

Remembering now, she says, "I was surprised how cold it was at night. I thought the desert would be hot, but didn't understand about altitude. I remember thinking I wasn't going to see very many stars because I needed to go inside and warm up. But I was so enamored of everything we were observing that I ended up being one of the last to go in."

She has a wistful look on her face, lost somewhere decades ago in her memory.

"Zero chance we are missing that detour stop," Walton responds, clearly registering the significance of the place for her. "It sounds like kismet. Maybe you were meant to revisit this chapter from your past on the way to whatever it is we are embarking on."

"Do you believe in things like that? Fate or the universe or God or whatever?" she asks.

They're suddenly engrossed again in conversation, picking up where they left off before, this time delving ever deeper into philosophical concepts, unpacking the inner workings of each other's minds and hearts.

They spend the rest of the day driving through some of the most beautiful landscapes that Aarya could recall seeing. When the alarm beeps to indicate that GPS has gone offline again, they realize self-driving is no longer an option. Walton agrees to do the driving, although Aarya admittedly has no experience managing an Atlas.

Nonetheless, they detour through Zion, driving up a zig-zagging road and then through the mile-long tunnel, marveling at the view out the gallery windows. Aarya's heart is so full from all the natural beauty and views, it feels as though it will burst. But they must press onward. They drive northward toward Salt Lake City, skirting the edges, then continuing northward more.

When they reach the outskirts of Jackson, the vehicle pulls through a grassy meadow as sunlight dips behind a ring of mountains.

"Bison!" Walton exclaims at the same time her eyes work out what she is seeing. And not just one, there's another, now three more over here, and then more, until she realizes it's an entire herd moving through the grasses.

"Pull over," she instructs the car, forgetting herself and that Walton is still driving. "As you wish," he says, pulling the car to a gentle stop on the shoulder.

"Sorry, that sounded so bossy," she looks over at him sheepishly. "I forgot the car wasn't self-driving."

"I figured, it's okay," he says, brushing it off. "Anyway, it was urgent," he says, pointing toward the herd across the other side of the road.

She steps out of the vehicle as quietly and carefully as she can. She walks further up to get a better view, wrapping her arms around herself in the warmth of her cardigan, to ward off the cool humidity that has settled in the valley as dusk lowers around them. Her hair is whipping around her face in the breeze, and she inhales deeply, taking in the pungent scent of manure mixed with moist soil and decaying grass. She is close enough to hear the animals moving methodically across the ground, somehow light and nearly silent, despite their hulking masses.

"I've never seen any before." Walton is at her side, taking in the unthinkably beautiful scene, a look of awe and wonder as he confesses this to her. "Careful!" He grabs her elbow, catching her just as she nearly falls into a gopher hole.

When she loses her balance, her weight shifts into him and she finds herself grabbing him around the waist to stay upright. She can smell traces of his aftershave, and she notices for the first time how it's the crinkly lines around his eyes that give him that soft, always-smiling look.

He reaches down to brush a lock of hair off her face, and she pauses in his embrace a heartbeat longer than necessary. When she pulls away, she's surprised to find her heart is racing.

"That was a close one," she says, looking away and brushing grass off her pants.

"You okay?" he asks.

"Yes, I'm fine, just lucky you were there to catch me. Looks like the sun is just about to drop behind those mountains, we probably had better get back on the road."

"Right, yes, of course." Walton is all business now, heading back to the car. Avoiding each other's eyes, they assess the remainder of the route ahead of them, discussing whether to stop for dinner or press onward and try to catch Professor Williams as he is heading out of his last lecture of the day.

Aarya pulls out her phone to assess the proximity of nearby restaurants and realizes she has missed three calls from her mom. Also, Ravi has sent four messages. His most recent message seems to imply he knows she wasn't at work today. "Just let me know you're okay, please." She wonders if Leonard has noticed his car missing, or if anyone has made the connection that both she and Walton didn't show up for work. She's not ready to talk to her parents or Ravi and face the questions she can't answer. She checks the camera app for Bumbu, and verifies his weight, water dish levels and food levels all look to be within normal range.

She puts her phone away and suggests, "I'm feeling in the mood for a little ambush! Let's try to catch him post-lecture."

"Yeah? You sure you can hold off eating dinner for a little longer?"

"Yes, I don't have much appetite now that we are so close to finding this guy and putting the pieces together."

"Same here actually," he grins over at her. There's a sizzle of electricity between them as the shared excitement and realization of the risk they've taken on brings them back to reality. Aarya distracts herself with reviewing the map, asking Walton questions about the plan and how they're going to convince the Professor to work with them.

As the car pulls away, her phone flashes another incoming call alert. Aarya sees her father's face briefly on the screen before pocketing it.

"Do you need to get that?" Walton asks. "Are people worrying about you?"

Aarya wonders if Walton has anyone worrying about him. She hasn't noticed him checking his phone. She didn't even bother to bring up the topic during their conversations.

"I'll call them after dinner tonight. I'm guessing someone at work called to see why I didn't show up."

She ventures to ask, "Who would they contact for you? For your emergency contact person?"

"My sister. Our parents are both gone now, so she's always my emergency contact. She lives only a few miles away and we joke about how she's also my same blood type and she owes me at least a kidney for the way she treated me growing up."

Aarya exhales.

"I messaged her this morning to let her know I was leaving town for a bit, just so she wouldn't worry."

Of course he did. Considerate, always thoughtful Walton wouldn't just run away from those who love him.

Was that what she was doing? Running away? She hadn't given it any thought until now, since she was so focused on the idea that solving the Solar Storm patterns and working to prevent more damage was such a noble endeavor.

But then, why didn't she say anything, or tell them where she was? For the past nine hundred miles she's had ample opportunity to respond to their messages, to check in and be accountable. What's stopped her?

"Look there's Parking Lot C," Walton says. "His lecture hall should be just up over that hill. If we're lucky, his class will be getting out in the next ten minutes."

Thoughts of Ravi, her parents and her job conveniently vanish.

Duty calls, she thinks. For now, anyway.

KLARA
Military Base, United States

Aino looks up as I enter the room, her icy eyes optimistic. Her face is so open and innocent; I feel like I can see into her soul. Her hair is plaited into intricate braids, and she somehow manages to look like a fairy elf and a fierce Nordic warrior all at the same time.

My stomach is fluttering, and I feel edgy, wondering what strange, painful, or unexpected thing might happen. After the drone swarm, I have barely been in the same room with any of the others, except the day LT attacked Luz. Since then, I feel different, like something has shifted in me.

I recall feeling like this after my father's death. I thought at the time it was shock. But recognizing it again now in myself, it feels supernatural almost. It's like the blood in my veins has been hardened. My body feels capable of more. I've tested this out in different ways when I've been alone in my cell. It isn't that I feel no pain at all, but it's almost as if I can choose what pain to feel. Sometimes I pinch myself, first feeling a mostly normal sensation. Then I harden my senses, pinching again, feeling nothing. It's so odd that I'm frightened by it. I've begun to wonder if I have some sort of nervous system disorder. I can still feel hot and cold. I don't have a tingling, pins-and-needles sensation anywhere. It's just this hardening against pain. But I am terrified of yet another change, another phenomenon I don't understand.

Now Aino is looking at me hopefully, expectantly. I fear I have somehow taken on the role of savior for this group, and I know that I need to be strong for them. I reach out to squeeze her hand reassuringly and she gives me the warmest smile. It's like a sunrise over an icy lake, melting a little of the fear and hardness on the surface of my heart. If I can't control the fact my body is able to do these things, then maybe I can choose to do what's required of me, if it means providing this comfort to the others.

I take a seat in the chair next to her, noting there are three other empty chairs circled up in the center of the room.

"Another test, I suppose?" she asks, pointing her head at the chairs.

"I guess so." I shrug.

The door bangs open and Jonah escorts Luz into the room. She keeps her head lowered so the shelf of dark hair covers much of her face. But it doesn't obscure her from me entirely. I notice dark rings under her eyes. I wonder if the attack from LT has put her on edge so much that she hasn't been sleeping.

She shuffles over to the furthest chair and slumps down, looking at her folded arms. Aino and I share a glance, worry exchanged in our eyes.

I am distracting myself by pinching my arm when Jonah escorts Penny into the room. He takes a seat in one of the chairs, but Penny stops short, a couple of feet from my side. She is watching me with a keen fascination, some realization or discovery washing over her face. I stop what I am doing and look up at her, quizzically. She turns her head to look at me square in the face but says nothing. Then silently, meaningfully, she reaches down to pinch her own arm. Just once. We lock eyes, instant awareness taking place in this brief encounter. Almost imperceptibly, she half shakes her head, giving me a warning.

She turns and walks to the chair in silence. I bite my lower lip, wanting to ask questions, but taking my cues from her that this needs to remain our secret.

Thankfully, Jonah has missed all of this because he is flipping through some notes on a tablet and calibrating the equipment in the room. Luz probably wouldn't notice if a truck crashed through the wall right about now. But Aino is all over us both with her eyes; her mouth open as if to ask a question. I quickly and carefully lay one hand on her forearm and try to convey a message without words.

Before she seems to fully understand, I ask, "What's in store for us today, Jonah?"

He looks up from his tasks, excitement in his eyes.

"We might be onto something pretty major!" He's almost manic in his energy today and it feels contagious. I stop myself just short of getting excited too, recalling what our past 'accomplishments' have involved.

"The last time you were all together, Klara was able to see all the doors, right?" He addresses us as a group, though Luz is hardly an engaged participant here. Aino is nodding and Penny squints her eyes with suspicion.

"Did you ever open any of those doors, Klara?" The intensity of his gaze makes my stomach flip. Why does he have to be so damn handsome?

I shake my head.

"No, that's right. We got caught up in the excitement of it all, but we missed a really important step here." He looks down at his watch and records a time on the tablet.

"Okay, this time Klara, you are going to open another door. Just pick any other door to open; it doesn't matter."

I nod my head, wary and begrudging, unsure what will happen if I do this, and whether I am even capable of opening other doors.

"Oh, and just open one. Whatever happens, just a single door for this exercise, okay?"

I nod again, exhaling through my nose.

He guides me over to the corner against the wall, bracing me. The others stand in a circle around me and for the first time today I get a little eye contact from Luz. She looks concerned for me, and I give her a reassuring nod back.

"Ready?" Jonah asks, his eyebrows shooting up in his face with visible glee.

I nod once more and this time I close my eyes. Reaching inward, I'm there in an instant. The hallway is becoming more familiar to me. I consider walking farther down but decide to keep this quick. I reach for the first door handle to my right. It's a dark, brushed bronze handle, warm to the touch. I grasp, then turn. It gives way and turns in my hand. I inhale sharply, then pull to open. Suddenly a wave of heat is blasting through the open doorway, and I stumble backward, but this time I don't fall over. I attempt to walk over to the door, but my legs are heavy, and it takes what feels like an eternity to get there. I reach for the handle, pulling the door shut.

When I open my eyes, I'm covered in sweat, but I'm still upright in the corner. Jonah is hunched over his instruments and tablet, recording information and moving at a frenzied pace. Aino is squatting by my side, a hand on my shoulder to brace me should I fall. I look over and see Luz on the floor, Penny cradling her head in her lap.

"What happened? Is Luz okay?"

Penny nods reassuringly at me, brushing Luz's hair out of her eyes, then calmly stroking her head. "She's okay. She fainted, but I was able to catch her. I think she's just very exhausted." Luz's eyes are closed, and she appears to be in a very deep, tranquil sleep. She almost looks peaceful lying there.

"Jonah?" I demand, my voice carrying to him across the room. "What just happened? I only opened one door, just like you instructed."

He puts down the tablet and comes over to us. "I'm pretty sure the door you opened was Luz's." I look over at her again, recognition snapping into place. He continues, "It would explain why she fainted. The readings I am getting are stronger than anything we've registered before!"

Aino looks up at him. "What do you think this means?"

"We'll need to do more tests, but I think it means Klara can unblock any of you by opening your door. And when she does that, you channel together, multiplying your power."

I look down at my hands, trying to take this in, recalling the feel of the doorknob in my hand, thinking back at how each doorway and knob was slightly different and unique.

"That's a game-changer!" Penny declares. "We really can stop the Black Dragon, and this will all be over." Her eyes are intense, and her body is protectively wrapped around Luz.

"We're more powerful together?" Aino asks, as if she is a step behind the rest of us.

"Yes," Jonah replies, a single answer to both questions.

Another hour later, I've managed to identify and open the doors of Penny and Aino, ultimately opening both at once. Jonah confirms the readings are triple of any we got when individually channeling.

When he asked me to open Luz's door again, along with the others, I refused. She is still resting on Penny's lap, and I don't want to put her through anymore effort today.

"We know enough," I had said to him. "We know how it works. We've given what you needed from us for today."

I worry LT will come in and force me, but he never shows up. I hold my ground.

We finally wrap up the session and Jonah walks me back to my cell. I look over at him, trying to assess what he might be feeling in this moment.

"I hope you don't get into trouble for not testing with all of us at once." I am genuinely concerned for him, not fully understanding the hierarchy here, or the level of authority he has.

"I'll be all right" he reassures me. Then he says, "You were pretty amazing again today, Klara." His eyes are soft now and I feel warm inside as I feel this praise settling in.

"Do you have any idea how special you are?" I know he is referring to my special abilities, but a part of me secretly hopes he means more by it.

"Do you really think we'll be able to go home soon?" I ask.

He places a hand on my shoulder as we stop in front of my cell. "I really do. I'm going to report back our findings from today and start to work up a plan of action with LT and the Committee. Hopefully, the next time you see me, it will be to carry out our final act and put this Program to bed."

I smile at him and fight the urge to reach out and give him a big hug. I'm already wondering if it will be the last time I see him, if we'll ever have contact again once this is over.

It's only after I'm alone in my cell and I hear the echo of his footsteps down the corridor, that I recognize new words he hasn't used before. Committee. Program. Has he been keeping things from me? Or have I just not been listening? I want to be relieved at this new discovery and the hope that this will end soon. But there is something menacing in the formality of those words he used. Something structural that I am just starting to recognize.

I reach down and pinch myself. Oddly, I can't feel a thing.

Later that night, something else begins to change. I'm as sick as the last time I had food poisoning. But this feels different somehow.

The next morning, after being up all night, barely sleeping between bouts of vomiting, I am depleted and exhausted. I have pulled myself into a modified upright position along the wall when I hear a polite knock on the door of my cell.

Jonah enters.

"I heard you didn't eat your breakfast," he says.

Still clutching the blanket pulled up under my chin, I shake my head.

"Have you been able to keep down any water?" he comes over and pours me a cup of water from the canister on a low table.

"Sips. Anything more just comes back up." I sit up and take the cup from him.

"I think we need to get you to the infirmary, to get some medication perhaps." He is assessing me more closely now, looking at my skin color, trying to get a sense of how bad this is.

"What medication will help this? I must be developing an intolerance to an ingredient in the food here." I've been getting sick like this more frequently, the sleepless nights more common all the time.

He sits down next to me on the bed and tilts his head to look over at me from an angle. His hands are pressed down at his sides. He looks away briefly, then back at me. I can tell he is thinking. He closes his eyes and shakes his head.

"There's something you should know," he says. "No one knows for sure, but there's a strong belief that for women like yourself, this special ability comes at a price."

"And… that's why I've been getting sick?" I ask.

"Yes," he says, and I can tell he's not just making a guess about this. I can tell there is more — a definite answer.

"Because," he pauses dramatically, "because they think your ability is caused by mutated cells in your body." His voice drops as he adds, "…a kind of cancer."

"Oh," I eke out, the sound trailing downward from my mouth as soon as I utter it, my mouth holding the 'O' shape, unable to let it go. Somehow the word is filled with weight, like an anchor. My eyes follow the sound toward my feet, no longer able to make eye contact. I think about how sick I have been, how my body hasn't felt quite right ever since that first night I had the dream. I'm trying to work out how long it has been and assess the speed and severity of this illness. I'm afraid to ask questions, not wanting answers that can't be unsaid.

He seems to understand my silence. "I wish I could tell you how serious it is, or what sort of treatment might be available, but this is all pretty new information. I'm on a need-to-know basis, so I really don't know much else."

I swallow hard and set down the cup of water.

"I'd like to take you to the infirmary today, at least to get some anti-nausea medication, and probably get an I.V. started. I don't think the clinic staff will know much or be able to tell you more, but I need to make sure we do everything we can for you."

I instantly feel a clash of conflicting feelings toward him, and they churn inside of me as my guts threaten to spill out all over again. My thoughts are at war. On the one hand, here he is, this kind man, checking in on me, telling me what he knows, helping me. And yet, I despise him for not knowing more, for not finding out as much as he can, for not telling me the instant he knew about this.

I'm too exhausted to unpack my paradoxical feelings. All I can say is, "I'll go to the infirmary." After a pause, I add, "thank you."

He exhales as if relieved, as if worried I would say no or react violently to the new information.

The wheels start to turn in my head, and it occurs to me to ask, "What about the others?"

His lips purse together. I can see he was hoping to avoid this question, and he's disappointed that in spite of my exhaustion and mental state I've thought through the likelihood that I'm not the only one who is sick.

"Does it happen to all of us, or just some?" I say the word 'some' as if it means 'me,' hoping for an answer that doesn't make this so much worse.

He inhales; his mouth twisted in a shape that indicates the words he is about to utter taste bitter on his tongue. "From what I heard, there haven't been any exceptions," he says. "Luz is showing the worst symptoms of those of you here on base. She's actually back in the infirmary now for a third time. I'm really sorry, Klara."

I nod. Then he adds, "You know, maybe Luz will be cheered up by your visit to the infirmary. She probably wouldn't mind some company."

I look at him as these words come out of his mouth and I think he sees the ridiculousness of what he said reflected back in my face. In a split second it hits him that Luz will understand more of our dire situation simply by knowing that I'm also ill.

He claps his hand on his forehead, slightly covering his eyes. "I'm sorry," he stutters "I, don't know why I said that. This is awful, Klara. I really am sorry. For you, and Luz and the others."

I can't keep the edge out of my voice now, my energy returning to me as the heat of anger fires up within me. "Then find out more," I demand. "Find out how bad this is, find out who is working on a treatment. Find out why this happened to us in the first place!" I'm almost yelling now, my voice hoarse from being sick the past nine hours. Tears spill down my face and I realize how helpless I am here and how hopeless it all feels.

"I've been trying, I have," he says defensively. "I don't have clearance for a lot of things I've tried to access. I have to be careful. If they catch me looking where I don't belong, I can get into a lot of trouble."

He won't be any help to me if he gets removed from this assignment, but somehow, I question whether that's as much his concern as protecting himself.

Acceptance of the limitations of our circumstances holds my anger at bay. I need him, we need his help. "Just, see what else you can learn and please tell me." I wipe the tears from my face.

The questions begin pouring out of me. "Do you think I'm going to die in here? Will I ever get to go home? Why did this happen to me and not someone else?"

He looks sympathetic to these questions and says, "I wish I knew. I'll try to find out more." He squeezes my hand. Instead of letting go, he looks closely at it and pulls it into the light.

Red and purple half circles are scattered across the back of my left hand. "What's this?"

I run the fingers of my right hand over the marks. "If I tell you, can I trust you to keep it a secret?"

He thinks for a moment, "Yes, okay, I won't say anything. What's going on here?"

"I'm not entirely sure," I begin. "A week or so ago, I started to feel different. I mean, I've been feeling all sorts of things since this began, but this was strange because I could control it. I noticed that if I saved up a little energy after channeling, I could access it later."

His brow is furrowed and he's trying to follow. "Like charging a battery?"

"Yeah, something like that. I could access it for myself. When I wanted to protect myself from something, I found I could tap into that little reservoir and make myself numb. It's never enough to make my whole body numb, but I've been practicing a little to see how much coverage I can get and for how long."

He looks down at my hand again. "And this is what practicing looks like?"

I nod.

"How long does it last?" he asks.

"Not long, the most I've been able to get is an hour and that was only for my arms. Expanding beyond that just reduces the time significantly. You won't tell LT or your leadership, will you?" I ask.

"No, this is our secret."

He helps me out of bed, and I lean on him, keeping my arm around his waist the entire time we walk slowly to the infirmary.

Just as he said, Luz is there too. She's hooked to an I.V. and is sleeping. She looks so pale, and I can tell she's lost weight. She's so out of it, she has no awareness I am here.

Jonah helps situate me in the bed next to hers and comes back with a nurse. I lean back against the pillows. Once the nurse gets the drip started, it's not long before I feel sleep coming for me.

As I fall into sleep, and into trust that Jonah will protect what I've told him, I dream of frozen lakes ringed by beautiful tall evergreens, of my home and life so far away. As I soar over my hometown in dreamland, my psyche wrestles with the question of whether trusting him was the right idea. I have to trust him if I'm ever going to get out of this place, but it's dangerous, and my unconscious mind is aware of the risk. In the dream, trust becomes a frozen lake and I'm carefully putting one foot and then another onto the treacherous surface. Risking trust on another person, it's like being on a frozen lake. Once you're out there in the middle, your sanity depends on believing it will hold you.

MACK
Boston, Massachusetts

"Tell your client to add another zero to that offer, or we'll see you at trial!" Norah ends the call abruptly, swiveling her chair away from a row of windows.

It's been raining in Boston for three days straight, the results of a tropical storm that came up the east coast ruining weddings and graduation parties for the past week. When Mack arrived, he looked uncharacteristically windblown and out of sorts. The natural curl in his hair is more obvious today, somehow both aging him and making him look more grounded.

"They said this storm system would move off by now, but here we are, in the thick of it still." He dabs self-consciously at the damp sections of his khaki pants, holding a sporty rain jacket about a foot away from his body as if the wet from it would infect him if allowed any closer.

"Let Meggie hang that up for you, Mack." Norah summons her assistant to remove the offending article of clothing, while Mack settles into the modern and tasteful accent chair across from her desk. It's one of a pair, angled inward and separated by a low table.

The assistant returns, efficiently producing two mugs of steaming coffee, and silently departing just as quickly as she entered.

Tucking a piece of dark, blunt hair behind her ear, Norah stands and walks over to the credenza, lightly touching a framed photo. It's a group of people, featuring her in the middle, arms linked together, triumphant. The smiles on the faces of the people around her are notably tinged with a sadness at their eyes, a holding back. It was only three years ago, this bittersweet photo. Miraculously, thanks to her dogged determination and skillful prosecution, this photo was taken outside the courthouse where she had just won a major victory for the family members of victims killed in the Spyrock fire.

It had been record-setting, history-making, both the scale of destruction, as well as the judgment awarded and sentence handed down. West Coast Energy was convicted of the deadliest homicide ever committed by a corporation on U.S. soil. And yet the photo was missing one man. His life was destroyed by the events; his wife and daughter literally ripped from his hands.

"I sometimes still wonder about him," she says.

"Who?" he asks.

"Luke, the one who disappeared. I think they called him LT?"

Mack sips his coffee, recognizing in her the same empathy he feels for his patients. It's not something she shows often, this buttoned-up woman. In fact, he's the one who nicknamed her "Queen of No." Sure, the first two letters of her name spell the word, but the moniker was more befitting of her hardline approach to life.

"I'll never forgive myself," she says. "I should have tried harder to convince him to give a victim impact statement; at least come for the sentencing. I'll always wonder what happened to him."

"I knew you had done well for yourself, Norah. But I never realized what an operation you had going here." Mack runs a hand through his hair as his eyes wander around the office. He thinks back to the luxurious lobby through which he entered, passing by several layers of personnel, first security guard, then front desk receptionist, then finally to Meggie. The light fixtures in her waiting room alone must have cost more than Mack and Georgia's recent vacation.

"Thanks," she graciously responds. "You know, some days I'm so proud of it all, but other days I feel the weight of responsibility.

There was something scrappy and liberating about the time when I was hanging on by a thread but had no one counting on me."

"We all counted on you," he says, his voice quiet. "Even then, Norah. Most especially, the victims."

She purses her lips wryly, seemingly unable to accept the praise.

"Well then, I guess I'm keeping up with my end of the bargain again on this one." She raises her eyebrows, one arched slightly higher than the other.

Mack inhales sharply and leans forward in his chair. "You found something?"

She nods. "I might have."

He exhales. There's a glimmer in his eyes and excitement has crept over his demeanor. He looks young again, like a schoolboy heading out to the play yard.

"It's only a clue, a slight thread we could pull to unravel what might be there," she cautions.

"But still, it's something. And if you found it, your instincts are so sharp, it must mean something."

"Well, judge for yourself." She hands him a stack of papers.

"I have a source at OHRP that helped me on a past case. This took some serious digging to find anything that could remotely be connected, and I have to be careful to protect my source."

As he flips through the papers, she explains. "It was over twenty years ago, but a prominent cancer research lab in Baltimore reported unanticipated side effects on human patients in a clinical trial. The effects were minor on the adult female subjects, but nonetheless a change was noted."

Mack flips through the pages, his eyes latching onto key findings in the papers. "A change in electromagnetic activity, in human bodies?"

"Yes. But for some reason, only to women. The trial was halted, and no long-term damage to the subjects was noted."

"The timing seems odd. It was so long ago. And nothing since then?"

"The timing is perfect," Norah purrs. She's the Cheshire Cat with a secret.

"Perfect… how?" he asks skeptically.

She cups the mug of coffee in her hands and leans back in her chair. "Shortly after the study was halted these Aurora women were conceived. They are all roughly one month apart in age, actually."

"But they weren't born in Baltimore!" Mack protests. "They're from places scattered across the globe. Surely not all their mothers were in this clinical trial. That would be an insane coincidence."

"Yes, definitely, you are correct on all counts." She has that smile again, like she is intentionally doling out answers slowly, threading the needle with meticulous patience.

"Why is this significant then? What is the connection to the Auroras?" There's a slight edge to his voice, recognition that she is playing a little cat and mouse. He's eager for answers.

"A lab assistant anonymously reported something alarming," she says, reaching over and flipping to a memo in the stack of papers.

"Here," she points, a carefully manicured fingernail tapping near a paragraph on the page.

"The assistant reported that electromagnetic changes were detected in non-subjects, women in the lab and even women participating in other trials who had come through the building?" Mack's eyes are wide as he reads the notes aloud, his face incredulous.

"But that's not all," she says, reaching again to point him to another document.

"Unrelated to this clinical trial, several years later, this news story out of Austin, Texas," she says. "It got almost no traction. Just an oddity, a fluff piece. A female child was believed to have electromagnetic forces strong enough to interfere with the Wi-Fi at home and school."

"And you think this is connected to our present-day Aurora women and their powers?"

"Well, as I said," she leans back and crosses her arms, "it's just a small crumb on a trail, maybe it's totally unrelated. It's all we could find. But as far as records of electromagnetic changes in women, this is the earliest information we could locate. It could be how it all started."

Mack takes off his reading glasses and pinches his nose, as if to squeeze out the thoughts. "And it somehow spread all the way to Texas, other countries, and to another generation of women not even born at the time of the clinical trials?"

He is thinking now, the wheels spinning, not exactly skeptical but puzzling out loud.

"But then, why are we only hearing about these handful of women dispersed all over the globe?"

Norah shakes her head. "I certainly don't profess to have all the answers. And even worse, it seems unlikely we will be able to get our hands on any intel about the Auroras that could help us piece this together."

The rain is splattering hard and fast against the large windows behind her chair, painting an ominous backdrop.

"Well, it's honestly amazing, Norah. Much more than I could have hoped you would turn up."

She gives him a self-satisfied smile, and the Cheshire Cat look slowly returns to her face.

"Is there something else?" he asks, already knowing the answer.

She nods. "Maybe. We think so. I had my P.I. do a little digging and she cast a very broad net. She found this online platform where scientists have been posting their observations and theories about the solar events."

"How does that connect to these women?"

"It's a very thin, fragile thread we are pulling here, Mack."

"I hear a 'but' coming," he says in a sing-song accusatory voice.

"But," she laughs the word out. She pauses, then he laughs, and they both laugh together, a relieved sort of collective laughter.

"It's a wild goose chase, I am sure. But… Jenny, my P.I., reached out to an astronomer on this platform who posted an interesting theory just a few days ago. It seems plausible, although we have no scientific evidence around things like this whatsoever. We are in virgin territory here."

"And the theory goes?" he leans in again, gazing up at her from under his thick eyebrows.

"The theory goes something like the solar storms were caused by these women, and there's an energy loop between them and the Sun. Each time they release energy, the solar storms flare up. This feeds their energy, causing them to flare back, and so on, and so on."

"The scientists, they think there's a causation to it?" he asks.

"That is the current working theory. A few other scientists have started to chime in on this thread and it may be gaining traction." She reaches to the side of her desk to pick up a note card.

"If you want, I had Jenny create an account for you on the Underground so you can login and monitor the comments. It's a very recently unfolding theory, so we expect new information to continue being posted. Maybe it will gain some traction, or maybe it fizzles out."

He takes the card from her, almost reverently, turning it over in his hands. Then he hands her back the file folder of documents.

"Where do we go from here, Norah?" he asks, looking back up at her. "You must have some inkling of a case you can make if you've done this much digging. Is there someone culpable who could be held accountable?"

"It's plausible, I suppose." She swivels to the side in her chair, looking at the window now and taking in the scope of the storm that has been raging just a few feet from their conversation.

"I have some thoughts on a different direction I'd take things, though. If I was to pursue anything at all." Still facing away from him, she continues, "I did this as a favor, Mack. I'll keep Jenny on the trail for now and continue digging. But if you want to monitor the scientists and try to get them to talk, it won't impact anything I'm doing."

She has a look on her face that Mack recognizes. He can tell there is something more, this 'different direction' she mentioned is much bigger than what she is alluding to. Her ability to sniff out a big case is truly a gift and if she has caught the scent, he is certain she will hunt it down.

"I can't thank you enough, Norah. You never cease to amaze me."

"And you as well, Mack. How you picked up on this, and the fact that you decided to do something about it, well you are a marvel.

Keep up your good work for your patients."

He is halfway out the door when she adds, "And please, say hello to Georgia for me."

Back out in the luxurious lobby, waiting for Meggie to retrieve his rain jacket, Mack fondles the note card containing his login credentials for a brief moment before stuffing it deep into his pocket to protect it from the rainy onslaught he will face when exiting the building.

Within minutes, he is back out on the sidewalk, shoulders hunched, and his head bowed under a tightly cinched hood, rain pouring off him in long, ropy waves. As he makes his way toward the train station, his thoughts turn to Georgia, and Lynelle, and how excited they will be to discover all that he has learned in such a short time. As he walks, his fingers curl around the edges of the note card in his pocket, tracing a line of thoughts, a line of hope in his mind.

AARYA
Jackson, Wyoming

"You asked me before if I believe in fate or God." Walton is sipping hot coffee under bright fluorescent lights in an all-night diner.

They have been debriefing from their encounter with Professor Williams, but returned to the recently discovered well of conversation that now exists between the two of them.

"I believe we make our own destiny, if we're open to see it, and willing to take the risks." He has a meaningful look on his face, as if sensing she has been holding back and playing it safe.

"As a scientist, I find myself resisting anything that defies logic or definition," she confesses. "And yet..."

"And yet there is a part of you that thirsts for an experience that transcends into the unknowable?" he finishes her thought.

"Wouldn't it be such a betrayal of my field, of my area of study, if I ever voiced such a desire? Don't you think it would undermine every ounce of credibility I've spent years building?"

"You want to know what I really think?" he leans in. "I think you are capable of accomplishing things most of us could never dream of. But you hold yourself back. You make yourself small, to fit into the size and shape of a life that you think others expect for you. You follow logic instead of your heart."

She is struck by his candor, his openness with her. What he is saying feels true to her, painfully so.

He goes on, "I think your heart knows what you deserve. Leaving with me on this trip is your first step down the path that fate wants for you."

"Do you think…" she inhales deeply, her breath shaking ever so slightly. "Do you think, maybe what we think about as fate is just our inner spirit guide or intuition? Something inherent in all of us that knows what's right for us?"

She tries to think of a time when she ever listened to that voice, ever gave into that tug pulling in another direction. But all that comes up is a long list of memories where she denied the existence of that voice. She's suddenly and acutely aware of all the times she muscled through a decision that looked good on paper, gained approval of others, and ended up feeling unfulfilled and disconnected.

"You want to know what I believe?" he says. "I think intuition isn't just blind belief. I think it's micro-assessments our brains have learned to make that we don't consciously register. There are plenty of studies to back this up." She's struck by this line of thought. Could she have spent her life silencing a scientifically helpful voice? And if Walton has bridged the gap between the mystical and scientific with his views on this topic, in how many other ways does he transcend the two worlds? Something feels inherently right to her about embracing both worlds and finding a way to integrate them.

She pulls out her phone, scrolling through the missed calls and messages from Ravi and her parents. She's trying to reconcile the life she's been living with this concept of what her life could be, envisioned through the eyes of someone like Walton.

"They want you to come back, don't they?" Walton asks.

"They are so angry and disappointed. And things with Ravi have been, well, less than ideal."

"I know you're taking a chance and heading in a new direction, but I can't imagine you'll feel good about yourself if you don't at least respond to them. I know it's uncomfortable for you to disappoint them. But if you let them know you're okay, tell them why you're not coming back, I think you'll respect yourself so much more."

With tears running down her face, she nods silently. Reaching over, she grabs his hand across the table.

"Will you sit here with me while I do this?" she asks.

"I'd be honored."

Twenty minutes and two more cups of coffee later, Aarya feels a weight lifted off her shoulders. She's explained herself to her parents as best she can, though their worry for her job and sanity came through loud and clear. She decided to leave things somewhat open-ended with Ravi. They'll have a good long talk when she returns, and maybe they'll decide to end things, or maybe they'll fix what's been missing. Regardless, she finds that she's surprisingly comfortable with the uncertainty of it.

"So where do we go from here, with the hypothesis of Professor Williams?" Walton asks.

Their ambush of the Professor was as successful as it could have been, Larry Williams being at first, surprised and worried they had sussed out his secret identity as Lone Wolf. But after the initial shock wore off, he invited them back to his office, sharing the detailed graphs and charts he had put together, allowing them to download electronic copies.

"I think we have to figure out how to prove that the three events in the baseline series really were caused by the Auroras, and nothing to do with solar activity," Walton says, stabbing a fork into pancakes, enjoying the breakfast-all-day menu items. "I'm trying to work out how we can get the data about these women. We need it in order to make that connection."

"We know at least one of them was a U.S. citizen, right?" Walton begins scrolling through Underground posts and notations on his tablet.

"True. Do you think the U.S. military might have information about when she was discovered and when she caused some of the outages? Didn't one of the posts mention they were being weaponized?"

Walton's face lights up, "Here it is!" He points to a post. "Posted by a user from Fayetteville, North Carolina."

"The details are a little sparse," she says, while reading. "The person posting is probably worried about being outed and is trying to minimize the specifics. But the dates and locations — here!" She points to the information then locks eyes with him.

"We really might be onto something," Walton says.

"Could two individuals like us, going rogue on our agency, risking our careers, be able to unlock this whole tragedy?" Aarya has a confused, bewildered look. "Is it ever really that simple?"

"Yes." He answers plainly. "Yes, because that's why whistle blowers have so much power, and deserve so much protection. We see it all the time in the news."

"If we weren't willing to put our necks on the line, do you think anyone else could or would piece this together?"

"I don't know. Maybe?" he says, hopefully. "But at minimum, it would take a lot longer for someone else to put these pieces together. We're in the right jobs with access to the right information to help figure this out. Right now."

In the morning, after a brief, but restful night's sleep at a cheap motel, they are back at the very same diner. The motel thankfully had a room with separate beds. But it was awkward trying to give each other privacy. And the sound of another person's breathing so close by was a strange distraction.

"I had a maybe ridiculous thought," Aarya says, reaching over to grab the syrup. "When I looked at the data points again, I wondered if somehow the Auroras be exacerbating the solar activity."

Walton ponders a moment, looking over the data again more closely. "An upcycling of solar maximum, you think?"

She leans in and points to a few key items on the tablet. "Not exactly. But I think there is some interaction. After the first Aurora incident, you see here where it scaled up such a significant amount?" She pauses to take a bite of plant-bacon.

"Then here, here and here." She shows him, punctuating each point on the screen with her fork.

"What if these women are heightening the effects of the solar storms?" he asks.

She pauses, the wheels turning while she chews, letting the hypothesis firm up within her gray matter. Then she exclaims. "Like a Wi-Fi booster!" Aarya's eyes are wide.

Walton ponders this briefly then nods his head solemnly. "It can't be unrelated, these women and their abilities just happening suddenly now in the middle of the largest solar storms recorded in history. You think they are somehow channeling the energy from the Sun, the electromagnetism?"

"I do. I think that's a possibility. Especially when you look at the locations where activity spiked and think about how it didn't align with traditional predictions. The challenge in proving this is going to be that we don't have good details on whether the women are moving around."

"Or being moved," Walton adds, ominously.

"Ugh. True." Aarya slumps back in her seat a little, at the thought of larger forces controlling women, somehow making things worse for society by taking advantage of the situation. "So it seems like it's going to be just as important, after we get the data from Lone Wolf, that we can find some sources of information on these women." Aarya begins typing, filtering entries on the Underground.

"I think that's right. We're going to have to pull both pieces of this puzzle together." Walton sits back in the booth for a moment.

It's not long before Aarya raises an index finger in the air, as if she has identified something important. If they were playing Charades, it would be her impression of the 'Eureka' moment. It's surprising how much more expressive she is around him.

"There was a story on the news, not too long ago. A boyfriend of one of these women had banded together with other family and friends. They are mounting a search effort." She shows the tablet to Walton. "One of the women's sisters has been posting on the Underground."

As they review the posts, talking through the connections and details, Walton pauses, pointing at the screen. "You have a new message!"

"Oh?" Aarya pulls it close, examining. "I haven't been messaging anyone directly. I wonder why someone would contact me?" She clicks and reads to herself.

"Who is it? What do they want?" Walton asks, exasperated.

"He's a medical doctor," she pauses, reading the lines again. "Says he thinks he knows what caused these powers in the women. He's interested in our theories."

"Should we respond?" he asks. "What does your intuition tell you?"

PENNY
Military Base, United States

She is sitting on a chair close to Luz. Close enough to almost feel the heat of her body, but far enough to avoid suspicion. She wants to reach out and touch her elfishly small hand. She wishes she could just tuck that errant piece of hair behind her ear. And, more importantly, to repeat back the words from her note, to tell her she loves her too. To point out all the reasons she is worth saving, to explain how much light and beauty she brings to this world.

Since she read the note, they haven't had any communication or interaction. Just sitting next to her in this room, Penny feels more alive than she has in days. There are so many things she wants to know. How did her penmanship get to be so fluid and floral? Why does she always smell like buttercream frosting? What made her say she is not worth saving? Penny is hungry for all the details, dark or delicious, bright or sour.

But sitting here in this sterile room, none of that can happen. Those thoughts are fuel for her plan, knowing that together they will share secrets and heal each other's wounds, once Penny gets them out of here.

Jonah has been talking for a little while now, going on about how

Klara's ability to multiply the powers is going to set the stage for a final act that will end the "war." Penny puts air quotes around that word in her mind every time he says it. It's not her war. It's not even a real war. But apparently plans have been laid. Jonah has used this new information to refine his AI tool that helps them detect the location of other Auroras. More women are being "recruited." Yes, air quotes on that one too.

He's filled them in on the messages from the Underground, how he contacted Ryen to let him know that Klara was okay, and a post that helped him get in touch with Aino's sister.

He's cautioned them not to mention the Underground or any of these communications around LT, and though Penny sees Jonah as part of the problem, she can also see that he's putting himself in danger to do what he can to help them.

It's no surprise that everyone is stiff and silent the minute LT enters the room. Even if they weren't keeping secrets from him, that guy could suck the life out of any room. Given his lack of softer skills, she's amazed he has gotten so far up the chain of command. But then again, she thinks about the phrase that people are promoted to their highest level of incompetence. Well, at least men are, she thinks.

They've rearranged the circle of chairs to make room for LT, and he sits among them now, clearly uncomfortable with the equality suggested by their circular seating positions.

"Now that Klara can tap into the powers of all of you, even those who aren't here with us, now is the time to send a message." His eyes rove over each of them, assessing, attempting to impart a sense of his authority over them. "We are preparing to attack a target in China, one that could destabilize the Three Gorges Dam and undermine large swaths of the power grid."

"We'll be traveling to China, then?" Penny asks the obvious question.

"Ding, ding, ding!" he chants tauntingly. "Three points to the mouthy red head for guessing the correct answer."

Jonah flinches at LT's degrading tone but says nothing.

"Don't worry, you can take your blue booger along if that's what you're worried about."

It's as if the eyebrows on every face sitting around the circle are synchronized, when they all raise at once and the faces to which they belong simultaneously point in her direction. Luz gives her a quizzing look, with the slightest amount of warning not to endanger herself. How can a person's face, one so arrestingly beautiful and innocent convey all of these things in a look?

Penny's face is giving a death stare to LT, and she breathes through her nose like a bull staring down a matador.

"Oh, you thought I didn't know about it?" He laughs at the surprise on her face, delighting in her pain.

"Did you really think you could hide anything from us in here? If you have something in your possession, it's because we allowed you, no– strike that– I allowed you– to keep it." In spite of the obvious message in his words, intended to demonstrate his power over them, Penny wonders for a moment if the others have similar items or if she is the only one with a strange object from a painful past.

Ironically, their past is more similar than he knows. But neither he nor Penny is aware how much the scars on their body resemble the other's.

"Do you want to tell us what that thing is? That bizarre, melted plastic, precious thing you carry around with you?"

At the word 'melted', Jonah tilts his head, looking from Penny then slowly over to LT. The wheels are turning, and he's making a connection that no one else could have. He remembers now the details from her chart in the infirmary, and the story he pulled up online in the news archives later that night, featuring two shockingly different photos side by side. One was a picture of bright-eyed little kid with the wildest red hair practically standing on her tiptoes to show off the first-place prize. The other photo, a mangled and charred vehicle along the roadside drenched in water next to a firetruck.

He's thinking out loud, piecing the clues together, when three words quietly slip out of his mouth "...the Blue Ribbon?"

Penny jerks her head up. But for a split second, before her guard was up, there was a vulnerable look to her that he'd never seen before. Had she really kept that melted prize all these years?

Picking up on the fact that this conversation could only go from bad to worse, Aino with her soft and sweet voice jumps in. "What does any of that have to do with China? I want to know when we are leaving and what we need to do to prepare."

LT is curious about the story behind Penny's 'blue booger', but the mention of China snaps him back to reality and pulls him out of bullying mode. He is nothing if not eager to be in command of the tactical planning. It's enough for now to pull him away from his curiosity and back to logistics.

Roughly an hour later, LT has relayed the plans to them and prepped them with the timing, layout, and contingencies. They will leave in the morning with just a small team to support the Auroras. In addition to the squad of armed personnel, each woman will carry two handguns and a knife. The weapons training they've each received over the past weeks will be required for the first time in a field operation and they are deemed ready. Though whether any of them is willing to shoot at a human being, that's another question entirely.

AARYA
Kansas City, Missouri

She tucks loose hair behind her ears and checks the messy knot on the top of her head. Running her hands down the front of her terracotta-colored cardigan for the third time, Aarya attempts to smooth invisible wrinkles that don't exist. She is anxious and tired, road weary from the fifteen-hour drive.

"What if he doesn't show up?" she asks Walton, voicing the fear she's been swallowing down. Late yesterday, after messaging and sharing high level details, they arranged to meet the doctor they contacted on the Underground. Unbelievably, he agreed to come all this way.

"I can't see why he wouldn't. He's probably just running late." Walton says. His hair is combed neatly, almost stylishly today. It's obvious he has put effort into his appearance.

"What if this is some kind of a set up?" Aarya is looking down at her hands, unable to make eye contact in her frazzled state.

"She seems legitimate, based on the details she was posting. Is it possible that you're more anxious about what might happen if she does show up? What if we can be part of changing all of this for the better?" Walton pats her shoulder.

Aarya takes a sharp inhale of breath through her nose and deliberately, slowly blows it out of her mouth, in an audible rush of air. She thinks about what he's said. For him to intuit so much about her state of mind, her fears and hopes, she realizes how closely he has been paying attention. She thinks about how it's an interesting turn of phrase, to "pay" attention. As if it costs the person something. She supposes, in a way, that it does. And this thought sends a warm feeling through her chest.

Feeling a bit calmer, she responds to his question, "Yes. Maybe I am more afraid of that. Earlier this year, if you had told me I'd be here, skipping out on my job, taking risks meeting strangers, getting involved in possible government conspiracies, I'd have said you were totally mad. I'm still getting used to this idea of breaking the rules."

"I know. But those rules were made by the system that created this problem. That system wants you to stay quiet and make yourself small." He reaches over to squeeze her hand.

"Let's make new rules, then." Aarya's eyes are glistening as she grasps his hand.

"Sure," he agrees. "I think the first one is no more hiding the truth, even if there are people who don't want to hear it, or it feels safer to keep silent."

Her breath shudders as she inhales, then she lets out a long slow breath and nods her head. "Yes. The world deserves to hear my truth. And I deserve to give it voice."

"I like the sound of that!"

To an outsider just walking into the shop, they would look like a couple, leaned into each other, locked in an exchange. But the moment is broken by a jangling, when the bells over the door to the coffee shop alert them to the entrance of another customer.

To say the woman who walks in is petite would be an understatement. She looks almost juvenile and for a few seconds, Aarya thinks it cannot be her. But then she is followed by a man, the one whose photo she recognizes from his profile on the clinic website, and Aarya knows this is Dr. Mack. So the diminutive woman with him must be Jenny, the private investigator, she surmises. She thinks how easy it must be for her to fly under the radar in her job, looking the way she does.

The woman's hair is just long enough to cover her ears, with the portion in front too long to be officially considered bangs, but slightly shorter than the rest. It covers her head in somewhat of a bird's nest shape, and Aarya can't decide if it's hip and cool or just really messy bed hair.

The tiny woman and Dr. Mack come over to the little foursome of armchairs angled inward. They make introductions and the anxious mood of too much anticipation is finally starting to fizzle out. Mack offers to get coffee for Jenny. Walton and Aarya already have their drinks and send him off to the counter to order.

Jenny gets to work pulling a tablet out of her rucksack and organizing herself. Aarya notices that her nails are nicely manicured, a bold, black-and-white pattern splattered across them in a striking, artful design. The messy hair must be intentional then, she thinks, taking in this eccentric, tiny little woman who is nothing like anyone else in the world.

"Love ya old school cahdigan," the woman says, not even looking up from her bag of items. Her Boston accent is thick and unmistakable. Aarya wouldn't have thought she had a chance to look about, but the comment reveals that somehow, she's taking in the details around her without seeming to. It must be a terribly valuable skill in her line of work.

"Thanks, I collect them. It's a little hobby of mine to save them. I think of them as rescues." She sits up a little straighter in her chair as her index finger strokes the single button at her collar. She looks over then at Jenny's cardigan, cropped, modern and somehow giving off a punk librarian vibe. It's so wide across the shoulders that it looks as though it may slip off at any moment. Large, studded buttons angle down asymmetrically from the left shoulder, rather than making a neat line down the center. The thick, black yarn is held together in a loose swooping knit.

"Yours is so unique, it's really incredible." Aarya says, her eyes running over the garment, drinking in each intricate detail.

It's the first time the other woman looks her in the eyes, and she sees a sparkle as the compliment lands. "Ah, thanks. It's my own creation! I re-purpose and restore them. My online shop is called 'Can Ya Cardigan.'"

Walton snorts, looking back and forth at the two women, eyes wide in surprise. "What?" they remark at him in unison.

He's shaking his head, "How is it possible that we have two of the greatest cardigan aficionados together in one room?"

Mack has just returned with a hot tea and steaming mug of coffee, setting the drinks carefully on the low table. "Cardigans?" he asks. "Did I hear that right?"

Three heads nod up at him gleefully. He shrugs his shoulders and grins back at them before taking his seat. "Well, it's nice to know we've already found some common ground." He sips from the mug and leans back, a contented look on his face. "I'd say we have a lot more in common, though, based on recent conversations and research." He looks meaningfully over at Jenny who nods and smiles.

"Well, we're certainly happy to share the data we obtained, and discuss our theory," Aarya eagerly offers.

"Yes, we want to get to that, but perhaps a little background on how this all got started?" Mack looks over to Jenny, a signal to begin.

Jenny walks them through the theory about the human research trials in Baltimore two decades prior and the little girl in Texas. As she unpacks the pieces of the story, she talks fast, words blurring together.

"We had the idear about checking patent office filings," she says, her Boston accent peeking through between words.

"And then I found this." She points to a record on her tablet. "Jonah Larkin submitted it several years ago. It's a patent filing for an artificial intelligence program to detect changes in electromagnetic patterns, across geographically dispersed areas. Essentially, it collects energy signal patterns from the Internet of Things."

Aarya tilts her head to the side quizzically. "Do you mean, like my Bluetooth waterless dishwasher could inform someone of a change in EM patterns?"

"Something like that, yes." Jenny confirms. "It's an ingenious way to collect data when you think about it. It skirts privacy protections too because EM data isn't personalized to humans. Or, at least— it wasn't."

"And who is this Jonah guy?" Walton asks.

"We weren't sure at first." Jenny responds. "It seemed like he was probably unrelated as an individual player. We thought maybe his program was stolen or appropriated by the government. But then we found postings on the Underground that look like they could have been created by him. A little more background indicates he dropped out of his graduate program shortly after the patent filing, and we can't get a permanent address for him since that time. Not only do we think he's involved in the program that abducted these women, but he also seems to be dropping breadcrumbs for us to follow."

"Intentionally so?" Aarya asks.

"He's a pretty sophisticated guy, involved in a very high security operation." Jenny explains. "The fact we were able to pull as much detail off the postings as we did suggests to me that he's taken active measures to reveal these clues."

"And when you say 'clues'..." Aarya asks, using air quotes hopefully.

"Yeah, we think we might know where the women are being held." Jenny says.

"Okay, this is a lot to digest." Walton says. "You think you know how and when the mutations began, and you've located the Auroras. Have you gone to the authorities with this?"

"Not just yet, no." Jenny answers. "We only landed on the location yesterday and wanted to meet with you first. If what you know can help these women, we want that information before someone goes looking for them."

Walton leans back in his chair, fingers steepled in front of him. Thoughtfully, slowly, he says, "If you could find them, then the government could too. This is all just a little too obvious." He says it as a statement, but it's clear he's thinking and questioning.

Mack jumps into the conversation now, for the first time since they sat down. "I said the same thing to Jenny yesterday." His left eyebrow is raised, as if to acknowledge the thought Walton has yet to voice.

"The government isn't looking for these women, despite statements to the contrary?" Walton asks.

"Why would you look for something you've already found?" Jenny answers rhetorically.

"This changes everything," Aarya says. "The government could try to stop what we're doing." She looks around the coffee shop suspiciously. "I mean, they could be monitoring our online activity, our credit card transactions!"

"We checked the plates of the cars in the parking lot," Jenny assures her. "There's no one here to be worried about at the moment. But you're right, we'll need to start being more careful."

"Leonard's car!" Walton exclaims. Aarya's mouth is agape. Jenny and Mack look over at the two of them with confused expressions.

"We kinda stole our boss' car." Walton groans. "It's charging outside."

Jenny shakes her head, clearly surprised at their spontaneity, intuitively knowing it's so unlike these buttoned-down characters.

"Okay, listen. You're going to make sure it's fully charged and then program it to head back when we're done talking here." Jenny instructs. "I've got burner Sat phones for all of us. Are you on the Wi-Fi right now?"

They both nod. "Disconnect. No more Wi-Fi. I've got a clean hotspot we'll use from now on and you'll come with us once the car heads back. You don't need to panic. But you're going to have to make some changes."

They nod in unison, eyes wide.

She pivots her train of thought, asking, "So what is it that the two of you wanted to tell us about? You have a theory about a connection with these Auroras and the solar storms?"

Aarya nods, then begins. "We originally thought the solar storms could be causing the changes in these women. That they were somehow picking up and channeling that energy. We realized that wasn't exactly right, but you've filled in some missing pieces for us. It makes perfect sense now."

She goes on to explain how they weren't sure the initial cause of changes in the women, but from the data Professor Larry shared, they figured out the women have been channeling the solar electromagnetism.

"We feel confident that the three baseline events were either caused by or exacerbated by the women, based on the data and the news stories. It's more than likely that ninety percent of the power outages wouldn't have occurred at all without these women. If you look at the patterns, there just wasn't enough impact from the solar storms alone for the rolling outages to occur. Once we knew something else was going on, we pieced the timing together."

"You're saying without these women, the outages might not have happened?" Mack asks.

"They'd have been minor, at best, from what we can tell. The current solar cycle is more active and powerful than average so it's an outlier for sure. But honestly, it's not that different from cycle ten when the Carrington Event happened. The only real difference this time is the magnification caused by the Auroras."

"Wow," Jenny says. "If it wasn't for the Auroras, our lives could go back to normal at some point? This isn't like the end of the world as we know it?"

"Exactly," Walton says. "Solar maximum is approaching in three months. If we can figure out how to neutralize the effects of the women, somehow stop them from channeling, after the cycle peaks, things could be normal again."

"You think we can find them." Aarya holds up her index finger. "But then what? How do we stop them?"

"And this is where Dr. Mack comes in." Jenny emphasizes the word doctor, and gesticulates toward him, her arm extended like she is ushering them to seats in a theater.

He pauses, looking over his shoulder. "Listen, I don't mean to be dramatic, but I am a little worried about this notion we could be followed. Can we return that car and get ourselves on the road? I'll fill you in on the medical part of this in the car."

"On our way to the Auroras?" Aarya asks eagerly.

"Yeah," Jenny says. "Let's put this place in the rear-view mirror."

LIN

Military Base, United States

She takes a tiny, careful sip of water, hoping it's a small enough amount to stay down. She needs to get some liquid into her system, but she's been so sick the past few hours that everything has come back up.

Leaning back against the pillow, she closes her eyes, remembering the key card and the woman, thinking and planning. The next time they take her out of this cell will be her best chance to find an opening, to work out her plan of escape. She'll have to be ready and alert. But right now, she is too depleted to think or plan. She's never been this sick before.

Reaching down, she grabs a tiny bit of flesh on her arm, pinching it between her forefinger and thumb, confirming what she has suspected. There's no sensation from her wrist all the way to her elbow.

"It is working," she whispers aloud, incredulous that another power is available to her.

But how can this help? She wishes she had thought to numb her pounding head so she could think. She closes her eyes, slowing her breath and trying to rest.

In an instant, her eyes snap open. Yes, that's it. She'll numb her whole head, her face, and as much of her shoulders as she can too. It's so obvious and simple.

After another tiny sip of water, she slides down onto the mattress, closing her eyes as a small grin pulls at the corners of her mouth. For as miserable as she feels, this is the closest to happy she has felt in over a month.

Two hours later, after she's managed to drink an entire cup of water, she rolls onto her side. There's movement outside the door of her cell.

When the guard escorts her down the hall, on the way to the room with all the equipment, Lin looks around again, stealthily, taking in the details. Passing by the cafeteria, she sees a worker pushing a dolly of soda and candy to refill the vending machines.

She realizes this creates an opening for her plan. It has to happen today. For once, she hopes the asshole—the man she has learned is called LT—will make an appearance. But if he doesn't, how long will it be until her next chance? She knows something is truly wrong with her, based on how sick she has been. She knows there's little chance she will be released when this is all over. And that understanding is motivation to take risks she wouldn't have taken before.

When the woman leads her into the room with the equipment once again, she's disappointed to see LT isn't here. It's just the two of them. The woman sets up the equipment and performs calibrations. Lin feels the panic rising up.

"No." She hears herself say to the woman's back.

She turns to look at Lin, "I'm sorry, what did you say?" The woman isn't exactly unkind in her response, more surprised and maybe a little annoyed at the interruption.

"We need the man today, the one they call LT," she hears herself saying. Stay calm, she thinks, trying to control her breathing.

The woman turns around, returning to her tasks. "Well, he's busy with some other things today, why would you want him here anyway? He's such a goddamn prick."

Lin starts the numbing process, thinking of her grandmother, trying to be brave at a moment when she is more afraid than ever in her life.

"There's something new, he needs to know. I can use the power differently than before."

The woman sits down and crosses her legs. "Why don't you tell me. I'm right here."

No, Lin thinks. Too many minutes have already passed, and she doesn't know how long it will take for LT to get here.

"I will tell no one but him." Her face is steely, and she crosses her arms, revealing nothing of the frantic thoughts racing through her mind.

"He must come fast," she adds. "If he wants me to show it. The new power it comes and goes."

The woman narrows her eyes, sensing something is off. After doing some mental math, the woman presses a few buttons on her watch, then uncrosses her legs.

"All right then. He's on his way. This had better be worth it. That man can be madder than a hornet when he's summoned away from his other projects."

"That man is always mad," Lin states. The woman grins ever so slightly and chuckles.

Lin reaches up to touch her face, attempting to be casual about it. The numbing isn't complete yet, but she hopes it will be enough.

He comes to the room faster than Lin expected, slightly red in the face, nostrils flared.

"What's this crap about needing me to come over here?" He looks from the woman to Lin.

"She said she wanted to tell you herself. Something about a new way to use the power, I guess."

"What a waste of my time," he mumbles, a disgusted look on his face.

"Out with it then. What's so important you had to interrupt me?" he demands.

Lin tilts her head slightly, blinking as slowly as she can. She musters up the matriarchal persona she has witnessed in her grandmother over the years.

"I changed my mind. You can go." She speaks in an authoritative tone, waving her hand dismissively.

She sees it in his eyes, the flash of dark anger. This seems to have done the trick.

"No, I'm not leaving, you little shit!" He grabs the front of her shirt and slams her against the wall. "I just got here, and you'd better tell me what this is all about. And fast!"

Although the back of her head was knocked against the wall, she feels nothing. She fights the urge to submit, to give him what he wants just so he'll leave. The next part has to go exactly as planned, or she will have incurred his wrath for no good reason.

She steps forward from the wall, antagonizing him, and carefully placing herself next to the seated woman.

"I said you should go." Lin repeats, shifting her weight imperceptibly.

"You bitch!" he roars, swinging a hand up to her face, almost exactly where he hit her the last time. Just as planned she thinks, a sick smile on her mouth right as he makes contact. Yet, she feels nothing.

In spite of this, her legs buckle under her, and she falls onto the woman, collapsing the two of them onto the ground. It's only a split second, but it was enough. Lin deftly uncurls the lanyard and slips the keycard up her sleeve as the woman attempts to push her off.

LT grabs her by the shoulders, yanking her up. "Tell me what's going on here, or so help me God, I will smack you into next week!" His face is so close to hers that little droplets of spit land on her cheeks.

"I feel nothing." She states blandly to him. "The experiment worked." She points to her face, already red and inflamed. "I can numb myself with the power, see. I feel nothing here," she points to her eye where it has started to swell. "I thought better to show you."

He releases the grip on her, allowing her to fall back on her heels. The woman has righted herself now and is on her feet next to him.

LT's anger is waning, as he processes the new information. Though he clearly is angered at being manipulated like this, his greed for more power and information is taking over. There's a slight gleam in his eyes. "You wanted to show me." He shakes his head, almost smiling. "Points for style," he adds.

"All right, Mary," he looks to the woman. "Take her up to medical and have them run some tests to see if what she is saying checks out. I want a full report." He shakes his head again as he leaves. The door is about to close behind him, when Lin reaches out and grabs it, then holds it for a few seconds to be sure he is gone. Then, pointing to the woman she says, "We go now. Before it wears off."

She can't believe it worked, and she grabbed the door in time, so Mary won't have a chance to scan her no-longer-existent keycard.

"Sure, yeah," the woman says, following out. The door closes behind and they start down the hallway. Thankfully, there is no sight of LT in the corridor. Just as they pass the cafeteria, they come to the elevator that requires a card swipe before it will allow them to select the floor for medical.

"Damn," the woman exclaims, looking down, realizing now the card is missing. "Must've lost it in the scuffle."

"Better hurry," Lin advises. "I'll wait here, we need to get there fast, or we won't get the full report like he wanted."

The woman contemplates her options, seeing the door to the room just ten yards away. "Okay, wait right here." Lin nods demurely.

As the woman walks in the direction of the room, Lin silently and carefully follows her, walking on catlike footsteps, veering off into the cafeteria just as the woman enters the room. She won't have long, she thinks.

Amazingly, the man with the vending machine supplies is still there. He's hunkered over the machine, struggling with something. Lin grabs the ballcap he's set on top of his clipboard and shoves it on her head, tucking in her hair. Silently, she grabs the dolly of empty green soda crates and wheels it toward the exit on the other side of the room. She can't go out the way she came in.

Rushing through the door, she finds herself in a hallway along the back of the building that she knows is very close to an exterior exit. She swipes the keycard containing Mary's photo, and the door beeps as the lock releases.

As expected, there's a guard at the counter, just before the final doorway to freedom. Miraculously, he's immersed in a book and doesn't look up as Lin floats past and scans the card once again. She quickly uses her power to disable the exterior cameras as she tucks the card back into place.

Blinding sunlight greets her as she exits the building that has been her prison for over a month now. There isn't time to celebrate or enjoy the feeling of the breeze on her skin. She must act fast before Mary sounds the alarm.

Ditching the dolly, she runs over to a row of side-by-side vehicles. But panic immediately sets in. Of course she will need a key. She curses herself for not thinking of this, for ruining her chances by acting so rashly. As she sits in the driver's seat, she's about to give up when something glinting in the sun catches her eye. One of them has a key still in the ignition! She rushes over to it and starts it up. She's inhaling gulps of air, brushing her hair out of her eyes as she drives over the curb toward the woods. She remembers seeing a dirt trail just past the tree line and can only hope the greenery will give cover long enough for her plan to work.

A branch slaps her in the side of her still-numb face as she navigates the vehicle into the forest. The sound of an alarm blaring rings out behind her and she pushes the accelerator pedal as fast as the vehicle will go. She's not sure if the trail goes through, but she remembers seeing a vehicle charging station about a quarter mile from the building when they were driving back from an outing. Bouncing through the woods, she pulls the vehicle up over an embankment and that's where she sees it. The green and yellow logo of a charging station is the happiest sight she has seen in a long time.

KLARA
Three Gorges Dam, China

We've been planning the trip for the last few weeks. LT said it was finally time, and I wondered if he was rushing because of how sick I'd gotten. I know this illness isn't going to slow down, and I imagine he knows that too.

They told us we were going to the Three Gorges Dam, to cause a massive power outage on mainland China. It seemed outrageous, a clear act of war. And yet, the visa paperwork was submitted with a cover story that we were visiting as a tour group. LT was very nonchalant about the whole thing. Apparently, arrangements were made for a local guide in the country to take us around to the tourist sites. The plan was to visit several cities and locations during our first week, then to strike at the dam when we were supposed to be taking a tour.

The trip and the tourist activities have been utterly exhausting. They gave me anti-nausea medications for daily dosing, and although I slept during most of the flight, and have slept on the infuriating tour bus as we pretended to visit the sites, I am tired in my bones.

When the day arrives, and we are finally in position about a mile away from the dam, I feel like I could close my eyes at a moment's notice. We have been like this, just outside the security perimeter for about fifteen minutes now, and I'm not sure why we are still waiting. LT hasn't given the signal, so there must be a reason. I'm anxious to get this over with. The longer we wait, the greater risk that we will be discovered or that something goes wrong.

Instead of a signal from LT that it's time to begin, I see his crouching figure making a slow path toward me. Just the sight of that man makes me cringe. It's bad enough this wasn't in the plans, but to have to interact with him just makes it all that much worse.

"There's a guard two hundred yards off, on the northeast tower," he whispers. "I'm going to get closer so I can cover you when it's time to move. You'll wait for my signal, then start the sequence. Check that your handgun is ready if you need to use it." He points to my hip.

"I checked it when we deplaned, I'm good."

"Well goddamn it, check again!" he barks, still whispering.

I give him a look, but know better than to argue, especially in this dangerous situation. I smoothly remove the gun, check the magazine, turn off the safety, and place it back in the holster.

"Happy?"

He nods curtly, then ducks behind a retaining wall and slithers off. I see him choosing the location he mentioned and getting settled, and I take the gun out again. This time I point it in his direction, finding him in my sights. Just checking, I tell myself. Making sure, I can defend myself if needed, just not in the way he means it.

I put it back in the holster, taking a few deep breaths to focus. It's the first time I've had a chance to think about what we're doing here and whether I have any choice in the matter. Would I choose not to participate if I knew all the facts? I don't have a lot of time to decide. I could pretend that I wasn't able to access the power, create some excuse. LT knows I am sick, maybe I could blame the illness. Who am I helping if I go forward with the plan? And who might I hurt? Would LT punish me, punish the others? A chilling thought crosses my mind. If we don't fulfill our purpose for the Program, do they have any reason to keep us around? The weight of responsibility weighs heavy on me.

I'm lost in a tangle of confusing "if/then" thoughts when the signal comes through to begin our sequence. Instantly I know it's safer to go along with the plan, but this will be the last time.

I close my eyes and immediately I'm in the hallway. To my left, I open a door, and a wave of energy pushes me back. We've been practicing this, so I'm prepared. I take a minute to regroup and turn to my right. Repeating the sequence, I move from door to door, but this time there are so many more. I can't quite seem to reach out. The handles to each door are just slightly out of reach. I think I feel one in my grip, but am I just holding a rock on the ground? I have no sense of time, but I can feel, distantly, that this is taking too long. I'm so drained, I feel both heavy and light at the same time.

I feel a tugging on my ankles and realize I'm moving. Weakly opening one eye, I can see the back of LT crouched low and it hits me that he's dragging me. He shoves me into the van.

In an instant, the vehicle is in motion and bouncing along the barely paved service road. Jonah's hands are on me, holding me down to prevent me from being tossed about. "What happened?" I croak, realizing the others are all here.

"We did it! You were great. But when you didn't respond, we realized something was wrong. LT had to come and get you; you were out cold. We'll be at the air hangar before you know it."

I fight to keep myself awake. I can just overhear LT's voice in the front seat of the van. He's talking to someone on the phone, getting initial reports of the damage we caused. I can't make out much, and I'm only privy to half the conversation. But the words "rolling outages" and "in the dark for months" come through. I think about families unable to keep their groceries fresh for meals. I remember the businesses that haven't been able to make payroll because they had to shutter. It hits me then, the impact on regular, everyday people, this thing we've just done. How can it be right, to cause so much harm to innocent civilians?

I reach a feeble hand up, grasping Jonah's forearm. "What have we done?"

I'm dozing during the return flight, drained from the effort, fighting back the waves of nausea, and riddled with guilt. I'm lost in the cobwebs between consciousness and sleep, and my mind pulls up the vivid image of LT in the sights of my gun. It wouldn't technically have been self-defense. Honestly, it would have put me in more danger at that moment since I needed his protection to get out of there.

But recalling the chance I had, seeing the image in my mind, pulls up a dark memory buried deep in my subconscious. My thoughts are swimming as I recall the feeling of a gun in my hands. The memory comes to me fully, and this time it's the true story, the whole story. It's not the version that Jonah read in the news story about me, the one I told the social worker that night. It's the truth, floating to the surface like a buoy cut from its anchor.

***

It's dark, and bitterly cold out. I'm eight years old, in my bed in Lutsen. Tucked tightly under the blankets, I'm covering my ears. But still, I can hear the gasping. The awful sound of sucking air. Half asleep I know that sound. I would know that sound today. It's the sound of my mother unable to breathe.

I can hear it from rooms away. Terrible recognition sets in. I sit up in my bed and clench the sheets around me. "Please don't kill her," I whisper.

I know where to find the gun in the front closet. It's got bi-fold doors, the kind that you pull out and the door panel splits in half on a hinge, folding back on itself, like flaps of an accordion.

Once opened, I use the stepladder to reach the box of shells on the top shelf. I know what to do, but my small hands are shaking so hard I can barely load it. The gun is nearly as long as I am tall, and it's unwieldy in my arms. In my parents' bedroom, the picture of the last supper over their bed is knocked off-kilter. The lamp is on the floor, casting ugly shadows across the carpet. The bedspread is tangled around my mom and her face is a ghostly shade of blue. That gasping, rasping sound barely ekes out of her now and I see her limp arms flailing, the fight almost gone. Tears streaming down my face, I swipe the arm of my pajamas across my eyes.

"Stop, Daddy please!" I scream at him, shakily pointing the gun at his back.

He makes no indication he hears me or knows I am here. I see the life going out of her. She is literally fading in front of my eyes. He is going to kill her this time. This time it will be too much.

"Stop!" I repeat. It's not a command; I am pleading with him, begging. My vision is blurred from the tears, but I can see his mass hunkered over the limp form of my mom.

The gun kicks and I fall backward hard against the floor. The specter of a ghost takes shape in front of me, as the smoke gathers. It smells like pennies and the taste of copper is in my mouth.

Dad is laying on top of Mom, blood spreading out across his back, slowly soaking his shirt. She is silent and unmoving under the weight of his body.

There is a rasping. This time it is Dad. He begins moving around and starts moaning. He rolls onto his side and cries out. Hands pressing against the exit wound on his abdomen, he looks up at me, shocked and confused.

"Klara, what the hell?"

The rage in his eyes pierces me. He is indignant even as my mother lays immobile next to him. Blood is now seeping out between his fingers, and he throws his head back. "Aaaagh!" he cries out in agony.

Afraid to go near him but wondering if it was too late for my mom, I carefully sneak over to her side of the bed. Caressing her face with my small hand, I see that the skin around her neck is red and hot. "Please," I beg. Snot is dripping from my nose, and I can taste the saltiness dribbling into my mouth.

"Please don't be gone."

My head snaps backward. A bloody hand grasps the edge of my collar as my father flails around. Soaking the mattress with his blood, he continues the awful moaning.

I tear away from his grip.

A gasp.

Then her eyes fly open.

I help her sit up and her eyes grow big with surprise as she takes in the gory scene around her.

"No, Klara," she says. Shaking her head, the words are a plea, coming too late. I see the depth of remorse sinking in. She sweeps her gaze across the room, landing on the gun. She imperceptibly nods her head, her lips hardening into a thin line across her face.

She walks out of the room and returns a short moment later. Bending low, she carefully picks up the gun, looking at it as if she has never seen one before. Ejecting the spent round, she deftly reloads and points at the writhing figure of my father on the bed.

"Klara, get out," she orders sternly.

Recognizing what she is about to do, I lock eyes with her. "No, Mom, don't," I beg.

"It's already done, Klara. I'm giving him mercy he doesn't deserve now."

I take one last look at my father. A cough shudders through him and blood spurts from his mouth.

Backing out of the room and huddling in the door, I take in the scene and terror grabs hold of me, as I realize what I've done and what's about to happen.

"Go on. Do it, Hannah." He glares at her, daring her with menace, his wheezing mouth agape.

Needing no further encouragement, my mother squeezes the trigger.

His head flies backward into the wooden headboard. It lands at an awkward angle, his chin unnaturally resting against his chest.

The ghost of smoke has reappeared, swirling in the space between his body and my mother. I retch on the carpet near my feet.

Ben runs past me to my mother, short flannel pants flapping at his ankles. "Mommy!" he cries out, grabbing her around the waist.

As Ben runs over to me, we hug tightly, terror knitting our bodies together.

A moment later, Ben and I are still clasped together, I hear Mom on the phone. "I shot my husband; he was attacking me."

A pause.

"No, he's not breathing."

***

Back in the present, on an airplane somewhere between Asia and North America, I allow the memory to crash over me, to wash me clean, to rub me raw. The truth of my past crashes like a freight train into the reality of my situation. The thin wisp of relief that I didn't take the shot at LT is like a tiny ray of light in a cold, dark room. I'm ashamed to know what I've been a part of. I'm ashamed I let Ryen walk out of my life. I've been so afraid of the truth, of unmasking myself as the monster in the story, that I've run in a big, arching loop back to exactly the thing I was running from. Are we just migratory birds, meant to return again and again to the thing that haunts us?

Mixed with the shame is something harder around the edges, something sharp and searing. It's rage. At LT. At my mom. And my dad. And the police, for all the times they could have done something, could have prevented that innocent eight-year-old from the burden of what she was forced into.

There's an ocean of rage inside of me, enough to go around. Enough for myself too. How could I allow this to happen again? How have I become a pawn in someone else's master plan? I've allowed myself to be the aggressor again, in someone else's story. And worse, I've helped LT orchestrate this.

It's like an existential mirror I am looking into for the first time. Seeing myself and what I've become.

My eyes fly open, and I sit bolt upright.

As I look around, I overhear Penny and Aino whispering darkly. Aino says, "Did you hear how awful it's going to be for the people here now? I can't be a part of this. I don't care if they torture me. They can kill me!" The last sentence comes out in a shrieking hiss, louder than a whisper.

"Well, it's already killing Luz." Penny says. I look over and see Luz has been hooked up to an I.V. bag, lying flat between the seats of the airplane. She looks colorless, almost transparent. Her clothes are swimming on her slight frame, revealing just how much weight she has lost since this all began.

I touch her forehead and ask Penny, "Did they give her anti-nausea medication today?" I reach into my pocket, pulling out a spare tablet.

"Why do you have that?" Penny asks, accusation vibrating off her.

I take a deep breath. It's time to come clean. I'm going to need their help. And we all deserve to know the whole story.

"I have something to tell you both. I don't think Luz knows either. The thing that allows us to access the power, it's caused by a genetic mutation. We basically have cancer and that's why we can do the things they need from us."

I can see Aino is mulling over all of this, realization sinking in, distrust rising to the surface. "How do you know this?"

"Jonah told me." I pause, then add, "About three weeks ago."

"Why didn't you tell us?" Penny demands, her face a landscape of betrayal.

"I didn't see what good it would do," I say weakly. "I thought it would just make this so much worse for all of you. It's felt so hopeless."

"You had no right!" Aino's eyes are alit with fire. The soft, demure creature I've come to recognize is gone, replaced by a tigress. Rage radiates from her entire body.

"I was trying to protect you," I say, weakly, already seeing how wrong I must look through their eyes.

"Protect us from the truth?" Aino is incredulous. "We deserved to know this!" she stabs a finger at the air in my direction.

"You know," Penny jumps in, with darkness in her voice. "Hiding the truth is just another form of control." Menacingly, she adds, "You're as bad as the rest of them."

I see myself, my actions, through her eyes for the first time. The reality of her words hits me like a tidal wave, knocking me back. I've had so many realizations, so much inward facing scrutiny in the last hour that I can no longer defend my actions.

Aino softens a bit, offering "Well, she's not as bad as them. Not as bad as LT." She darts a look in his direction.

"No, she's right," I offer. I think carefully as the words take shape in my mind, and then in my mouth. "Truth-telling is the most powerful way to show love." As I give voice to the thought, I absorb the power of it, unearthing all that has been hidden. The lie I told myself, that I was protecting them, has been spreading inside of me, just like the cancer in all of us. Truth is the light, and I've been living in the dark, where shame and fear have been feeding the cancer. I couldn't see it until now, but I can't unsee it, I can't unlearn this. I've crossed a threshold, passed through a portal into a different land. I know nothing can ever be the same.

"Trying to protect you, that's me making a choice for you," I admit. "For us to be equals, for this to work, I can't hide things from you anymore." Correcting myself I say, "I won't," the promise of the words solidifying inside me.

Penny says, "One way or another, we're all going to die if we don't do something. Either they decide we know too much and can't risk letting us just walk away when this is over, or if we ever do get released, it will be directly into the hospital where our days will be numbered."

"Or into prison," Aino darkly suggests. We both look at her questioningly. "For all we know, we're the bad guys here. We have zero information. We don't have any solid reason to think that we're working on behalf of a legitimate government operation. After today, the damage we caused, and now this cancer bullshit, I'm done. I'm going to find a way out."

"Me too," Penny adds. "We have to save Luz." The look on her face as she glances over at Luz almost breaks my heart.

And that moment is the one that cracks open and tears apart the lie I have been living. It's as if I am an astronaut on a distant land, and my oxygen tank just ran out. Taking off the mask, ready to die, I inhale deeply only to learn the air here is breathable. All my life, I've believed I was in danger and there's no one who can help me. Yet here is the stunning reality right before me. I don't have to be the hero, and I don't have to do this alone.

I look around at the women and see them with fresh eyes. Together, we can protect each other. Each is a heroine on her own, yet we can work collectively, combining our strength.

This is the secret power in us, I realize. Not the ability to channel energy on command. No, we have the power to combine forces and resist. To help one another and band together. This is the power of humanity, and feminine power. It's how we will bring down LT, someone who works on his own, for his own purposes. And his ego, his singularly self-focused aim, that's exactly the weakness we will exploit. The truth of it has been here all along, if only I had trusted enough to unmask the lie.

As the wheels of the plane come down, the jarring sensation of the ground coming up to meet us is the force that knocks the last piece of my plan into place. As we disembark, I walk with the exact knowledge of how we are going to get out of this. We will end what started so many months ago on that frozen lake.

AARYA
En Route

The foursome drove through the night, making their way east. After sending Leonard's car back as far westward as it could be programed to go, they had climbed into Jenny's "cold" rental vehicle. Without going into detail, Jenny explained the vehicle could not be traced to her and would make it hard for anyone to track their movements. Aarya found a sense of comfort in knowing that they were in the company of someone so capable at navigating this dangerous situation they had placed themselves into. In the back seat, as the sun was dropping lazily behind the horizon, she nodded off, her head coming gently to rest on Walton's shoulder.

She awakens to find herself curled into his lap, her cardigan draped over her, just as the vehicle rolls to a stop at a charging station. The city is blanketed in total darkness and the three other passengers appear to be coming out of their own slumber.

"What time is it?" she asks no one in particular, pushing herself up into the seat. Mack looks at the clock on the GPS dashboard and replies, "A little after 3:00, according to this clock. But with the clock drift from satellite outages, it could be more like 3:30. I think we should get snacks, and a bathroom break here, then try to make the rest of the trip in one final push.”

As the ChargeBot comes around and starts re-charging the vehicle, Jenny carefully makes payment to the SnackBot using some untraceable form of payment she had explained as Aarya was nodding off.

“No purchases in the shop,” she cautions as the others head in to use the restrooms. “I’ll be here waiting for ya.”

Aarya feels sheepish next to Walton as they walk into the station store, remembering the warm feeling of finding herself curled up against him, recalling the safety of his arm draped casually across her shoulders as she slept. She sneaks a glance over at him in the too-bright lights of the station and finds herself surprised at what she is feeling. She rolls her shoulders and breathes deeply, thinking it must be the excitement of adventure, the closeness of their time together that is clouding her feelings. She didn’t leave things on a good note with Ravi, but he is waiting for her back home, with the life that she is meant to live, the version of her story that is acceptable and expected.

But as they assemble back into the vehicle, she conjures up an image of Ravi, trying to remember the safety and affection she felt with him in the early days of their relationship, but the only image that comes to mind is a disapproving, parental version of Ravi. It’s the one that was mortified to learn of her quick departure with Walton, the one who chided her for sharing information instead of trying to garner acclaim. She shakes her head, trying to shed the image, trying to remember the life waiting for her back home.

All four of them are awake now, driving in the darkness and heading further east.

Walton looks to Mack, “Want to fill us in on what you think will stop the effects of the Auroras?”

“Sure,” Mack says turning to face the three of them. “Now, mind you, it’s only a theory and can’t be tested in advance. But I worked with my colleague, Lynelle Jandry, and she pulled in some pre-eminent cancer researchers we’re connected with in the scientific community.”

“Cancer?” Aarya asks, puzzled. “What does that have to do with anything?"

"Valid question," he responds. "The effects we described, likely escaped mutations from the human trials, seem to behave like cancer, in that they are cellular mutations. As the mutations spread, their powers have likely increased, but I'd expect the women are experiencing a range of symptoms, growing sicker by the day." Mack can't hide his own sadness, speaking of the sick women, both as a physician who cares deeply about his patients, but also from a more personal place. There is a heaviness in his face, in the lines around his mouth.

"God," Walton sighs. "Until the posts about the family and friends of these women trying to locate them and bring them home, I really thought they were nefarious, acting of their own dark motivations." His brows are furrowed, lips pursed slightly. "Now, this. The cancer and the illness they must be dealing with. I just see them so differently. I'm sort of angry at myself for the assumptions I made when I knew so little."

Aarya is touched by his self-correction, the ability to look inward and re-examine where he went wrong. It makes her think again about Ravi, and the contrast is harshly apparent. Confident, self-assured, sometimes arrogant, Ravi, whom she realizes now has never openly corrected himself or attempted to gain more insight into a situation that could be more nuanced than he might have initially understood.

This ability of Walton's to look inward, this introspection, she has seen it in him before. It's the thing that separates people in her life into two groups, she thinks. She's read about it in articles, but it's sinking in for the first time. Walton has a growth mindset, she realizes. He can evolve, improve, and change. Sure, Ravi has changed, gained more knowledge and skills, but it's not the same kind of growth. The spiritual, existential growth she craves, that she recognizes in Walton, it requires an ability to look critically at oneself, and one's beliefs.

And more to the point, it's the reason he could see what she needed to change, what she needed to release, in order to be her truest self. "That's love," she says, to the shock of herself and the others.

Jenny looks at her quizzically, not quite following the chain of thoughts only known to Aarya. Walton loves her, she realizes, taken aback. That's love, wanting someone to grow and improve and become the best version of themselves. When Ravi says he loves her, how can it be true, when he doesn't even see her, when he wants her to be a restricted, conformed version of herself?

Snapping back to the reality of the conversation, she sees the need to address her out of context comment. "I just mean, both of you are looking at the situation with so much empathy, or love, I guess." She's blushing now, her fumbling explanation doing little to cover for her outburst.

"Yes, I suppose so…" Mack agrees, somewhat tentatively. "Walton is right anyway, that these women are victims on so many levels. And they need our help."

"What does that look like?" Walton asks.

"AI nanobots" Mack says. "It's an emerging area of cancer treatment but has shown tremendous efficacy in the past year during trials. One of our colleagues is leading a trial that just concluded."

"I've heard of nanorobots," Jenny offers. "Are they like microscopic robots that go inside you? Seems so creepy to me."

"Yes, that's not a terrible way to describe them, I guess. But now we've coupled them with artificial intelligence to help them evade the immune system response, so they can be utilized longer-term for maximum impact. In fact, in some ways, this AI could be attributed to this Jonah fella that filed the patent for the AI model used to detect the Auroras. It's a derivative of one of his earlier AI computational models he worked on with other students for their university project."

"What does the AI do exactly?" Jenny asks, a suspicious look on her face. "Do the nanobots act on their own then, making choices without humans? Could they take over someone's body?"

"They are self-organized, and the AI can predict outcomes and make certain decisions without a human giving the green light. But that's not a bad thing. It's not like robots taking over the world. They can remember past encounters, and the neural network helps predict exactly when they need to be cleansed or adjusted, for each specific human host."

"Human hosts!" Jenny shudders. "Just listen to how that sounds. Keep them out of my body. I think I'd prefer cancer."

Mack looks sympathetically at her. "A lot of my patients feel the same way. Unnatural interventions can have unintended side effects. But when we are fighting cancer, we need all the help we can get. Chemotherapy and radiation aren't natural either. And look how much damage they do, in an effort to treat or cure the patient."

"This colleague of yours," Walton asks, "could they like just give us some of these little robots? How does it work?"

"Yeah, sure, I've got some in my duffel bag actually," Mack says.

Jenny jumps, pressing her body as close as possible to the car door.

"Kidding, I'm just joking," he says, hands splayed out apologetically. "You can't take them out of the controlled lab environment at this point, not the ones that are hooked into the neural network. We'd need to transport the women to the lab in Boston for supervised treatment. And obviously, the nanovehicles haven't been used against their particular type of cellular mutation, so there is a risk it may not be very successful. So far, there are fifteen specific cancers the trials have focused on, with remarkable success. But certainly, the Aurora variation is a novel cancer, with unknown characteristics."

"It sounds like the best shot they've got," Aarya says. "I mean, the AI could theoretically 'learn' about their unique illness, right?"

"It would certainly be able to do that much faster than human computations and predictions ever could."

"Ok, I'm with Jenny on feeling a little creeped out by the, what did you call them, nanovehicles? Eww," Walton says.

"Nanoparticles, nanovehicles, nanomaterials, nanobots, it's all the same." Mack says.

"Right, well the 'nanos' I guess you could say, they give me the heebie jeebies. But it sounds like we need to get the Auroras to that lab," Walton says.

"I agree." Aarya chimes in. "How are we going to free them? And do you think they'll come willingly with us?"

"I think we can get a message to them, through Jonah," Jenny says. "If they know they are sick, I think they'd come with us. Especially if Jonah helps convince them."

"That's great!" Aarya says, encouraged by Jenny's resourcefulness.

"But what about Aarya's first question?" Walton asks. "How on earth will we get them out of the military facility? It's going to be heavily guarded. And don't tell me the nanos are going to march in there!"

Mack chuckles. "No, the nanos won't help us here. We are going to need a diversion."

For the next seven hours of driving, none of them sleeps. Instead, as the flat, open plains fall behind them, opening up to gentle rolling hills and eventually the beauty of Appalachian Mountains, they talk through different ideas and options, brainstorming and calculating.

As the trip time dwindles down, it seems their options are slipping through their fingers, like sands of time in an hourglass. Just slipping away, bit by bit. By this point, they have one idea they all agree is terrible and their least favorable approach. And they also have two others that are only slightly better. They've agreed any plan will require luck and risk-taking. Walton, being someone who appreciates a well-thought plan, and who doesn't believe in luck, is clearly unsettled by the ad-lib style of approach they seem forced into.

Yet, there is one promising aspect of the plan, which incidentally was revealed by Mack almost as an afterthought. It came up when Aarya interrupted a particularly wild thread of brainstorming, one where she would pose as a news reporter demanding answers, then pretend to faint. "I just thought of something." All eyes are on her, Jenny's eyebrows arched in a question.

"Let's say one of these hair-brained ideas actually works. How are we going to get very far with the Auroras if the operatives clearly have a fool proof way to locate them?"

Walton's face falls. He has tried to stay positive, to throw as much caution to the wind as he can possibly tolerate. But Aarya's question brings crushing reality back down around him, the exhaustion of events, and amount of time spent outside his comfort zone finally catching up with him. He physically slumps in the seat, looking crestfallen.

"She's right," he says. They found these women all over the world. How can we prevent them from just finding them, and us, again?"

"Oh right, that." Mack says, almost dismissively. Aarya's eyes thin out into slits, skeptically eying him, wary of his casual tone.

"I can't believe I forgot!" Mack exclaims, now looking a bit sheepish after taking in the reaction of Aarya and Walton. Jenny makes a face, her lower lip pulled back to expose her teeth, and Walton thinks she looks like that old emoji of "toothy grimace" he used to send in grade school when emojis were still a thing.

"Canya believe we didn't think of it soonah?" Jenny asks Mack.

Navigating to the Underground site on his tablet, Mack opens a recent message thread. "I mentioned to you about the group created for the family and friends of the Auroras, right?"

Aarya nods her head, a little sidelong as she's trying to assess where he is headed with this.

"This Ryen fella. He's the boyfriend of the Aurora abducted from Minnesota. I've chatted with him recently. He's been looking for ways to help, to free the women. And he just so happens to be a welder. It's quite remarkable, since there aren't many left who learned the trades."

"Right, Ryen the welder. Sounds like a character out of a Tolkien book. He has what exactly to do with us and our problem?" Aarya asks.

"Yes, sorry, long thread to pull here making that connection. It's just that he's built a Faraday Cage van. You all know what a Faraday Cage is, I'm sure?"

Walton nods, rolling his eyes. "We are scientists, remember?" he says, pointedly enunciating the word.

"Of course," Mack continues. "He's fashioned the cage, or maybe it's a shield, I can't remember, but it covers the interior of a passenger van. If we transport the women in this van, their electromagnetic signals will be blocked, and we're fairly certain they can't be detected."

The simplicity of it sinks in. "Have you contacted him to ask him to meet us? How do we get him here in time?" asks Aarya.

"He's already here," Mack says. "He's been waiting at a nearby campground. He's got replacement license plates so he can swap them out after the getaway. He even managed to get some magnetic panels from a friend who owns a mobile dog grooming service."

"It almost sounds too good to be true," Walton says.

Over the next several hours, they drive in the direction of the campground, continuing to refine the plan, and deciding on Plan B and a fallback position for both. They pull into a charging station not far from the rendezvous location, and everyone gets out for snacks, bathroom and a stretch.

As Aarya walks out of the station, heading in the direction of the vehicle, she spots movement out of the corner of her eye. It's a flash of black, maybe a cat, she thinks, wistful for the comfort of her sweet Bumbu waiting for her at home.

But, getting a closer look, she realizes it's not a cat at all. It looks like a human head. She cautiously approaches the row of bushes along the parking lot and hears a sharp inhale of surprise.

"Are you okay?" She asks the nearest bush, taking in the small white flowers that coat the dark green sphere.

"I need help," a meek voice whispers up at her, a branch waving slightly as if it's the one speaking.

Well, this is not part of the plan, Aarya thinks, knowing the time spent and attention drawn helping this woman may just derail everything they've laid out. But she knows she can't ignore the woman's desperate plea. Maybe, she thinks, we can call the police and leave before they get here. Maybe there's a way to do both?

"Okay, stay there and I'll get my friends. We can call the police."

"No! Please, no police." The top of the woman's face is almost visible now, dark eyes peering insistently up at her. Aarya can only imagine the kind of trouble the young woman must have gotten into if she doesn't want the police involved.

"They'll just take me back," she explains, emotion audible in her voice, as it nearly cracks.

Oh no, is she a prison escapee? Aarya thinks, looking desperately around, assessing her surroundings. She looks toward the car, trying to catch Walton's eye.

"A consulate maybe?" the head is poking up a little higher now, making eye contact. "I don't know where I am, but is there a Chinese consulate nearby?"

Getting a better look at the young woman, Aarya's eyes go wide in recognition. "Black Dragon?" she asks, realizing a split second after it comes out how awful it sounds. "Lin, I mean, I think that's your name, am I right?"

The young woman nods eagerly.

"Stay here," Aarya instructs. Less than a minute later, she has Jenny at her side, having agreed that the entire group or the men approaching Lin in her fragile state could scare her off.

"Hiya Lin," Jenny says in the general direction of the bushes. "We're not gonna call the police. We just want to help."

The pair of eyes peer through the greenery, taking in the diminutive and eccentric woman standing next to Aarya.

"Will you take me to a consulate?" Lin asks.

"Sure, yes, we'll take you wherever you need to go. Can we pull over the vehicle so you can hop in? We need to get out of here fast, so you're not spotted."

Lin ponders this, considering her limited options, and whether the women can be trusted. After a brief moment, she nods. When the car pulls up next to the row of bushes, the door discretely opens, and Lin hops in with lightning speed and agility. The door closes as fast as it opened, and the car careens out of the parking lot and onto the roadway.

Silence hangs heavy over the group in the car as they drive off, wondering what sort of danger they have invited, wondering what sort of a wrinkle this introduces into the plan.

"I looked up the nearest Chinese consulate," Jenny says, the first to break the silence. "It's up in D.C., a little over four hours' drive. We need to get you into our vehicle, or we'll be followed and caught wicked fast."

Lin is curled into herself in the back seat, looking hopefully at

Jenny.

"But maybe, there's something else you'd want to do first? I have some information that might be important for you to know." Mack looks meaningfully at Lin, the young woman clearly overwhelmed and weary. "Are you by any chance not feeling well, have you been sick?"

Lin nods weakly, a look of puzzled surprise on her face.

"We know a doctor who can help you, and she can help the other women too. Did you know there were others like yourself, with these powers? Did you see any of them at the facility where you were held?"

Lin only shakes her head slowly from side to side.

"You're not the only one, Lin." Aarya explains, cautiously placing a hand on her leg. "We're on our way now to rescue all of them, and we'd like to take all of you to get medical treatment. Will you come with us?"

Lin nods her head, still silent. Then she surprises them all by saying, "What about LT?"

Jenny's eyes go wide, and Mack's mouth falls open. "You know about Luke?" Mack asks.

"The bald man they call LT? Yes. He was my main captor. He's in charge of the experiments and the outages."

"This is incredible," Jenny says. "Could you identify him if you had to?"

"Yes," Lin confidently replies.

As they pull into the campground, Aarya's mind is churning, processing the information and wondering about Lin's experience in the recent months. She thinks she has an idea, but it hasn't fully formed in her mind.

"It will be around the bend here," Mack says. "Number eighteen; I think I see the van."

They pull in through evergreen trees and park on a packed patch of gravel next to a fire ring. A variety of happy, active birds are chirping overhead, a few flitting back and forth between the trees and branches.

The group is met by a handsome, young man who appears to be

both strong and also very Joe Average. Aarya thinks he has kind eyes, although they are somewhat shielded under the brim of his ballcap. She notices his Minnesota accent is strong when he speaks and it instantly gives him an approachable, likeable air. He explains the Faraday shield design to them, pointing out various aspects of the structure and she notices the callouses on his capable hands.

Aarya realizes that their situation has changed quite drastically in less than an hour's time. Not only have they picked up two more allies for their small contingent, but their options have improved significantly. She is feeling more optimistic than she has since the meeting in the coffee shop, which already feels like a lifetime ago.

As they explain to Ryen how they intend to break the women free, the skepticism is nakedly clear on his face. "I can't see that working. You might find one of them with that approach, but by that time, the guards will have tripped the alarm and you'll be caught."

"He is right," Lin speaks. They turn to her, surprised at her contribution to the conversation. "That plan will not be successful."

Aarya is about to disagree, to point out how they can neutralize the guards and escape undetected when Lin continues. "I will go in with you. You're going to need my help finding the others and I know my way around."

Everyone looks at each other for a few seconds before Ryen says, "That sounds a lot better than anything else we've come up with. She's our best hope."

"This all sounds crazy," Walton says. How will we find them, how will we get them out? There are guards and cameras and secured doors."

"I had time to think about these things, when I came up with my escape plan," Lin says. "I can neutralize the camera system for about thirty minutes, if I channel my power."

She explains the different vendors who will come this afternoon for deliveries. "There is one that looks similar enough to you." She points at Ryen. "But, he has a mustache. Can we get a fake one?" They discuss a nearby costume and magic shop that might have just what they need, but they'll have to double back into town.

It is decided that the best option is for Ryen to intercept the delivery truck on its way to the facility, and overpower the driver, steal his delivery truck, and take his credentials.

"We'll need to get zip ties," Jenny says, "so you can restrain the delivery driver."

"Yes," Lin agrees. "We will need them also for LT."

"And how exactly do we overpower LT when he's in his own facility, possibly armed?"

Lin smiles and it's a devilish look, one that is either manic or childlike, and possibly some bizarre intersection of the two. She points at Walton. "Your right arm, are you able to move it?"

A look of sheer terror overcomes Walton, his left arm reaching over to reach the right arm that hangs limp at his side.

"It won't last very long. But I will numb both of his arms long enough that he can't reach for his gun or radio. You'll have to be fast with those zip ties." She looks meaningfully at Jenny who nods in acknowledgment.

Aarya thinks that Jenny looks a little too eager and might be surprisingly good with zip ties.

"We will take his key card," Lin says. "I think I can lead you to the other women. Are there four?"

"Yes, there are four of them being held at this facility," Mack confirms.

She nods, "I didn't know, so I couldn't understand it before. But I realize now that I have been sensing them, with the power. That's how I knew there were four. I can find them."

Aarya marvels at how quickly and easily this plan has come together. She is nervous and excited all at once. She looks over at Walton, thinking he must feel as out of place in this as she does. They are academics, after all, not secret operatives or soldiers.

But when she looks over at him, he is holding his head high and there's a gleam in his eye that she has never seen before. He practically shouts, "We are doing this!"

All five of them laugh in unison and Aarya wraps her arm around his shoulders, squeezing him and shaking her head.

Out of nowhere, a hawk screeches and swoops down to land on

the picnic table in the clearing. The others turn, shocked and intrigued. But Lin appears to have been expecting this and addresses the bird. "Grandmother," she says. "I see you approve."

The bird fixes a single predatory eye on her, seeming to nod its head. Its broad wings make a whooshing sound as it takes off.

"I am ready to claim my birthright," Lin says.

KLARA
Military Base, United States

Since the trip, we've had very little time together to discuss the plan. Our best opportunity is when Jonah is overseeing our testing, and even then we are usually being observed. He has to be careful. We need him, so we can't let him get caught helping us.

He's come up with a way of passing notes between us, which makes for slow and stilted communication. Yet, the ability to communicate and work together is thrilling. Despite the obstacles, I feel freer than I have in a long time.

I share what I know about the numbing and learn the others have discovered aspects of it too. Together we practice how to control it, how far we can take it, how long it typically lasts. Penny was the first among us to realize it could be used on someone else. Jonah even let her practice on him, to help us test the limits.

We've devised a plan for me to escape, to go to the media and get help. I argued with this, back and forth for days, not wanting to leave them. "What will they do to the rest of you when I'm gone, and to Jonah?" I wrote in my secret note to Penny.

"You can't worry about that. Just get out and get help," came her scribbled answer.

So today is the day. We're supposed to be running more tests with one of the scientists on staff. I'm going to claim to be too sick, to get them to put me in the infirmary. It's not a far stretch, given how weak and ill I've been lately. From there, I'll have a better chance of numbing the nurse, fleeing through the stairwell, and making my way to the exit that Jonah will be guarding. He can buzz me out. If we disable the cameras, hopefully they won't be able to prove he helped us.

Realizing the day for our plan has come, I'm a bundle of nerves. My breath comes too quickly and even though I try to calm myself down, my mind continually focuses on what can go wrong. I rehearse the sequence in my head, thinking through each step, each decision point. But the morning has gone by in a flash, and all I can think is that I need time to go more slowly, to think and be prepared.

Once I've been transported to the infirmary, a male nurse starts my I.V.

"Let's get you settled here," he says. I wait for him to return to the bank of computers along the wall, so he will be farthest from me when I numb him. As he sits down at the computer, I'm about to begin when he says, "Your blood pressure and heart rate are extremely elevated."

As he spins around in the chair to type up his notes, I attempt to start the numbing, calculating how long it will take and how much energy I will use. But I realize I'm feeling warm, heavy and soft around the edges. He says, "I've added a sedative to your med cocktail this time. It will help you relax and get some rest."

Horrified, I try to fight it, to reach over and rip out the I.V. But it's too late. Too much of the drug has already gotten into my system. As I drift off, all I can think about is Jonah sitting at the guard desk downstairs, waiting for me.

PENNY
Military Base, United States

Pain searing through her shoulders and arms, she forces herself to complete another set of push-ups. Waiting and wondering was sending her into monkey-brain mode. The physical exertion and repetition is helping, but she can't go on like this forever. Klara should be outside the facility perimeter now, making her way to safety. How long before they hear any news? Will they hear news, or will it just be the appearance of the police, FBI, or some other force come to release them? Will it be calmer than all that, with a new guard coming to simply tell her she can go home?

There are so many 'what-ifs' flying through her brain. This was the real reason she had to start moving her body, to do something. What if she was caught? What if no one believes her? What if the government really is behind all of this and those who are supposed to come help them are the ones holding them captive?

She decides to lay down on the cot, to focus on reading one of the few novels they have been given. She has read it before, but what else can she do?

And then she hears a noise outside her cell. It's too soon. This can't be good, she thinks.

"We're here to help, but we have to hurry," a woman's voice whispers. Penny detects an accent, maybe Chinese. This is off, something is wrong here.

In seconds, the door is opened and before her stands a middle-aged man and a young Asian woman. Shocked, it takes her a moment to register. "You're the Black Dragon," she says accusingly. Penny backs away from the door, hands outstretched defensively.

It's the man who responds, "She's one of you. She was forced into this too. We're taking all of you to safety."

"Why should I trust you?"

"What choice do you have?" he answers. "Listen, there's no time. Either come with us or stay here. But we're going to find the others."

Her mind quickly focuses on a single word, a singular thought: Luz.

She pushes past them and heads down the hall. "Follow me."

"I think one of us is up ahead, just there," Lin points. "I can sense her."

Penny nods. Outside the door to Luz's cell, Mack swipes a keycard.

Lin gasps when she sees her. Penny rushes to her side. Luz is barely able to raise her head, weakened and pale. "She's been really sick," Penny tells them, almost in tears, her face contorted.

"Can you stand?" she asks. But without waiting for an answer, she reaches under Luz's arms and lifts her up. Mack comes over to help and they carry her over the threshold.

"Are there two others?" Lin asks Penny.

"Just Aino," Penny responds. "I think Klara got out this morning."

"One is out in the truck already, but there's another still here, upstairs on level two."

"The infirmary?" Penny asks. "Something's gone wrong."

Lin pivots, "I'll go upstairs and find her. You get to the van." And in a flash, Lin disappears down the hall.

Turning a corner, Mack inhales sharply. A guard is approaching rapidly, beginning to draw his gun. "Can you numb him?" he asks Penny.

But it happens so fast, Penny has no time to react, no chance to think. There's a popping sound. Luz cries out.

"No!" Penny exclaims, looking over at her, tiny red dots seeping through her shirt, blossoming into ink blot sized stains. Luz slumps in their arms.

She's not thinking, she can't see, all she feels is fiery rage and a prickling, electric heat pulsating through her. The guard drops to the ground, completely immobilized. She didn't think, didn't focus, just sent a wave of rage in his direction.

Mack is pressing on the wound with one hand, trying to pull both of them now. "Let's get her out of here!"

They shuffle around the unconscious guard and Mack holds them back behind a corner, peering around. "It looks clear, let's go! It's that doorway down there."

It feels like slow motion. No matter how fast they go, it isn't fast enough.

In the back of the delivery truck, a man and woman help them lift Luz. "Put pressure on that wound," Mack commands, removing his polo shirt and pressing it down. "Keep it there, just like that."

Tears are streaming down Penny's face. "Let's go, we have to get her to a hospital!" her voice is strained, her hands shaking.

"Klara is still in there," Aino says. "The Black Dragon and a short little woman are in there looking for her. Jonah said she never made it out."

"We can't wait!" Penny moans.

"Shh-hh," Luz is weakly reaching for her, grasping at her. A bloodied, weak hand touches Penny's face and for just a second, the Earth stops spinning. Time stands still. The touch of her hand is everything, it is her whole life and every sunny day, and every drop of rain. Luz looks angelic staring up at her with glassy eyes.

"You can't leave me," Penny croaks. "I need my Luz."

"Don't be sad. I am not feeling pain. Just hold my hand."

Penny grasps her hand, stroking her hair. "This never should have happened. It's all my fault."

"No, amor. None of it ever was. But you saved me when you loved me. When you saw me. Just me. All of me, exactly as I am."

Penny is shaking her head. How is this happening again? How is she so close to tragedy, unable to stop it?

"Save me again, one last time. By holding me, looking at me the way you do. You thought I was your Luz, but it was always you lighting me up. The light you saw in me, it was just a reflection of your own. You are beautiful and brave. You're a survivor."

She slumps back.

"My Luz, my light, don't go," Penny cries.

And then she is gone. Her eyes gently close. She has slipped away, like a wood nymph returning to the forest.

There's a rustling as Jenny and Lin appear dragging an unconscious Klara toward the truck. The two men jump out, helping to hoist her in.

"That's all of us," Mack says. Lin rushes to the cab of the truck and they are instantly pulling away.

It's total darkness in the back of the truck. Penny is cradling Luz in her lap, crying silent tears. As they come to a stop, she overhears Jenny saying something about Lin numbing the guard at the exit.

It's a blur, but they are moving again. Penny can't think about and doesn't care about any of the logistics or details. It doesn't matter anymore if there is a guard, if they even get away.

There's more talk about Klara, unconscious, but according to Mack, stable. Discussions about a van, a facility where there is a cure. She doesn't know some of these people, doesn't care to ask their names. She may as well have died with Luz, wishes she had.

The truck comes to a stop again.

"There's no time to swap the plates, we just have to hope no one noticed the van," she overhears.

Then the truck door noisily slides upward, and the light is blinding. Hands reach for her, to pull Luz away. "No!" she screams, not letting go.

Somehow, the collective hands have moved Penny still clutching to Luz over into the Faraday van.

They are bumping along, pulling onto a main road. She hears Mack say, "She's gone. A hospital won't help now."

"We should stick to plan, head to Boston," another voice says.

"We know we'll be safe there."

Somewhere along the way, hands pry Luz from her, carefully wrapping the body in a blanket. Penny looks down to see she is holding a piece of blue, hardened plastic. Tragedy has found her again; history on repeat.

KLARA

En Route to Boston, Massachusetts

I am aware of movement, vibrations of the road and subtle bumps registering in my body, as my mind slowly grasps that I'm no longer in the infirmary. My eyes flutter open, and I take in the scene passing outside the window. A glimmer of orange sunlight warms the edge of the horizon, out past an idyllic cornfield.

"Hey sleepyhead." It's Ryen's voice. I would know that voice anywhere. I shut my eyes and feel a tingling sensation spread all over my body. I feel in my nostrils sensing that tears are threatening to spring forth. I open my eyes and turn my head, hoping I'm not dreaming, or if this is a dream, hoping I don't wake up.

"It's you," I say, disbelief and astonishment nearly taking my voice.

"And it's you," he says, reaching over to take my hand.

"How?" I ask, then add, "Where?" I look around, taking in the van full of passengers. Aino, Penny and a handful of people I don't recognize fill the vehicle, most dozing, others in a daze staring out the window.

"There's so much to tell you," he says. The joy in his face is evident as he tries to blink away tears. But I can tell that something

211

is off, that some of what he wants to tell me isn't good news.

I look around again, registering that Aino is in the back row, curled and asleep, and Penny is nearly catatonic, staring out a window. "Luz," I say, softly, as I look down at a blanket covering what I know must be the missing member of our group.

Ryen nods. "There was an incident, with a guard. Penny hasn't eaten or spoken a word since we left."

I look at her again and recognize the shock still has its grip on her. I remember that feeling, when my dad was killed. I remember the grief too, but I know Penny's grief has augered through her to a depth I've never felt. My heart aches for her, for all of us. For the injustice of what we've been through.

I turn back to Ryen, taking in this bittersweet moment, feeling safe and secure for the first time in months. He fills me in on all that happened leading up to and during the process of freeing us. He points to each of the individuals in the van, telling me their name, how they got involved. A young, dark-haired woman he calls Aarya is one of the few awake and smiles sweetly at me as he makes the introduction.

The rest of the trip to Boston went by in a blur. After several more of the group began to wake up, and realize I was awake, a buzz of conversation started, though the energy was muted, forcibly stifled in recognition of the silent member in our midst.

During the moments of silence, I felt a whirlwind of mixed emotions. Sitting next to Ryen while he drove through the night, we held hands, cried, apologized, and spent time explaining what had happened since we saw each other last. Knowing he'd been in a hospital in Canada when I was out looking for him filled me with so much regret. If only I had called that particular hospital. If only I had convinced the police to help. He shared so many of his own regrets, about our argument, about my capture, how I had been treated, what I'd been forced to do.

I found myself in awe of his actions to help find us, to help with the rescue. Having spent my whole life unable to accept the help of others, here was this man who loved me, and literally saved me. Looking back at the passengers, I realized they had all come together to help save me.

I felt loved in a way I never had before. I felt able to receive love in a way I never had. I was a part of something now. I had friends, allies, and support. I was terrified and liberated at the same time. The feeling was like being in a freefall, jumping off a cliff. One moment, a crushing fear would come over me, and in the next, I'd remember I wasn't alone anymore. I would remind myself, the safety net is down there, waiting to catch me. I could accept help and trust in it.

Arriving at the medical facility in Boston, there was a lot of discussion among the group, regarding what they called the Faraday Van and how to ensure we wouldn't be detected. We were finally escorted in where we received a full medical workup.

I'm sitting now in a hospital bed, I.V. in my right hand, holding a tablet in my left hand. A team made up of a male and female doctor have just finished explaining the nanobot treatment, how long it will take, possible side effects, and what my long-term prognosis will look like.

"There's one last thing," the woman says, pausing to look at the other doctor. He nods ever so slightly, and she continues. "Once the bots repair your cells, and as your body regenerates, well, you won't have access to the power any longer. By correcting the mutation, the ability will also be abated."

I look down at the tablet, bearing a waiver document, with signature lines and consent boxes awaiting my confirmation. The formality of it is what strikes me. I didn't choose this. I never wanted any of this. The power made me vulnerable in ways I never could have expected, putting me and those around me in danger. As my hand hovers over the screen, I think about how the word vulnerable can have positive and negative connotations. I was vulnerable to those like LT who wanted to use me for their own gain. But I've also become vulnerable, I realize, in other ways that will benefit me for the rest of my life. I've let my guard down and accepted help from others. I've realized how much Ryen means to me and that my independence was part of my psychological armor keeping everyone at just enough distance that I felt I couldn't get hurt. But that just hurt me in other ways. I had been hurting for a long time before this all began, but I was familiar with that pain, ready to accept it as mine for a lifetime.

This unfamiliar vulnerability, the unfamiliar fear that I've opened my heart and left it exposed, it feels like the right pain to have chosen, if faced with a choice between the two. I know it won't be easy, after a lifetime of guarding myself from this exact experience. But I have to try.

I flick my fingers across the screen, checking one box, then another, then signing with my fingertip. A momentary feeling of grief passes through me, knowing that to sign away my illness, I have signed away a part of me that I'll never get back. But this is my choice now and having that kind of control feels good.

Just as the two-doctor team leaves the room, I look up to see a striking woman leaned against the door frame, her dark hair and intense eyes taking me in. She comes over, hand outstretched.

"Hi, Klara," she says as I take her hand in mine and feel the firm, resolute grip on the other end. "I'm Norah." She smiles at me and sits in the chair next to my bed. "I'd like to be your attorney, if you decide that's what you want."

She goes on to explain that she's been working with a team of attorneys, capable and talented people who have been building a case. "There was never government approval for the program that Luke Tierson established."

"LT?" I ask.

"Yes. He was working for a para military group privately funded and lacking oversight. What happened to you, should never happen to anyone." There's a ferocity to her, an intensity that would be frightening if I didn't know she was on my side in this.

"And I don't just mean the abduction and time you spent in that North Carolina pseudo-military base." She shakes her head and continues, "The mutation that you and the other Auroras suffered from, it was released during a human experiment in a lab that wasn't following protocol and failed to properly report what they knew. The harm you suffered, not once but twice, was the direct result of improper oversight, negligence, and outright willful disregard for your rights, safety and well-being."

I am envisioning this woman in a smartly tailored suit, addressing a jury, pounding her hand into a lectern with righteous indignation.

"Yes, and yes," I respond.

She looks quizzically at me.

"Yes, I was wronged," I say. "And yes, I'd like you to represent me."

The curiously small woman I know now as Jenny comes into the room at Norah's beckoning, carrying a tablet containing another set of forms requiring signature.

"Did ya tell her," Jenny asks, "About Jonah and LT?"

I look up as I hand back the tablet, asking "Tell me what?"

Norah nods at Jenny, who says, "LT is dead."

Hearing this, I feel something in my gut unclench.

"What happened?" I ask. "I was told he was just zip tied and restrained while we made our getaway."

"Yes," Jenny nods. "But when he got free, he was a raging bull. He blamed Jonah and went at him. Jonah didn't have a choice," she says.

"You mean — ?"

"Yeah, Jonah shot him, point blank." She looks down at her hands. "He's real torn up about it."

The thing that unclenched inside me tightens back up again. I think of Jonah's kind face, his attempts to help us. I remember that he saw LT as a father figure and try to put myself in his shoes, having to do what he did. And picturing that, it's just too close to home for me. In an instant, I am emotionally undone. I feel the weight of agony, responsibility, grief, anger. It all slams into me like a tsunami wave of everything I've held back. I'm tasting snot and salty tears before I realize that I'm crying, fully weeping. This is the kind of ugly cry that looks as bad as it feels. I allow the feelings and the tears to wash me clean. I think of what he will bear for the rest of his life, what I've had to bear all these years, of being put in the position of having to pull that trigger. The person who should have sheltered, protected and mentored me having been the same person who caused me to do the worst thing in my life. And it's happened again, but this time to Jonah. I can picture his face when he carefully asked questions about my story, about my father. I try to picture his face as he must have looked when he pulled that trigger.

Jenny is handing me tissues and Norah's hand is on my shoulder. I can see in their eyes that they can't understand why this news has caused such an outburst. I should be relieved or at least feeling something like closure, not a sobbing mess.

I ask, "Where is he now — Jonah?" And I see a moment of recognition flash in their eyes, registering that my anguish expands to someone beyond LT. "He helped us you know. I want to make sure they know how much he helped us."

"He's cooperating with the FBI. I can't speak to his current whereabouts, but I'll try to find out more. And I'll pass along this information. When they come to fully debrief you, you'll have a chance to share what you know."

Jenny chimes in, "He planted breadcrumbs to help us find ya." Her face is bright and tilted a bit, as if she is just recalling this fact. "It's pretty clear that LT lied to him, too."

"LT was a victim in his own right," Norah adds somberly. "It's the age-old story, but pain begets more pain. He lost his wife and daughter in a wildfire. I did my best to hold the power company accountable, but it's never enough. He was a wounded and angry man who was wronged. The real villains here, as usual, are greedy corporations." Her eyes are glowing, and I can see she is just getting started.

"That's why we have to take this to the public. Wait just a moment," she says to me, then steps into the hall to speak with Jenny in private. I'm confused when they both leave in separate directions, and I'm left alone for the first time since we arrived at the facility.

Before I've had time to think about where they've gone or what they might be up to, Ryan sheepishly appears at the door to my room.

"You're looking better already," he says, making his way over to me. He touches my hand lightly, careful of the I.V. "You're getting some color back. How do you feel?"

I look into his kind eyes, and I think for a moment, since I haven't had a chance to digest everything or assess how I'm feeling.

"You know, it's the first time in weeks that I haven't felt nauseous. And it sounds like I can get started with the nanobot treatment later today."

He smiles and I see the relief on his face, and it registers how scared he must have been for me. He leans down to kiss me, tenderly, but passionately, and I place both of my hands on the side of his face. It feels exactly like home.

"Oi, get a room!" Penny's voice snakes into the space and I look over to see her being wheeled in by Jenny who looks to be quite adept at handling the I.V. and wheelchair at once. Close on her heels is Aino in another wheelchair, with Norah looking much less capable as she pushes and wrangles in.

"What's this all about?" I ask, looking around at the small gathering.

"I mentioned taking this to the public," Norah says. "I've arranged for a press conference this afternoon, before you begin the treatment."

"No," Penny says, her voice low and steely. She's locked eyes with Norah and it's clear she is not interested in this discussion.

"We've all been through so much," Aino pleads now. "I don't want to go in public and talk about any of this. I want it all to go away, forever. I just want to go home."

"I understand," Norah gently explains. "But it's very important that the public hear your story and understand how you were manipulated. We go on the offensive here in explaining what happened, or you could all easily be vilified, and possibly held accountable for civil or criminal charges. This is your best chance to make sure the public knows the truth."

And there it is again. That word: truth. In that moment, I realize it's exactly what we need to do.

"Truth is the light, and truth-telling is love," I say. "As much as anyone, I want to avoid publicity and go back home to pretend none of this ever happened." I look down at my hands, "But the public, our family and friends, they deserve the truth. Luz's family deserves the truth."

I look over at Penny. She's shaking her head, and I can see tears glistening in her eyes. "If you were them, wouldn't you want to know her story, from those who loved her?" I say.

Penny cries in earnest now and wipes at the tears. She tilts her head in my direction and ever so slightly, nods her head just once.

"We'll do it," I say to Norah.

AARYA
Los Angeles, California

Aarya's feet are propped on a pillow on her coffee table, Bumbu curled sweetly in her lap. "Hurry!" she calls.

Walton appears, a glass of her favorite Roussanne freshly poured in his hand. Reaching over to give it to her, he gently kisses her on the forehead. "Oh good," he says. "You've got your sweater."

She officially called it off with Ravi when they got back from Boston. She realized he was all wrong for her, even though he was right for her 'on paper.' Her parents were even more disappointed than Ravi, who seemed to have known what was coming. But after everything she had been through, their approval didn't matter as much as her own happiness.

She looks over at Walton, seated next to her now, and thinks how this awkward man she has known and worked with for years has turned out to be exactly her match. He was right under her nose all this time, and she was lucky enough to figure it out.

"Here, the clip is ready!" he exclaims.

Leonard's face appears on screen.

"He changed his hair color again," Aarya squeals.

"And Mr. Pakkala, we understand you went so far as to loan your vehicle to the astronomers who were part of the rescue mission, is that right?"

The reporter points a microphone at him, leaning in. "Yes, I knew this was history in the making. After I discovered the connection between the women and these events, I just knew we had to act."

"Bullshit!" Aarya and Walton scream at the screen in unison. A little of her wine splashes out, absorbed quickly into her cardigan, one of Jenny's latest creations.

"And what about the solar storms? We're hearing that the solar activity has already started to lessen. What's your prediction?"

"Yes, we've reached solar maximum, so the Sun activity should begin to subside. And of course, now that the Auroras have been treated, they are no longer exacerbating the events. We'll still see more Coronal Mass Ejaculations in the coming months, but the decline will be noticeable as we begin to return to normal."

Aarya looks at Walton, seeing the smile play at his lips. His nostrils flare as he tries to bite back his reaction.

"Did he just say… ejaculations?!" They burst out laughing, faces red, wine spilling over, Bumbu jumping off in surprise.

KLARA
Lutsen, Minnesota

It was several weeks before we were given the green light to go home. Norah explained that the investigation would be ongoing, likely for months if not years. We were instructed not to speak to the media, or to anyone, without our attorneys.

And so, remarkably, I awaken to the blinding beauty of the lake facing me from the floor to ceiling windows in my cabin back home in Minnesota. The nanobots are still inside me, hard at work. My symptoms have already improved significantly, and they tell me the treatment will be finished in another month.

I look down and see that I'm tucked into that same quilt, one square a bright red cardinal, another a gleeful black and white chickadee, and so many other local birds splashed colorfully across my shoulders. I never got to enjoy it, that morning so many months ago, that feels now like a different lifetime, a different version of myself in this place that hasn't changed.

As I look over at Ryen, I pull the quilt up around me. It's hard to imagine a time when I would have pushed away this man, would have prioritized my autonomy and my own version of my life over letting someone in. It was impossible to see it then, but it's so painfully obvious now, after everything I've experienced. I realize that I had never faced the demons living with me after I shot my father. I had never forgiven my mother for putting me in that position. I wonder if I ever would have or could have faced all of that. If I had never been abducted off that frozen lake, so many months ago, I wouldn't have this amazing group of friends, I wouldn't have been liberated from my past, and I probably wouldn't have Ryen.

I listen to his deep contented breathing, a cadence as comforting to me as the sound of the waves lapping outside on the rocky shore. The light glints off a scar across his left temple, still red and purple along the edges. I envy that, the visible, external display of the trauma, the journey he has lived. I think of Penny and her Phoenix tattoo and realize this must be part of it for her, to have physically recorded such a major event, to carry its story with her on her body. I will go back to that tattoo artist in Duluth and have him memorialize my journey across my shoulders, to grant me a permanent and visible record, and to help me remember not to go back to my old ways. I envision one of the birds on this quilt, flying free from a cage, the door flung open.

I shudder when I realize that in the end, abduction was my liberation.

EPILOGUE

Norah was captivating as she spoke before congressional hearings on human experimentation and detailed the impact on the Auroras and their health. She spearheaded programs to identify other women displaying symptoms and arranged government funding to pay for their treatment. An international program took longer to coordinate, but Congress eventually recognized the dangers of focusing exclusively on U.S. women, when another Black Dragon could emerge again. Treaties were signed and monitoring programs were implemented. An international scientific panel was formed.

It was several weeks before the mechanical damage at the Three Gorges Dam hydroelectric plant was repaired. Restoring power to the grid took a full month, during which time more than five million businesses and households were forced to manage a range of outages including rolling blackouts, and brownouts.

LT was vilified by many, but Norah made sure his story wasn't one-sided. He had acted on orders from his corporate board, whose mission was presumably authorized by the Department of Defense. And she reminded the public that he had, after all, been a victim too.

Losing his wife and daughter in a wildfire caused by the local power company had forever changed the trajectory of his life. She pointed to his story as another example of why big corporations must be held accountable for their actions. Although a contingent of legislators attempted to push for stronger oversight and transparency of privatized military programs, only slight modifications were agreed upon and passed into law.

Despite all of this, there were factions who chose to believe it was a hoax. A blonde, belligerent member of Congress used her time during hearings to grandstand about how embryonic gene editing was the real reason the women developed powers, rather than an underground experiment gone rogue.

Penny fought with herself when the cure was offered at the facility in Boston. She didn't think she was worth saving, after twice watching someone close to her die, being impotent to change the course of events. Her survivor's guilt was immense, especially when someone as bright and loving as Luz was snatched from the world too soon. But she heard Luz's voice in her head. "The light you saw in me, it was just a reflection of your own. You are beautiful and brave. You're a survivor." For Luz, and her memory, Penny decided to undergo the treatment. Several months later, she traveled to Bariloche, in the Rio Negro region of Argentina, in the foothills of the Andes. She met Luz's family and friends and collectively they arranged a memorial. They installed a sculpture of a flame in the center of town, dedicated to Luz, welded by Ryen and incorporating a mesh Faraday component. Luz's body was donated to science, to help with research on the mutation.

They heard that Aino, after returning home, realized she was still in love with her high school sweetheart. Two months later, and against all odds, she discovered she was pregnant. Dr. Mack helped formulate a medical advisory group to monitor her pregnancy and follow the child's development, looking for any clues of the mutation resurfacing. Aino decided to name the baby Leena, meaning light, in tribute to Luz.

Walton was re-hired back to his original position, where his work included an ongoing study of solar storms and devising new methods to predict and deflect their impact. But Aarya knew she couldn't return. Jenny helped make connections for her to find a position working with an online collective formed out of the Underground, dedicated solely to sharing research findings. In her free time, she set up a program to locate and rescue cardigans to send to Jenny for re-purposing and re-homing. Together, they expanded the business to include up-cycling and re-use of many other types of clothing, textiles and items destined for landfills.

Although Lin was exonerated of wrongdoing, her father's shame was too much to bear. She decided to stay in the U.S. and was accepted into the Philosophy program at UCLA. Sometimes, while playing the cello, she still feels a connection to the power, even though doctors assure her the mutation was cured. She learned her grandmother had passed away shortly before the incident with the hawk at the campground. In spite of this, she speaks to her grandmother regularly, drawing on her strength and wisdom, as if she is ever-present.

Jonah was ultimately cleared of any criminal charges related to killing LT. His involvement in the program is still under scrutiny, and the investigation will likely continue for years. During conversations with Klara after they all returned home, he realized the heavy burden she had been carrying from killing her father as a child. They worked together to form a virtual support group for people who justifiably take the life of another. Having learned his AI technology was used to help cure the women, he decided to take a job at the lab in Boston in furtherance of their nano medicine program. He was subsequently featured as Boston's Most Eligible Bachelor.

Klara and Ryen decided to split their time between northern Minnesota and Tasmania, selling Ryen's welded sculptures and a new line of jewelry designed by Klara and brought to life by Ryen's metalwork.

Klara and Penny forged an unlikely friendship through their mutual enjoyment of hiking and time spent in nature. Attempting to unburden themselves of the guilt they both had carried since childhood, they enjoyed a six-day hiking trek on Cradle Mountain Huts Walk in Tasmania, followed by hiking three hundred miles along the Superior Hiking Trail. Each mile symbolized a week of guilt they had carried in their lives. Penny pointed out that if they were using kilometers instead of miles, their "guilt trip" would have already concluded. They decided to keep on trekking, writing a book about their journeys titled *Hike to Heal.*

ACKNOWLEDGEMENTS

Much gratitude to…

To my editor, Rachel Moulton, for your editorial prowess and encouragement. And for your patience with my snail's pace.

To Tricia DeMesquita for your enduring belief in me, and your ability to see the future with me.

To my husband, Josh, and our former neighbor, Evan Tsai, for technical input on guns and such.

To Stacy Zinken, for being interested in my work and believing in it. Thank you for all the laughter, silliness, troublemaking and spa getaways. You show me what it means to be a kick-ass woman. I'll always be trying to keep up with you.

To Cybil Solyn, Wendy at Copper Cat Books, and my book club crew, for your eclectic love of the written word, whether read or heard.

To Thomas J. Spence, for your incredible photograph, and providing inspiration through nature.

To Dara Barlin, for your constant encouragement and shenanigans.

To Megan Fraser, for helping me build a bridge to the future I deserve.

To Sue Metoxen, for website help and self-publishing tips.

To Beni Hassan, for self-publishing tips and amazing brows.

To Mary Z, for years of support, self-care, and encouragement.

To Mary Caroll Moore, for sharing your talents as a course instructor, in *Your Book Starts Here*, and the Weekly Writing Newsletters. Also, many thanks for connecting me to Rachel.

To all my family and friends, who fill my cup and allow me to pour myself into new creative endeavors.

9 781967 568017